A Veil of Vines

Tillie Cole

For those who have been struck from their senses by love.

TILLIE COLE

Author's Note

For many, many years the great nation of Italy was defined by its regal elegance. Kings, queens, princes and princesses ruled from their castles. People bowed at their feet.

Until they didn't . . .

In 1946, a republic was born. The royals and their extended families were formally stripped of their power. It was widely believed that Italy had finally been freed from the rule of the blue bloods. The aristocracy no longer had their titles, their heritage publicly shorn.

But in private, matters remained largely unchanged.

For ancestry and tradition were not forgotten, no matter how much the people of Italy may have wished it so. Centuries of upper-class ceremony and influence cannot be so easily erased.

Those Italian families who had once ruled supreme, who were once the beating heart of the sacred country they honored, steadfastly held on to their elevated statuses. In their elite social circles, nothing much changed. To the people who mattered most in their world, no titles disappeared. No wealth was lost.

Everything was as it had always been.

Time moved on. Many moons passed. Tradition and duty endured; royal blood continued to run through the veins of their heirs.

In modern Italy no titles exist, yet this centuries-rich ancestry has not been lost. There are still princes and princesses; there are still dukes and duchesses. Just as it has always been, they look to their own.

Marriages are brokered and arranged to ensure the fortunes of the elite families remain intact and prestige is added to their reputations. Their world is exclusive, tight-knit; to those born to this life such matters are the most important of all.

This is a story about what happens when this network of power and wealth is challenged.

This is a story about what happens when the heart trumps tradition.

This is a story about what happens when two souls merge—two souls that should never have even met.

A VEIL OF VINES

TILLIE COLE

Prologue

Upper East Side, New York
Fifteen Years Ago . . .

Caresa

"For me?" I asked.

He gave a small nod. "Why, thank you so much," I said. His smile was so big. My prince was tall and handsome, with dark hair and tanned skin. He had the brightest blue eyes. He was Italian, just like my papa. Just like me.

I rushed across my playroom to the dress-up trunk and opened the lid. I threw all of my dresses over my shoulder, looking for the one I wanted. "Ah-ha!" I shouted, pulling the dress from the bottom of the trunk, along with the matching veil. My nonna gave these to me last Christmas. The dress was my favorite dress ever.

I pulled on the dress, slid the comb of the veil into my hair, then turned back to look at the mirror. I stared at my reflection and laughed. I loved this dress so much! I twirled around and around, feeling the bottom of the long lace dress swirl around my legs.

I grew dizzy, so I stopped and looked over to the stuffed bears and dolls sitting on either side of my pretend aisle. They were waiting for the ceremony to begin.

Straightening my shoulders, I moved to the top of the aisle and clutched my invisible flowers to my chest. I waited ten seconds, then began humming the Wedding March. My feet moved forward slowly, one after the other, in time with the beat.

Then I saw him. My prince stood at the end of the aisle, dressed in a tuxedo. His back was toward me, but when he heard our guests get to their feet, he turned. I held my breath as his blue eyes met mine. My heart beat so fast I almost couldn't breathe. I was marrying him. I was about to become his wife.

He smiled. His eyes filled with tears as he saw me in my pretty dress . . . because he loved me.

My prince loved me so, so much.

My legs wobbled as I walked forward. I almost tripped over. But my prince held out his hand as I approached. He wouldn't let me fall. He would never let me fall.

I squeezed his hand in mine, and my heart felt so full. The congregation stilled, and the priest stepped forward. I held my breath, waiting for the vows to begin . . .

"Caresa. I'm here." I blinked and blinked again, staring at my reflection in the mirror. My papa suddenly appeared behind me.

"Papa!" I ran to where he stood. Papa kneeled down, and I wrapped my arms around his neck. "You're back!" I exclaimed as he kissed me on my cheek and squeezed me so, so hard.

"Si, carina," he replied and gently pushed me back so he could look at my face. His dark eyes swept over what I was wearing. "I'm back from Italia, and find you are getting married?"

"Yes!" I stepped back, picking up the hem of my dress. "You're just in time to watch me marry my prince!"

Papa's head tilted to the side. "Your prince?"

"Yes," I said proudly. "He is tall and handsome with dark, dark hair and the

bluest of blue eyes." I put my hand over my heart. "He is the most handsome man in all of Italy." I stepped forward and put my hand on my papa's shoulder. "You will like him, Papa. He is so kind to me. He smiles so big, and he loves me so, so much." I leaned in and whispered, "I think he maybe even loves me more than you."

Papa raised a dark eyebrow. "Does he now?" He screwed up his face and shook his head. "No, impossible! No one will ever love you as much as me."

I thought about what he said, then nodded. "Yeah, you're probably right. I'm your little duchessa, *right, Papa?"*

He winked playfully. "Right, carina. *No one will ever be good enough for my* duchessa."

We both sat down on the floor. I rested my head on my papa's shoulder. My papa gazed at the wall, lost in thought. Then he said, "So, you dream of marrying a prince?"

"An Italian *prince," I corrected. "Who loves me and I love him. And you will walk me down the aisle of a huge* duomo. *My dress will be beautiful and white, and I will have a super-long veil decorated with pretty silk vines, just like Mamma had at your wedding. Everyone in Italy will watch and cry and be happy."*

"Good," my papa said quietly.

He put his arm around my shoulders and pulled me close. He smelled of sky and sun and fresh air.

I closed my eyes, and I pictured the wedding dress I would one day wear. I pictured the cathedral, the flowers, the veil of vines . . .

. . . and my dark-haired, handsome prince by my side.

The one I loved with my whole heart. The one who loved me with his whole heart in return.

My happily ever after.

Chapter One

Manhattan, New York
Present Day

Caresa

I closed my eyes as the music pounded through my body. The air was sticky from the mass of bodies on the dance floor. My body swayed to the beat, my feet ached from the five-inch Louboutin heels I was wearing, and my skin was flushed from the copious amounts of 1990 Dom Pérignon I had consumed.

"Caresa!" My name split through the harsh sound of drums and synthesized piano notes. I rolled my eyes open and looked across our cornered-off section of the club at my best friend.

Marietta was sitting on an oversized plush couch, waving a new bottle of champagne in my direction. Laughing, I followed my throbbing feet to where she sat and slumped down beside her. In seconds, a champagne flute was in my hand and the bubbly was flowing once more.

Marietta sat forward, swishing her long blond hair over her shoulder. She raised her glass as though she was going to make a toast. But instead, her bottom lip jutted out into a pathetic pout.

5

I tipped my head to one side, silently asking her what was wrong.

"I was going to make a toast to the Duchessa di Parma, my very best friend," she shouted over a new but similar-to-the-last song. "To my best friend leaving me here in dull old New York to go marry a real-life godforsaken prince in Italy." Marietta sighed and her shoulders slumped. "But I don't want to. Because that would mean this night is almost over, and tomorrow I lose my partner-in-crime." A sudden sadness bloomed in my chest at her words. Then, when her eyes filled with tears, those words became a punch in the gut.

Placing my glass on the table before us, I moved forward and put my hand on her arm. "Marietta, don't get upset."

She put down her own drink and grabbed my hand. "I just don't want to lose you."

My stomach rolled. "I know," I said. Then I didn't say anything else, but I could see Marietta register my unspoken words. *I don't want to go either.*

Keeping my hand in hers, I slumped back against the couch and let my eyes drift over the busy dance floor below. I watched the throng of Upper East Siders losing themselves in the music. A pang of fear swept through me.

This really would be my last night in New York. In the morning, I would fly to Italy, where I would live from that day on.

Marietta shuffled closer to me and cast me a watery smile. "How are you doing?" she asked as she squeezed my hand.

"I'm okay. Just nervous, I guess."

Marietta nodded her head. "And your papa?"

I sighed. "Ecstatic. *Overjoyed* that his precious daughter will be marrying the prince he chose for me as a child." I felt a pang of guilt for speaking about him so negatively. "That was uncalled for," I said. "You know as well as I do, *Baroness von Todesco*" —Marietta scowled playfully at my use of her title— "that we don't really get a choice in whom we marry." I leaned forward and picked up my champagne. I took a long swig, enjoying the feel of the bubbles traveling down my throat. I handed Marietta her glass and raised mine in the air. "To arranged marriages and duty over love!"

Marietta laughed and clinked her glass with mine. "But seriously," Marietta said, "are you okay? Truly okay?"

I shrugged. "I honestly don't know how to answer that, Etta. Am I okay with the arranged marriage? I suppose so. Am I okay with moving to Italy permanently? Not really. I love Italy—it's my home, I was born there—but it's not New York. Everyone I know is here in America." Marietta's eyes softened with sympathy. "And am I okay with marrying Zeno Savona? The infamous Playboy Prince of Toscana?" I took a deep breath. "I have no idea. I guess that will become apparent in the next three months."

"In your 'courting period,'" Marietta said using air quotes, and snorted with laughter. "What a joke. What twenty-three-year-old woman and twenty-six-year-old man need a courting period?"

I laughed at her sassy tone, but then soberly replied, "Ones who don't know each other at all? Ones who have to see if they can stand each other's company before sealing their marital fates forever?"

Marietta shuffled closer. "You know as well as I do that you could hate this so-called prince, detest everything he is—and he you—and I'd still be your maid of honor at your wedding on New Year's Eve." She sputtered a laugh. "The very fact that the date has been set says it all. This marriage is happening." Marietta held up her glass, got to her feet and, with arms spread wide, shouted, "Welcome to the life of the European blue bloods of the Upper East Side! Drowning in Prada and Gucci, dripping in diamonds, but having no free will to call our own!"

I laughed, pulling her back down. She broke into hysterics as her ass hit the couch, spilling champagne all over the expensive upholstery. But our laughter waned as the house lights came on one by one. The last of the dance music drifted into silence, and the rich patrons of Manhattan's most exclusive nightclub began making their way to their limos and town cars. It was three o'clock in the morning, and I had six hours left in the city I loved beyond measure.

We stayed silent as the club emptied. Eventually Marietta rolled her head on the back of the couch to face me. "I am going to miss you so much, Caresa. You have no idea."

My heart broke as Marietta's tears fell hard and fast. Lunging forward, I hugged my best friend. In fact, I gripped onto her for dear life. When I pulled back, I said, "Don't worry, Etta. I'm sure your suitor will be coming soon."

"Don't remind me," she said through a thick throat. "My father already has a list of potential husbands for me. It makes me sick. Expect a call very soon, telling you of the pot-bellied, snobby, pompous lord or duke I've been betrothed to."

I tilted my head. "Well, you're kind of snobby and pompous yourself, you know," I said playfully.

Marietta's mouth dropped open in outrage, before she nodded in defeat and admitted, "Yeah, I kinda am." I huffed out a laugh, but the humor drained from me immediately, lost to my thoughts of Italy.

Marietta's head landed on my shoulder. "I know you're worried, Caresa. But you needn't be. I've seen your prince. As much of an arrogant, slutty tool as he is rumored to be, he's totally gorgeous to look at." Marietta tapped my leg. "And he's getting *you*. Not only are you the sweetest, kindest person I know, but you're equally as beautiful. That dark hair, those huge dark eyes and tanned Italian skin. He's going to be smitten the minute he sees you."

"Yeah?" I doubted that was true. I knew the rumors. Prince Zeno didn't strike me as a man who could get smitten with anyone that wasn't his own reflection.

"Definitely."

Silence stretched until I said, "I'm going to miss you, Etta."

Marietta sighed in agreement. "You never know, maybe I'll be married off to a fellow Austrian baron and sent there. That wouldn't be so bad, because you'd be near."

"No, that wouldn't be bad at all."

"Come on, Princess," Marietta said, getting to her feet. "Let's get you home so you can fly away bright and early to your prince's palace."

I stood and linked my arm through Marietta's. Just as I was about to head outside to my waiting limo, Marietta ran back and grabbed the barely touched bottle of bubbly. She shrugged. "Or we can continue getting trashed in the back of your limo as we take one last farewell tour of Manhattan?"

I smiled, a sense of relief settling in my veins. "That sounds perfect."

An hour later, with my head through my limo's sunroof, Marietta and I drinking in the bright lights of New York, real fear began to set in.

I hadn't lived in Italy since I was six years old. I had no idea what to expect. So I carried on sipping champagne and laughing at Marietta, and I let myself forget about the prince, about duty and tradition.

At least until the sun rose again. When the next chapter of my story would begin.

Chapter Two

Caresa

As my papa's G5 began its descent, I looked out of the window beside me and waited for the plane to break through the clouds. I held my breath, body tense, then suddenly the burnt-orange remnants of daylight flooded the plane, bathing the interior with a soft, golden glow. I inhaled deeply. *Italia.*

Fields and fields of green and yellow created a patchwork quilt below, rolling hills and crystal-blue lakes stretching as far the eye could see. I smiled as a sense of warmth ran through me.

It was the most beautiful place on earth.

Sitting back in my wide cream leather chair, I closed my eyes and tried to prepare myself for what was coming. I was flying to Florence airport, from where I would be swiftly taken to the Palazzo Savona estate just outside of the city.

I would meet Prince Zeno.

I had met him twice before—once when I was four, of which I had no memory, and again when I was ten. The interaction we'd had as children had been brief. If I was being honest, I had found Zeno to be arrogant and rude. He had been thirteen at the time and not at all interested in meeting a ten-year-old girl from America.

Neither of us had known at the time that that our betrothal had been agreed upon two years prior. It turned out that the trip my papa had taken to Umbria when I was eight was to secure a forever-bond between the Savonas and the Acardis. King Santo and my father had planned for their only children to marry. They were already joined in business; Zeno's arranged marriage to me would also strengthen both families' place in society.

I thought back on my New York farewell of nine hours ago and sighed. My parents had driven me to the private hangar and said their goodbyes. My mama cried—her only child was leaving her for a new life. My papa, although sad to see me go, beamed at me with the utmost pride. He had held me close and whispered, *'I have never been more proud of you than I am right now, Caresa. Savona Wines' stock has plummeted since Santo's death. This union will reassure all the shareholders that our business is still strong. That we are still a stable company with Zeno at the helm.'*

I had given him a tight smile and boarded the plane with a promise that they would see me before the wedding. And that had been that.

I was to marry Zeno, and I hadn't protested even once. I imagined to most modern-day women living in New York, the process of arranged marriages sounded positively medieval, even barbaric. For a blue blood, it was simply a part of life.

King Santo Savona died two months ago. The shareholders of his many Italian vineyards, the stakeholders in Savona Wines, had expected his son, Zeno, to immediately step up and take charge. Instead, Zeno had plunged himself into the party scene even harder than before—and that was quite a feat. Within weeks my papa had flown out to Umbria to see what could be done.

The answer: our imminent union.

I knew I had been fortunate—for our social circle—to get to age twenty-three and still not be married. That had been no decision of mine, even though it pleased me greatly. It had all been down to Zeno. The king had wanted his son to sow his wild oats. Get the "playboy behavior" out of his system before we wed. But no one had expected King Santo to pass away so young. We all thought he would be around for many years to come.

It was decided—mainly by my father, Zeno's uncle Roberto and the board of Savona Wines—that Zeno needed to grow up and become responsible. And quickly.

The date for our marriage was immediately set. The board was satisfied.

My stomach lurched as the plane dipped. I opened my eyes, trying to shed the deep unease I felt in my veins, and saw the twinkling view of the Florentine city lights below. I let my forehead fall against the window and stared, unseeing, out of the glass as the plane touched down and parked in the Savona private hangar. Antonio, the G5's air steward, opened the door of the plane and motioned for me to exit. A limo waited for me at the bottom of the stairs. The driver greeted me kindly, and I slipped into the back seat.

Before he closed the door, the driver spoke—in Italian, of course. I doubted I would speak a word of English from that day on.

"Duchessa Acardi, I have been instructed by the prince to take you to the Bella Collina estate."

My eyebrows knitted together. "In Umbria? I am to go to Umbria?"

The driver nodded. "The prince wants you to stay at his most impressive estate. He will meet you there. He has arranged dinner for your arrival." He pointed at the limo's lit-up bar. "The prince has organized refreshments for your journey. At this time of night, we should make it to the estate within a couple of hours. But he wanted you to relax and get comfortable. He anticipated that you would be tired from the journey."

I forced a smile and thanked him. He closed the door, got into the car and pulled away.

Bella Collina? I had assumed I would spend all of my time in the Tuscan palazzo. I'd imagined my days to be filled with nothing but lunches, charitable dinners and meeting the crème de la crème of Italian high society.

I shook my head and pushed my confusion aside. I made myself comfortable on the long black seat and rubbed my fingers along my forehead. I was still feeling the effects of last night. Marietta had made sure that I was sent off with a bang.

I smiled to myself, remembering her passed out in the backseat of the car after our spontaneous tour of Manhattan. I had let her be, relishing my last few moments amongst the hustle and bustle of New York alone.

I thought of Bella Collina. I knew that in Umbria there would be absolutely no hustle and bustle. Florence was a busy city; I had been there many times. But Umbria? It was sleepy and calm, completely serene—but no less stunning than its wealthier, more popular Tuscan cousin.

A true flash of excitement washed through me when I thought of the very exclusive estate in which I would reside. It was home to the famous Bella Collina Reserve. A red merlot wine so rare that the waiting list just to acquire a single bottle was years long, even despite its eye-watering cost. The process of making this wine was never spoken of in the tight-knit wine world. The entire enterprise was shrouded in secrecy. Most sommeliers in the world would sacrifice a limb just to be a witness to Bella Collina's production.

I wondered if I would be so fortunate as to see it.

All Savona wines were good, of course, but they were also mass-produced. The merlot was the shining jewel in their crown.

The more I thought of where I would be staying for the coming weeks, the more my suspicions grew as to why—I was pretty sure it was because the prince didn't want his betrothed "ball and chain" cramping his style on the Florence nightclub scene. He wouldn't be able to bring his nightly conquests to the Palazzo Savona with his *fidanzata* stalking the halls.

I sucked in my breath as I realized that I didn't even care. I didn't care about my future husband at all.

Thirty minutes passed, and I grew thirsty. I retrieved a bottle of *acqua frizzante* from the bar. I had just taken a couple of mouthfuls when I noticed a bottle of red wine that had been left to breathe on the shelf next to the cooler. A single crystal wine glass sat beside it. Then a flash of a familiar—but very rare—label grabbed my attention.

"No," I whispered, lifting the bottle of red into the beam of the limo's ceiling light. A smile tugged on my lips as I read the beautiful calligraphic font spread across the center. I noted the pencil drawing of an idyllic sprawling vineyard in the background.

"Bella Collina Reserve," I murmured quietly and brought the bottle to my nose. I closed my eyes. I inhaled slowly, savoring the unique notes of this exclusive merlot. Blackberries. Dark cherry. Vanilla. Black pepper. A gentle, subtle hint of tobacco.

Warmth filled my chest at the beautiful aromas, and I opened my eyes. I reached for the glass and poured out a small amount of the deep-red liquid. Just as I was about to lower the bottle, I caught sight of the vintage: 2008. Thought by many to be the most important year of this reserve. No one knew why this year changed the wine so much, but experts agreed that from 2008, Bella Collina Reserve went from being a fine wine to one of the world's greatest.

With this vintage as a gift, Prince Zeno was bringing out the big guns.

I sat back and took a tentative sip. The minute it hit my tongue, I immediately felt at home.

My family knew wine; it was our business. And I knew this reserve; it was my dream flavor. My favorite. A wonder to me. Over the years my palate for wine had grown strong. I had visited hundreds of vineyards, some of the best in the world, yet nothing could compare to this. As far as wines went, it was perfect.

By the time we had turned off the main thoroughfares and traveled along a winding road that led to an impressive stone entrance, I had managed to drink two glasses. The speaker linking me with the driver sprang to life. "Duchessa, we have arrived."

I opened the window beside me and stared at the illuminated entrance. I swallowed hard and placed my empty glass on the bar. Metal groaned, breaking through the twilight, as the massive black wrought-iron gates began to open. The limo slowly pulled onto the property's lane, and I drank in the thick forest that shielded the estate. I inhaled the freshness of the lush green trees. The unpolluted sky was thick with stars—not a single cloud in sight.

A few minutes later, the thick woods cleared, and I gasped. Acres and acres of gold and green vineyards covered the landscape. The scents of plump grapes and damp soil permeated the warm air. I closed my eyes. It reminded me of being a child. It brought me back to the days before I was taken to New York. I could still feel the heat of the Emilia-Romagna sun on my face, the deep smell of olives, grapes and flowers drifting in the breeze as I ran around our Parma estate.

I smiled a nostalgic smile and allowed my eyes to drift open again. I rested my arms on the window and leaned my chin on them as the limo drove on. There were several small villas peppered over the landscape, their lights twinkling in the distance. They must have been the winemakers' residences. It was not only the Bella Collina merlot that was made on this land; other reds were too—particularly the Chianti from the region's finest Sangiovese grapes. The Bella Collina olive oil was also up there with the best. But nothing compared to the famed merlot.

The limo turned right, and my breath caught in my throat. I lifted my head and stared disbelievingly at the property ahead. Bella Collina was a veritable Palace of Versailles tucked away in the Umbrian wilderness.

"*Mio Dio*," I whispered as I took in the imposing stone structure, the sweeping steps and the vast number of windows set in the building's walls. Large pillars of red-veined marble flanked the entrance. Cypress trees framed the estate as if it were the shining star of a fine Renaissance painting. Sculptures of famed Savona monarchs of old stood proudly on the manicured lawns, and strategically placed lighting illuminated the sheer perfection of every piece of topiary.

As a child, I had been to the Palazzo Savona in Florence. It was widely regarded to be one of the finest estates in all of Italy, if not western Europe. But this . . . this . . . there were no words. It was perfectly placed, as if it had always been there. As if it had grown naturally from the Umbrian earth just as sure as the vines and woods that kept this architectural treasure hidden from view.

The limo rounded the corner and glided to a halt. I took a deep breath as I looked up at the house that sat high above, made only grander by the many levels of stairs leading to its front door.

The driver appeared at my window and opened the door. He held out his hand, and I forced myself to abandon the safety of the car. The soothing sound of rushing water hit me first. A huge, ornate water fountain occupied a central position in the wide driveway. I had not seen it from my side of the limo. I walked toward it. The crest of

Savona assumed pride of place, towering like a spear thrust from the center, spotlights adorning the intricately carved marble shield with layers of soft light.

Lost in its ornate design, I turned only when I heard the sound of footsteps descending the main stairs. A man dressed in a dark suit slowly approached. The driver immediately stood to the side of me, dutifully, waiting for the gentleman.

"Is that . . . ?" I trailed off. The driver's reaction betrayed it was someone of importance.

"Prince Zeno," the driver finished for me. "Yes, Duchessa."

The prince approached at a leisurely pace, like a man who was used to people waiting for his arrival.

From this distance, I could barely make out his features, but the closer he got, the clearer they became. And Marietta had been right. He was extremely handsome, the epitome of Italian beauty. His black hair was thick, brushed over to the side and styled to perfection. His skin was olive and clear, his face cleanly shaven. His tailored navy-blue suit was most certainly designer, and it fit his lean, muscular body like a glove. I could see why the rumors of his handsomeness had reached the circles of the New York Italian gossipmongers.

When he was but a few feet from me, his blue eyes met mine. His jaw clenched briefly, as if he was fighting discomfort—*or forcing himself to be here,* I thought—but then a blinding smile pulled on his lips and a confident façade settled on his exquisite features. "Duchessa," he said warmly, bowing politely before reaching for my hand. Such was the duty of any aristocratic man; he gently brought the back of my hand to his mouth and grazed his lips across the skin.

He released my hand, and I dropped into a curtsey. "Principe."

When I stood, Zeno's blue eyes were watching me closely, roving down over my fitted knee-length Chanel dress and down to my Prada heels. His gaze rushed over my shoulder-length hair, which was styled straight and parted in the center. On the plane, I had applied a dusting of light makeup, finishing the look with a bold red lip. Five-carat Tiffany diamond studs sparkled in my earlobes—classic Italian glamor.

His eyes finished their journey, and I caught a slight flaring of his nostrils. A nervousness washed over me. I may not have had a long history of relations with men, but I could recognize one who liked what he saw. The knowledge should have pleased me. It surprised me to find that I was simply . . . indifferent.

Zeno's mouth hooked into a small smirk. Behind him, a few men dressed in the typical housekeeper uniforms of black pants, white shirts, black vests and smart black ties came down the stairs. Wordlessly, they moved to the trunk of the limo and retrieved the few suitcases I had brought with me.

"The belongings you had shipped arrived yesterday. They have already been put away in your room." The prince pointed to the men now carrying my bags. "These too will be ready for you within the hour."

Prince Zeno extended his elbow, gesturing for me to thread my arm through his. "That gives us time to eat the dinner I have had prepared to celebrate your arrival."

I gave him a tight smile and linked his arm. We had only taken three steps when I said, "Oh, excuse me a moment." I rushed back to the limo, grabbed the half-full bottle of Bella Collina merlot and hurried back to the where the prince was waiting.

His eyes narrowed as he noticed what I held. I felt my cheeks warm and explained, "2008 is such a special vintage of this wine. I couldn't let it go to waste. Especially because of how much it costs."

Prince Zeno smiled. "Your father mentioned your love of our most sought-after wine." *Ah*, I thought, *that explains it being left for me.* I wondered what else my father had schooled him on to impress me. "We can have the rest with the meal," he added.

Zeno pushed out his elbow once again. I linked my arm through his and let him lead me up the steps. With every step ascended, I couldn't help but look out over the gardens, to the rolling hills in the distance.

"What do you think, Duchessa?" Zeno asked, bringing my attention back to him.

I shook my head, searching for something to say. I could not quite put the beauty of this magical place into words. "It is . . . beyond anything I could ever have imagined."

"It is quite something," Zeno agreed.

"How many acres do you have here?" I asked.

"Bella Collina has just under ten thousand."

"That much?"

Zeno shrugged. "A great deal of that land is woods, orchards and olive trees for the oils. And, of course, the vines. About five thousand are used for the wines." I cast my eyes over the vast land below. "Most of our vineyards around Italy are of a similar size." He paused, then said proudly, "Though none produce wine like Bella Collina. Whether it be the soil here, the weather, or a mixture of both, no other winemaker in the world can compete."

I nodded in agreement. "So you spend a lot of time here?"

Zeno tensed momentarily, before schooling himself. "Not so much. The palazzo in Florence is my home." He cleared his throat. "My father . . . he spent much of his time here."

At the mention of the king, I felt a rush of sympathy. Pressing my free hand to Zeno's arm, I said, "I am so sorry about your father, Zeno. It must be difficult for you right now."

Zeno's blue eyes flicked down to me for a second before focusing back on the final set of steps. "Thank you. He spoke highly of you." Zeno's jaw clenched. Nothing else was said on the matter. It was obvious the subject was painful for him.

Silence reigned until we reached the house. I stopped and stared up at the mansion. "It is breathtaking."

Zeno waited for me to stop my admiration before gesturing toward the open doors that led into the house. The minute I entered the lobby, my eyes widened. Above was a domed roof, which reminded me of the Florence Duomo, the beautiful cathedral where our wedding would take place. Rich golds and reds adorned the walls and furniture. And in the center was a grand staircase, split into two. Impressive crystal chandeliers hung like diamonds from the ceiling, bathing the room in golden light.

But best of all were the oil paintings of all the Savonas of Italy. I walked to the long wall and smiled at the old monarchs who had shaped Italian history. It ended with a new painting: Prince Zeno. He stood in a proud pose, staring off to the side, the angle showcasing his strong jaw and dark features.

I turned away, stopping in my tracks at the sight of the huge painting that covered most of the wall. It was of a small vineyard nestled into the side of a hill. I moved closer. The vines ran in rows, green and browns, bustling with ruby-red grapes, thick and ripe. In the distance was a small villa. No, it was better described as a gray stone cottage, like something pulled from the pages of a fairytale—a hidden sanctuary tucked away from the busy world. An old-fashioned lamp shone above its door, welcoming anyone who approached.

I didn't know why, but I couldn't tear my eyes away. I was so entranced by the serene beauty of this small piece of heaven that I didn't notice Zeno had moved beside me until he spoke. "It was my father's favorite painting. He would spend hours looking at it." He shrugged. "I have no idea why. It is of a shabby villa in the middle of a field, only fit for paupers."

My stomach rolled at the hint of sadness in Zeno's voice. He must have felt my pity, because he immediately cleared his throat and gestured for me to follow him. He led the way through an ornate golden archway to another large room where several people in housekeeping attire stood waiting.

Zeno moved to my side and placed a hand at my back. "This is the Duchessa di Parma," he said to the estate's staff. "Duchessa, these are the people who keep Bella Collina in pristine condition, the men and women who will make your stay here comfortable."

I nodded and made sure to look each employee in the eye. "It's very nice to meet you all." I gestured around the beautiful room we were in. "You do an excellent job of maintaining the estate. I have never seen anything like it in my life."

The men bowed and the women curtsied at my compliment. Zeno placed his hand on my back again and steered me through a set of glass doors and out onto a large patio. The warm breeze rippled through my hair. To my right was a dining table set for two.

I made my way toward the table, but stopped when I saw the view. "Beautiful," I murmured as I moved to lean against the stone balustrade that bordered the patio. Beyond was a panoramic view of the vineyards, acres and acres of full and blooming vines. The moon hung low in the sky, bathing the countryside with its pale blue hue.

I heard the sound of a chair scraping stone. When I turned, Prince Zeno was holding the chair out for me to sit. Tearing myself from the view, I walked to the table and sat down. Zeno moved opposite and pointed to my hand. "Are you going to let go anytime soon?"

I stared at him blankly, unsure what he was talking about, until I saw that I was still clutching my bottle of Bella Collina Reserve. A surprised laugh burst from my mouth. I placed the bottle on the table. "I didn't even realize I was still holding it."

"Clearly you *do* like the vintage," Zeno replied with a hint of humor in his voice.

"I don't think *like* is a strong enough word."

"Then I'm glad I brought you to this estate," he said softly.

An awkward silence descended. Fortunately it was interrupted by a female server bearing water and a bottle of white wine. She made to take the merlot, but I put my hand over hers to stop her. "I shall drink this." She bowed and poured out the wine with an expert hand.

The next few minutes were occupied by servers bringing bread, Bella Collina's homegrown olive oil and balsamic vinegar, and finally our appetizer of *insalata caprese*. The servers excused themselves.

Once again I was alone with the prince.

Inhaling deeply, I scanned the grounds and the trellis climbing up the ancient stone walls. I shook my head.

"Something wrong?" Zeno inquired.

My eyes snapped to his. "No," I said. "This is all just . . . so surreal."

His head cocked to the side as his bright blue eyes focused on me. "The marriage?" he asked. His voice was tense, as if he were forcing the words.

I lowered my head and played with the stem of my wine glass. "Yes. But not just that." I pointed to the vineyard, the mansion, the food. "Everything. Being here is testimony to fact that the monarchy's abolition may as well never have happened. You are still the prince to these people. These magnificent grounds are worthy of a ruler."

"You are the Duchessa di Parma. You are not so unused to this life either." I looked at Zeno to find a single, challenging brow raised in my direction.

"I know that. Believe me. As a child in Parma I was always at royal functions. In New York, it was more so. We were the exotic Italian aristocrats who lived on Fifth Avenue. We were even more under the microscope, if that is at all possible."

Zeno sighed and tipped his head back, eyes focused on the blanket of stars above. "It is our life. The titles, the status of monarchy may have legally been revoked, but we both know we shall always be *someone*. You cannot erase that much history from a country in such little time." He batted his hand. "There will always be rich and poor. And whether they like to admit it or not, the lay public love to have a royal line to admire, to wonder what our lives are like and to look up to." He let out a short, dismissive laugh. "Or hate, as the case may be. The monarchy is officially gone, yet look at us—a dethroned prince and an American-raised duchessa arranged to be married by our fathers. You can't get more medieval than that."

I swallowed, and realized I felt a sudden kinship with Zeno. He didn't want to marry me either. I saw by his expression that he too acknowledged we understood one another . . . perfectly.

"Well, to those in our strange little world, you are about to become king."

Zeno seemed to pale. He sat straighter in his seat. "Yes," was all he could muster in response.

"I think my parents dream of coming home to Italy one day. They love New York, but home is always home." I tried to fill the suddenly tense air with idle chatter—it was a much better alternative to strained silence.

"The duke has taken our business to a level my father could never have dreamed of by moving to America. I know that my father understood the sacrifice your father made by becoming the distributor of our wines for North America." Zeno fidgeted with the napkin on his lap. "And now we must start again, from scratch. My father's passing brought unease to the investors. King Santo, the great king of both Italy and the vines, died, and the competitors that have always been pushed aside have reared their heads. They are already stealing business from us left, right and center—it began mere days after my father's death." His jaw clenched. "It seems the usual buyers don't think my father's Midas touch with wines has been passed on to me. I apparently make them nervous. Your father is holding down the fort as best he can in America. Italy is down to me."

I knew everything he said was true. It was not so much his father's passing, rather it was Zeno's reputation as a lothario and party socialite that required our swift union. He said the buyers weren't sure of him. I wasn't either; I was certain my father felt the same. Zeno was completely untested. Of course, I could not voice these thoughts out loud.

"However, you are here now. A Savona and an Acardi to make the business strong again." *And to convince the investors and buyers of the same thing*, I heard in my mind.

"Yes," I said. This time I had nothing left to say. I took a bite of my caprese. "I am to stay here for the duration of our courting period, not Florence?"

Zeno took a long drink of his wine. "I thought it would be best."

I narrowed my eyes in suspicion. "And you are to stay here too?"

Zeno met my eyes. "I have much business to attend to in our estates all over the country, many crisis talks to attend. I will often be absent. There is much to do now that I've been strapped tightly into the driver's seat."

"That would be a 'no,' then," I said, a sharp edge to my tone.

Zeno dropped his knife and ran a hand over his face. This time when he looked at me, there was no pretense. All I saw was agitation and frustration on his handsome face. "Look, Caresa." He paused, gritting his teeth, then continued, "We both know this whole marriage is for the business. It's nothing new in our world. Marriages have always been based on social bonds and securing family ties in Europe, since the beginning of time. Nothing has changed. I'm a royal, you're a duchessa. Let's not pretend this is anything beyond what it is—a contract to ensure that stability is clearly demonstrated to our business partners, and a solid, appropriate marriage for those in our social circle." He gestured to the house. "Ancestral money can only get us so far. To keep these estates thriving, we need money by modern-day means. There are no tithes or bribes bringing in the coin. We do what we must to survive and keep our lineages alive. Wine is our key. You and I joined in marriage is what will calm the stormy waters our families have found themselves in."

Zeno sat forward and took my hand. "I am not saying this to be cruel. But you seem like an intelligent woman. Surely you do not believe this charade is about *love*."

I laughed. I truly laughed as I removed my hand from his. "I don't,

Zeno. I am very much aware of what this 'charade' really is." I leaned forward too. "And seeing as I have just finished my master's degree in educational psychology from Columbia, I assure you, your assessment of my perceived intelligence is well-founded."

A smirk pulled on Zeno's lips. "Educational psychology?"

"Yes." I bristled. "Had this marriage not been arranged and I wasn't a duchessa, it is what I would have devoted my life to. Helping children—or adults—who have learning difficulties. Any problem can be overcome; we just need to find the best way for each person. I would have either worked in that field, or something with horses."

Zeno sat back in his chair, looking every inch the royal prince that he was. "Maybe I have underestimated you, Caresa."

"Maybe?" I retorted.

He studied me closely and said in a low voice, "You are extremely beautiful."

I tensed, unnerved by the sudden change of topic. He observed me closely, seemingly amused by my cautious expression. "We are a good match in every way that counts," he said. "Looks, money, status. We both could have done worse."

I laughed. Loudly. "So you believe yourself to be very handsome?"

Zeno took another sip of his wine. "There is no need for false modesties, Caresa. I'm very much of the opinion that we should always say exactly what we think. In private, of course. We both have reputations to protect."

The server came to clear our plates and, for the next hour, the prince and I talked about trivial things. It wasn't unpleasant, yet by

29

the end of the meal, my stomach was in knots. I hadn't expected a fairytale with this arrangement. For us to instantly fall in love the moment our eyes met. But neither had I expected things to be so clinical. So . . . cold and matter of fact.

When the last of the cannoli dessert had been eaten, I lowered my napkin and announced, "I am tired. I think I'll go to bed." I gave the prince a tight smile. "It's been a really long day."

Zeno got to his feet and offered me his arm once again. I threaded my arm through his, the warmth of his skin radiating through the fine thread of his suit. He watched me warily out of the corner of his eye. He was trying to decipher if he had genuinely hurt me. He hadn't, of course. I was just numb. Immobilized by sudden waves of sadness.

Zeno led me back through the house, up the steps of the left staircase and down a wide hallway. Imposing crystal chandeliers hung from the Renaissance-inspired painted ceilings. I wasn't sure how far back this home went, but it wouldn't have surprised me if those ceilings had been the work of Michelangelo himself.

The red carpet was plush and soft under my feet; the air was permeated with the fragrant smell of roses. That was no surprise when every six feet or so a large vase of the white flowers stood proudly on a glass table.

Zeno stopped at a set of gilded double doors at the end of the hallway. "These are your rooms."

I inhaled deeply. Forcing a smile onto my face, I looked up at him. "Thank you for dinner."

He gave a curt nod and, in the gentlemanly gesture that had been instilled in him, took my hand and brought it to his lips. He laid a gentle kiss on the back of my hand. "Sleep well, Duchessa. I will not be here when you wake. I have business to attend to in Florence."

"How long will you be gone?"

Zeno tensed, then shrugged. "I could be gone for many days. Maybe a week or two. Or more, depending on how things turn out." He sighed. "It is the wine harvest from this week, Caresa. I must go to the vineyards and show my face. I must show an active interest in all our vineyards. Then there are all the meetings with buyers."

I gave a tight smile of understanding. I knew the harvest was the most important time of the year for Savona Wines. Of course I did. It was when my papa was busiest in the US—securing buyers, promoting the new vintages, attending awards ceremonies, celebrations and dinners.

Zeno didn't look enthusiastic about his duties. Also, he did not ask me to accompany him. That fact had not escaped me.

"Okay," I murmured and turned to open my door.

"You will have some dinners and fittings, etcetera," Zeno said. I looked at him over my shoulder. "The festive season is almost upon us. We have several engagements to appear at together: the annual Savona grape-crushing festival, the winter masked ball, and . . ."

I wondered what he was struggling to say. Zeno rocked on his feet then cleared his throat. "And the coronation dinner."

Zeno's eyes met the floor. The coronation—his ascension to king. Of course, he was not yet the king. He was not really a prince anymore. But in our society, he was now *our* king, or soon would be,

31

after the coronation.

"Will that be here?" I inquired.

Zeno ran his hand over his forehead. "Maybe. I have not yet set a date, but it must happen soon. It" —he took a sobering breath— "it has all happened so quickly that I have not yet had time to contemplate arrangements. Business must come first."

He waved his hand theatrically in front of his face, signaling the end of the conversation. "I've kept you far too long." He began to walk away. "I will see you soon. Maria will be your personal secretary. She will inform you of all the engagements we have coming up and organize your new clothes, fittings for the ball, dinners and, of course, the. . . *our* much-anticipated wedding."

I gave a quick nod and went into my room, shutting the door behind me. I leaned against the coldness of the golden panel and closed my eyes. I counted to ten, then opened my eyes.

The rooms before me were no less grand than the rest of the estate. I walked through the large living space, taking in the elegant white-and-gold walls, running my fingers over the beautiful pieces of furniture. A large doorway led to a bedroom that boasted a huge antique four-poster bed. Floor-to-ceiling French windows opened onto a balcony with a view of the vineyards. But what I loved was that in the far distance I could see the picturesque town of Orvieto. For some reason, I knew it would make me feel less lonely.

The bathroom was luxurious, with its claw-foot tub and rain shower. My closet already contained my clothes. My toiletries, perfumes and cosmetics were already at the vanity.

There was nothing left to do.

Catching sight of the moon through the balcony doors, I walked outside and leaned against the balustrade. I breathed in the freshness of the air, only to hear the sound of a car crunching on gravel. A black town car was disappearing into the distance.

I expelled a humorless laugh. The prince was hurrying back to Florence.

He wouldn't even stay a single night.

Feeling exhausted, I took a shower and climbed into bed. As I reached over to the nightstand to turn off the light, I noticed a picture hanging on the wall beside my bed. A woman, dressed in a regal purple dress, posing for the painter. I didn't know why, but my eyes were glued to her image. She had the darkest of hair and beautiful brown eyes.

She was radiant: a former queen of Italy.

As my eyelids drooped, pulled down by the lure of sleep, I wondered what her life had been like as Queen of Italy. I wondered if she spent days here in the royal country estate.

But my last thought, as my eyes closed and my world turned to dark, was . . . was she ever happy?

Chapter Three

Caresa

Maria, my secretary, was just rising from her seat as I walked from my bedroom into the living area. I had been at Bella Collina for three days. In those three days, I had been fitted for evening wear and taken to lunches with the aristocrats of the Umbrian area, although not many resided this far out of Florence. And there was still no word from Prince Zeno.

Maria frowned when she saw me in my running leggings and long-sleeved top. I had thrown my hair up into a high bun and wore absolutely no makeup.

"I feel the need to get out of this house," I said as I sat down to tie the laces of my sneakers. "I need a run in the fresh air."

"Very well, Duchessa." Maria gathered her things. "I would keep to the garden paths if I were you. The harvest has begun and the vineyards are busy."

I nodded and walked toward the door; Maria followed behind. "I'll be gone for the next several days. I am needed in Assisi. You don't have anything pressing until your first ladies' luncheon." She cast me a wide smile. "You have time to relax and get to know the estate. The grounds are beautiful, and there will be lots to see."

"And the prince?" I asked, mainly because I thought I should.

Maria shook her head. "He has had to go to Turin today. I don't know when he will get back." She pressed her hand on my arm. "His father was a workaholic. I would prepare yourself for his son to be the same."

We reached the main doors and stepped out into the crisp fall air. Maria kissed me on each cheek then bade me farewell.

I cast a glance around the pathways and decided to go left toward the surrounding forest. I turned on my phone, put in my earphones and let the up-tempo beats of my jogging playlist hit my ears. I pushed my feet as fast as they would go, heart slamming in my chest with the sheer freedom of the run.

I thought back to yesterday. Maria had given me a stack of glossy brochures to look through. There had been no formal proposal, no engagement ring, yet the wedding preparations were already underway.

I ran and ran until the pathway gave out. It looped, trying to tempt me back to the mansion, but I wasn't ready. I looked beyond the pathway. All that lay ahead were fields of vines.

In an instant, a flash of memory from my childhood came rushing back to me. Of me running through the vineyards in my Parma home, leaves kissing my outstretched fingers as I passed. I picked up my feet and ran through the rows of vines. I tilted my head to feel the midday sun on my skin.

Song after song played. I kept on running, my speeding feet keeping time with the beat of the music. I ran so far that when I stopped for breath and looked around me, I realized I had absolutely no idea where I was.

I flicked the earbud headphones from my ears and tried to listen for signs of life. I could hear the harvest continuing in the distance, but nothing close by. I rose to my tiptoes, scouring the area for any sign of activity. Nothing but fields with their rows of green lay before me. Except for what looked like a small cottage about three hundred yards away.

Walking to the end of the row, I made my way toward the cottage. Hopefully someone would be home.

As I walked, at a slow, steady pace, a sense of peace settled over me. Out here, amongst the vines, I felt a sense of freedom I had not experienced since I was a child. The past three days had been a mixture of jet-lag and duty. Sleep hadn't come easily, and more than that, I was homesick. So very homesick that it felt like a hole had been carved into my stomach. My parents were excited for my upcoming wedding, so I hadn't told them how I felt. Marietta, however, had immediately seen through my façade. She told me the only thing she could—that I had to keep strong.

The ground began to slope upward. I trudged forward until I could see the cottage better. I stopped where I was and blinked. The vines that I had found myself among had ended. A plain grass field stood between me and another field of vines, but that field was protected by a large wooden fence.

Forcing myself to keep moving, I noted that this field of vines was much smaller than the others I had seen on the Bella Collina estate. Yet the vines were fuller somehow, different; the soil was a deeper color.

I edged around the fence, trying to see if anyone was there. I could see that the majority of the vines were around the back of the stone cottage. Checking no one was near, I walked through the small wooden gate up the path of a pretty, well-kept garden. Though small, the garden was bursting with vibrant colors, browning from their summer hues into the golds and oranges of fall. A trickle of water flowed from an old water mill at the side of the old cottage.

By the time I arrived at the stable-style red door, I was mesmerized. The place was straight from a fairytale. I stilled, my eyes drinking in the garden and the small quaint building.

I gazed at the Alice-in-Wonderland view. "The painting," I murmured. This place . . . this nook of heavenly peace was the painting from the main house. The one that graced the lobby.

"It was my father's favorite painting . . ." Zeno had said.

I was standing right before it.

I knocked gently on the door, but there was no reply.

Following the garden path that led to the back of the house, I continued to be awed. The back of the house was no less enchanting than the front. An oak deck graced the rear. From there I could see the mansion in the background. And if I was not mistaken, the view looked onto my rooms. It was far away, little detail could be made out, but I was sure that's what it faced.

Even though I now knew the direction of the main house, my feet kept moving. An imposing barn-type structure sat just beyond a sprinkling of tall trees. I narrowed my eyes but was unable to see exactly what it was, so I kept going.

Next to the barn was a fenced paddock with two wooden stables at its edge. A smile tugged on my lips when I spotted two horses grazing. If there was one thing I loved as much as the wine industry and psychology, it was horses. I had competed for years in show jumping and dressage competitions. In fact, I was the Hampton's dressage champion for five years running.

One complaint I'd had over the past few years at college was not being able to ride as much as I'd have liked. When I reached the fence, I clucked my tongue in my mouth, trying to coax the horses to join me. The one closest to me raised his head. The black gelding looked at me, his ears flicking back and forth as he tried to figure me out. "Come here, baby," I called, leaning forward when he carefully began to approach. He was at least seventeen hands, with long white feathers cascading down to his large round hooves. He had a thick neck and solid, heavy legs. If I wasn't mistaken, he looked to be a mixture of Shire and what could be Friesian. He was absolutely beautiful. His mane was long, a deep glossy black. It had a slight wave to the strands, as did his tail. When he stood before me, I held out an open hand, allowing him to huff and sniff my skin. After a few seconds, he ducked his head and gave me permission to pat his neck and rub the center of his head.

I laughed as he nuzzled my hand. The dull sound of a second set of hooves drew my attention. A slightly smaller, leaner horse drew up at the fence. My heart soared. She was an Andalusian—my favorite breed of horse. Better still, she was dapple gray. I had never seen a dapple-gray Andalusian in the flesh. Years ago I had a black Andalusian, Galileo. As a young girl, he had been my life. I had had him until he died just a few short years ago. I had been with him as the vet put him down, stroking his neck and laying kisses on his face when he had failed to stand up for the last time.

To many he was just a horse, but losing him had broken my heart.

This Andalusian mare was bigger than Galileo, perhaps fifteen-three hands, with a stronger, more robust frame. But she was no less beautiful than Galileo had been. Looking at her brought tears to my eyes.

It was funny how memories could sneak up on you and bring the most hidden, dormant emotions to life.

"Hello, little lady," I said as the mare allowed me to run my hand over her nose. "You're so beautiful. You remind me of someone I used to love very much." Her platinum mane and tail shone like molten silver in the bright sunlight. The long waves hung down to the top of her flanks. "What's your name?" I asked. Her nose searched for food in my hand. There was a stone bench beside me. On it were some already-sliced carrots. I took a few in my hand and fed each of the horses with my palms stretched flat.

The black gelding came further forward. I had earned his trust. I kissed him on the nose and asked, "What is this place, huh?" Realizing I had no more food to give them, the mare and gelding sauntered back to the center of the paddock to graze. I watched them for a while, then I noticed a small but full tack room to the left of the stables. *So someone rides them*, I thought. These two horses were exceptional breeds, expensive too. For them not to be ridden would be a travesty.

I glanced around, searching for any other kind of life, but none was present. I left the paddock to recommence my investigation, ducking under the low-hanging branches of the surrounding trees until my view of the rest of the land was unobstructed.

I gasped. Rows and rows of full-to-bursting vines were spread out before me, just like the ones at the front of the villa. There were only a handful of acres—maybe eight or nine—but the ripe grapes gave off an incredibly strong, heady, addictive musk. The fragrance of the fruit in this particular corner of the estate was much more potent than elsewhere.

It was quite simply the most beautiful sight I had ever laid eyes on—a landscape worthy of the finest oil paints and canvas. I could see why the old king had been so taken by this vista—a piece of heaven tucked away from prying eyes.

Pressing on, I walked along a small man-made path beside the high wall of the barn until I reached the main doors. They were locked. I exhaled, disappointed.

Just as I was about to walk away, I suddenly heard the distant melody of familiar notes drifting on the gentle breeze. I turned, following the lively sound of a chorus. I was three rows deep into the private, cornered-off vineyard before I recognized the music that seemed to be coming from the center of the field—Verdi.

I inhaled deeply as the *Dies Irae* from Verdi's *Messa da Requiem* filtered through the surrounding leaves. My heart beat faster. Being

from Parma, Giuseppe Verdi's masterpieces sang in my blood. Some
of my favorite memories were of me, as a child, in the Piazza
Garibaldi in the center of Parma, attending the opera with my family.

I followed the music until it led me to an old silver cassette player
sitting alone in the middle of a row. The music was straining from the
dirty, scratched speakers. I frowned in confusion as I stood beside it.
Who even owned a cassette player anymore, let alone cassette tapes?

Then, through the thick foliage, I saw a flicker of movement from a
few rows over. Someone was moving, presumably a worker bringing
in the harvest on this comparatively small plot of land. The breeze
around me chose that moment to pick up, and it grew colder, the fall
chill beginning to close in. I wrapped my arms around my waist,
trying to fight off the cold. I passed one row of vines, then two . . .
and when I reached the third, I completely froze in my tracks.

A man stood about twenty feet away. He was facing away from me,
but I could see that he was tall with broad shoulders and a tapered
waist. He had messy black hair and deep olive skin. He wore heavy
brown work boots, and a pair of worn jeans on his long, muscular
legs. I stood, mesmerized, as he reached up to a high vine to his left.

With meticulous concentration, he examined the bunch in his hand.
He ran his fingers over each grape, feeling the weight of the bunch in
his palm. Next, he leaned in and smelled the fruit. Finally, evidently
happy with whatever he was testing, he brought up the set of
secateurs in his hand and cut the bunch from the vine. He placed it
delicately on top of the already brimming bucket at his feet. The man
straightened, slowly rolling the strain from his neck. He tipped his

head back and drew in a long breath, pausing to take in a lungful of the crisp early-afternoon air. A shiver ran down my spine at the sight of his slightly sweaty skin shining in the bright sunlight.

Then I completely stilled when he bent down to lift the bucket . . . and turned directly to face me.

I was sure the wind was rippling gently and that time had not completely stopped, yet in that very moment, as my eyes gazed on a beautifully rugged face, I felt as if it had. A strong angular jaw sporting scruffy black stubble, smooth tanned skin lying over sculpted cheeks, one showcasing a small scar, and plump pink lips— they all stole my breath. But, most striking of all were his almond-shaped eyes . . . the brightest, bluest irises peeking from under long black lashes . . . eyes that I quickly realized had landed straight on me.

The man had stopped in his tracks, the bucket of grapes slung over his shoulder, hanging heavily down his back. His impressive biceps were tensed with the strain of the weight . . . and so were his almost-turquoise-blue eyes as they remained transfixed, in surprise, on me.

Swallowing hard, I forced my mouth to open and words to pass my lips. "Hello," I offered weakly, my throat still rough and dry from my run. I winced at the slight shake in my voice. The man did not move.

Clearing my throat, I took a step forward and pushed a smile onto my lips. The man's eyes crinkled slightly in suspicion. Unraveling my arms from around my waist, I said, "Sorry to disturb you. I found myself slightly lost and saw your house. I came to ask for directions, and" —I laughed nervously— "found myself mesmerized by your vines, gardens and horses." The man still didn't speak. He had not moved one hairsbreadth. I filled the silence with more nervous chatter. "You have the most beautiful home." I blanched. "I mean, I didn't go *inside* your home, I promise. I meant the building itself—the gray stone, the red roof—and the garden . . . and your horses. I just love horses. I used to ride competitively—" I cut myself off, gritting my teeth to shut myself up.

Taking a long, controlled breath, I walked the last few steps forward until I stood right before him. I held out my hand. "I should have started with an introduction. My name is Caresa. It's nice to meet you."

The man's blue gaze, which had been so firmly fixed on mine, dropped to my outstretched hand. I watched as his Adam's apple bobbed in his throat and his already flushed-from-work cheeks seemed to grow a little pinker.

This close, I could feel the heat from his skin radiating across the cool air between us. I glanced up and noticed, again, how tall he was. Maybe six-four? He was an inch or two taller than Zeno. And he was definitely broader than the prince. His torso was packed with muscle, and there was a scattering of dark hairs on his chest. There was not a part of him that wasn't muscled, but not in the manner of a body-builder. This man was fit, lean and toned, not bulky. He . . . he was . . . *breathtaking*. There really wasn't any other way to put it.

His sudden shift of movement caught me by surprise. The man, without looking at me, slowly lowered his bucket to the ground, dropped the secateurs and carefully straightened up. He wiped his dirtied palm on the worn jeans that hung low on his waist. A sharp, defined *V* led the way to his waistband. I felt heat rise to my cheeks as I noticed it.

Then his hand pushed out, and I stared at it as his warm skin met my palm. His rough fingers gently encased my own, and he said quietly, timidly, "Hello, Caresa. My name is Achille, Achille Marchesi."

His deep baritone voice wrapped softly around the syllables of my name. He shook my hand once, then let go.

"Achille," I repeated and gave a small smile. I looked into his eyes, finding him watching me with a nervous gaze. A thick strand of his black hair had fallen over his forehead, the ends covering the top of his left eye. "It's very nice to meet you," I said and wrapped my arms around my waist again.

He stood on the spot, head down, obviously not knowing what to do or what to say. "Your home," I repeated, "is extraordinary."

"Thank you," he replied. His head tipped swiftly upward, and he looked surprised at the compliment.

Achille glanced away for a moment. When he looked back at me, he said, "You are the Duchessa di Parma, yes?"

"You have heard of me?"

"We all—the workers here—were told of your imminent arrival. About your marriage to the prince." He drew in a breath. "That you would be staying here until the wedding."

"Ah," I replied. I didn't know why, but I didn't want to talk about that right then. Today was the first reprieve from this arranged marriage I'd had in three long days. I wanted the moment to continue. It was nice to talk to someone who wasn't advising me about luncheons or etiquette. Achille pointed into the distance. "The main estate is back that way. If you leave here and turn left, there is a direct path to the house. The grass is well worn from years of use, so it will guide you home safely."

"Thank you," I said. Achille turned and picked up the bucket of grapes. Spontaneously, I asked, "You are a winemaker?"

Achille must have assumed I had walked away, as he startled at my question. He looked at me over his shoulder, his dark eyebrows drawn down, and nodded. He lifted the bucket to his back again and gave me a stiff smile as he walked by. I closed my eyes in exasperation. *Caresa, what are you doing?* I asked myself. *He obviously wants you to leave.*

But I didn't listen to the voice in my head. Instead, I watched him walk, back tensed, toward the barn. When he disappeared from view, I took a final long glance at the vineyard. Seemingly he was only a few rows into his harvest. The first section was clear of grapes, but the rest of the vineyard was brimming.

A bird called out her song from a towering tree beside me. Her high-pitched notes snapped me from my thoughts, and I pushed my feet into action. I walked through a cluster of trees until I was back at the barn and stables. To my right, I saw Achille reappearing through the barn doors. The gelding in the paddock whinnied and trotted toward him. I watched as the merest hint of a smile pulled on Achille's mouth. My heart surged at the sight. It beat even harder as he moved to meet the horse, rubbing his hand over the gelding's nose, pressing a kiss to his head.

I took a step, my foot breaking a fallen branch on the ground. The sound echoed like thunder in the quiet surroundings. The gelding looked my way, quickly followed by Achille. He blinked, once, then twice, his questioning blue gaze not helping my racing pulse.

I cleared my throat. "A beautiful horse you have there," I called and approached him.

Achille nodded in agreement, his hand slowly running up and down the horse's neck.

When I stood beside him, I reached out to rub the gelding's nose. "What breed is he?"

Achille swallowed, ducking his head slightly, and answered, "His father was a Shire and his mother a Friesian."

I smiled and let out a single happy laugh. Achille's hand stopped on the gelding's neck as he watched me. The weight of his stare was heavy, and it caused a flush to sprout on my cheeks. "Sorry," I said, flustered. "I just guessed that mix when I saw him earlier."

Achille smiled at me briefly, minutely, but the small glimmer of amusement crossing his face was enough to launch a swarm of butterflies to swoop in my stomach. The silence stretched between us until the mare came over. In a way that only horses can, she pushed her head between us and nudged Achille's arm with her nose.

I laughed again, louder this time, as she flicked her hoof against the fence. "Rosa," Achille reprimanded, his voice raspy, yet deep in tone. His displeasure didn't last long. He sighed and ran his hand over Rosa's dapple-gray neck.

"And an Andalusian," I said. The gelding stepped back to give Rosa her turn with Achille and came over to me. I patted his neck, the heat from his coat warming my chilled skin.

"Yes. Purebred."

"I had one too. A black gelding." I paused and pressed a kiss to the gelding's nose. "He was my favorite horse." I felt Achille's eyes on me. I glanced up, and our gazes met.

"Was?"

"He passed away a few years ago."

Achille nodded and averted his gaze.

"And what is his name?" I asked, pointing at the gelding.

"Nico," Achille replied. "He's mine. The one I ride, I mean."

"You ride?"

"Yes," he said. "Mainly to check on the vines. Cars and trucks can affect the soil, so I ride." He shrugged. "I prefer it anyway."

I studied him, finding myself wishing he would speak more. He was incredibly shy and timid, that was for sure. I found it curiously endearing. In my life I had met very few men who were introverted and shy. Most were powerful, full of confidence, and, in some cases, full of their own importance.

Most behaved exactly like the prince.

"And who rides Rosa?" I asked. The movement was slight. If I hadn't been watching, I would have missed it. Achille's hand froze on Rosa's neck the second the question left my lips.

He inhaled deeply, then said softly, "My papa used to. She was his."

Was. The word stood out to me. *She* was *his.*

"I'm sorry for your loss," I said after a moment.

Achille's hand fell from Rosa, and he flashed me a tight, grateful smile. "I need to get back to work." I saw by the look in his eyes that he didn't know what else to say to me. Didn't know how to act around me.

"Okay," I said and, with a final kiss to each horse's nose, backed away from the paddock toward the path leading out of the garden. Achille was standing tensely, his eyes flickering to mine and then the ground. "It was nice to meet you," I said and waved my hand.

Achille didn't respond straight away, but then said, "You too, Duchessa." No sooner had he spoken than he turned and entered the barn. I sighed, feeling slightly disappointed. I would have liked to have seen what was in the barn, even talked to him about wine. But anyone could see he was not the type who engaged easily in conversation.

I left the garden and closed the kitsch wooden gate that framed Achille's house so perfectly. Just as Achille had directed, the well-worn path was there to guide me home. I jogged all the way back, only this time I did not listen to music. My mind was preoccupied with replaying my meeting with Achille.

My heart kicked in my chest as I pictured him. His shy, handsome face, his sculpted body—he was incredible. The dirt on his hands and the sweat on his skin only added to his appeal.

As I reached the doors of the mansion, I shook my head. I could not think of other men any longer. I was here to be married, not on a vacation. I was betrothed to Zeno, and that was that.

48

I went into the house and to the stairs to my rooms. I had just put my foot on the first step when a flash of color caught my eye. I walked over to the painting of the stone cottage and studied it closely. It was most certainly Achille's home. Though now I had seen it in the flesh, I realized that, as talented as the artist was, he could not do the picturesque scene justice.

"Do you like it, Duchessa?" I glanced to my right and saw one of the housekeepers smiling at me.

"Yes," I replied. "Very much."

The older woman nodded. "It is almost as beautiful as the wine itself, and nearly as sweet as the winemaker who lives there." As the housekeeper turned to walk away, her words sank in.

"What?" I asked abruptly. The housekeeper turned to face me. "What do you mean 'as beautiful as the wine?'"

"The merlot, Duchessa. Bella Collina Reserve." My heart fired like a canon in my chest. The housekeeper smiled. "This is the home of our famous merlot's winemaker. It has been in the same family for years. The son runs it now."

"Oh," I whispered. My eyes drifted back to the painting. I wasn't sure if the housekeeper was still there or if I was alone. Blood rushed through my veins, and my lungs strove to take in air. I stood as still as a statue, hypnotized by the painting of the small house, fairytale-meadow garden and full-to-bursting vines that surrounded it.

And I thought of Achille. Achille, amongst the vines, hand-harvesting the grapes with such deep passion in his eyes and such intense concentration on his face . . .

49

"Bella Collina Reserve," I whispered to myself. "Achille makes the Bella Collina merlot . . ."

I wasn't sure how long I stood there, staring at the painting. Eventually I returned to my rooms. I ran a bath and climbed in, letting the hot water envelope me and calm me with its lavender-scented vapors.

Achille was a private man, of that much I was certain. I didn't know anything else about him. But I sensed he had been uncomfortable with my presence, at my unwanted intrusion into his world.

I knew he would not expect to see me again. But as I closed my eyes and envisioned that small private vineyard and the beautiful man who ran it, I resolved to return.

I told myself it was to speak to the man about my favorite wine, to see and understand the process, to ask the many questions I had.

As Achille's blue eyes danced through my mind, I ignored the truth in my heart—that I also wanted to speak to this man again because of him. Not just the wine, but him.

I allowed myself to pretend the opposite.

I was betrothed to the prince.

I was marrying Zeno.

This was only about the merlot.

Nothing more.

Chapter Four

Achille

I stood in the center of the barn and listened carefully. She didn't move for a while, but then I heard the sound of her feet walking away. When her footsteps faded to silence, I headed out of the barn and turned right, walking through the trees until I was at the perimeter fence of my vineyard. The duchessa cast one last look at my home then followed the track toward the main house of the estate.

She was dressed all in black, her dark hair pulled back in a bun. She started to run, and in a couple of minutes she had disappeared down the valley, only for her distant silhouette to appear again five minutes later as she ran up the hill toward her home.

I leaned against the fence and watched until she was gone. My eyebrows pulled down. People hardly ever came to this part of the vineyard. The king had been strict with the other workers about where they could go—my small patch of the estate was strictly off-limits to most.

The king was always terrified someone would discover the secret of our merlot. So for years it had only been my papa and me. When Papa died seven months ago, it left only me. I didn't mind my own company so much. I had never been one for friends, and what little family I had lived in Sicily. I only saw my aunt a couple of times a year. The last true friend I had stopped speaking to me when I was younger, and I had come to the conclusion that he was only my friend because he lived on this land and there was no one else around the same age. Very few people had come by since.

That was just how it was.

Nico neighed from the paddock, the sound reminding me that I had to get back to work. But with every step I took, all I could do was replay the last hour. *That was the Duchessa di Parma. That is who the prince is marrying.*

Several weeks ago the prince's secretary had gathered the staff and told us of the upcoming marriage. I didn't know what I'd expected of the duchessa from America, but I hadn't expected her to be so . . . so . . .

I sighed, wiping a hand down over my face, shoving those thoughts far from my mind. My hand fell to my side, and I went into the barn. The oak barrels that the new wine would be aged in were stacked and ready for the end of harvest. I had only just begun to collect. The weather this summer had delayed the grapes' development slightly. If there was one thing my father had taught me, it was that the grapes could not be picked until they were absolutely perfect. I was a week or two behind where I expected to be, but the extra time had given me the most promising bunches of grapes I'd had in years. And considering the recent vintages were regarded as the best, I felt a heady rush of excitement swirl in my blood at the prospect of the most excellent wine this year's harvest might bring. It was the first year I would be completely alone in this endeavor, no experienced voice guiding me.

It both terrified and excited me.

I began tipping the buckets of grapes into the stomping barrel. By the sixteenth bucket, my stomach was growling. I cut off a hunk of the Parmesan cheese that was on the table beside me and drizzled aged balsamic vinegar over it. I also grabbed the last of the bread Eliza had brought me yesterday. Eliza was a housekeeper at the main house and the wife of one of the oldest winemakers on the estate. She and her husband, Sebastian, had been my father's best friends. Ever since his passing, Eliza had made sure my pantry was always stocked with food. Especially during the harvest. I had little or no sleep for a good few weeks each October, and things like food came second to the winemaking process.

But I loved it.

I lived for this time of year. Everything led up to this point. This was when I was most content.

This was when I felt most alive.

I inspected the grapes again as I ate, making sure each was perfect. As the sun began to descend in the sky, I poured the rest of the grapes into the barrel, only stopping when the final bucket was empty.

Kicking off my boots, I cleaned my feet, rolled up my jeans and stepped into the barrel. The grapes immediately began to split and spill their juice. The stems were hard under my feet, but they were essential to making the darkest, deepest red wines.

Many minutes passed by, and the minutes changed into hours. Once the grapes had been crushed, I felt my muscles begin to ache. They ached liked this at the same time each day, when I had pushed my body to the maximum.

I jumped from the barrel and cleaned my feet. For the next few hours, I pressed the wine and began the process of fermentation.

I looked up out of the doors to see a sea of stars shining in the cloudless sky. The moon hung low, illuminating the water from the sprinklers as they sprayed the vines. It was a light show of silver threads, green leaves and red fruit.

Bringing my hand to the back of my head, I walked out of the barn and closed the doors tight. Nico and Rosa saw me come out and immediately headed for their stables, knowing what was to come. I jumped over the paddock's fence, grabbed their buckets of feed from the tack room and carried them to the stables. The horses quickly ducked inside. I filled their water and put out some hay. When I came back, Rosa was standing in my way.

"Hey, beautiful," I greeted her, running my hands over her ears and along her neck. Rosa stood as calm and still as ever. That was all down to my father. He had a way with horses that I never would. Nico was mine; I rode him every day. Rosa was too small for my build, so she had to make do with being lunged and schooled in hand.

As Rosa walked away, I felt a deep pit burrow in my stomach. She seemed so lonely and lost without my father. As if she knew her purpose was exhausted with him gone. We used these horses for work in the fields. Without my father, Rosa was lost.

Her and me both.

Papa had trained her in dressage, spent time with her every day making sure each move was perfected and polished. I was sure Rosa missed dancing across the paddock with my father on her back. I had no such skill with which to help.

A wave of guilt crested in my chest.

I just love horses. I used to ride competitively . . .

I blinked as the duchessa's words suddenly came forward, drifting through my mind. I thought of her big brown eyes and soft smile as she had talked to me about Rosa and Nico. Remembered the awe and sadness in her voice as she spoke of her old horse.

I looked down at my bare arm. Shivers had broken out along my skin. I didn't feel cold, but the temperature *had* dropped, so I rationalized that must have been it.

I left the paddock and made my way home. Solar lights lit my way along the garden path. When I entered the cottage, I walked straight to the fire and threw on some newly cut logs. My muscles ached and I needed heat. As the fire sprang to life, I shed my clothes and climbed into the old shower. The hot water relaxed my tense neck and shoulders. The scent of burning wood hung in the air. I didn't move, head hanging forward, until the water turned tepid, then freezing cold.

I threw on some sweatpants, let my wet hair drip-dry and made some coffee in my moka pot. I took some ready-made fresh pasta from the fridge and poured myself a glass of my 2010 merlot.

Before I sat down to eat, I put a new vinyl on my father's old record player. When the needle scratched the vinyl, Verdi's *La Traviata* came crackling through the ancient speakers.

For a moment, as the opening bars filled the quiet of the room, I stared across at the single wooden chair beside the fire. Once there had been another opposite. If I closed my eyes, I could see my father sitting, reading his book—out loud to me, as always—his favorite opera playing in the background. From when I was a young boy, we had sat beside that fire each night after a hard day's work, and he had read his favorite stories to me. From the classics—my favorite being The Count of Monte Cristo, his being Sherlock Holmes—right through to fantasy—my favorite was The Hobbit, and his was The Lord of The Rings. But his absolute favorite, and my absolute favorite too, was philosophy. He would talk to me of Plato and Aristotle and their philosophies on love. He would talk about my mother, who he loved beyond measure. And he would talk about how she was the other half of his soul.

He would tell me how, one day, I would find my other half too.

Since he had been gone, the old house seemed devoid of life. The single, now solitary, chair beside the fire sat just as lonely as my heart.

I opened my eyes and stared into the climbing red and orange flames. I blinked away the sheen of tears from my eyes, refusing to let them fall.

The music reached a crescendo, and I went back into the kitchen to retrieve my food and wine. I brought them back to the front room and sat down on the seat before the fire. I ate my food quickly, then washed and put away the single dish.

Feeling exhausted, I turned off the lamps in my small home one by one. I made my way to my bedroom and, as I did every night, sat on the edge of my bed. With a deep breath, I pulled out the envelope from my nightstand and opened the back. As carefully as possible, I pulled out the three-page letter. With shaking hands, I let my eyes rake over the perfect cursive writing, studying every single word. And like every night, as I scanned each page, I felt my heart break in two.

A lump rose to my throat, and I felt like I couldn't breathe.

I inhaled deeply and skirted my fingers over the paper before folding it back up. I put it in the envelope and placed it back in its drawer. I got under the covers and turned out the lamp. The dark sky was visible through my open shutters, and I stared up at the bright stars beyond. The sound of the horses huffing and walking around the paddock met my ears, as did the whirring of the sprinklers watering the vines. As I closed my eyes, tiredness sneaking in, I found myself picturing a pair of large, kind brown eyes, and a soft, gentle laugh catching on the breeze.

Curiously, the image momentarily displaced the sinking-pit feeling in my stomach that had burrowed within me seven months ago, and made it easier for me to breathe.

*****

The sun had barely risen the next morning when I tackled the next row of vines. I had just filled three buckets when the sound of rustling leaves filled the two-second pause of the cassette player as it changed songs. Noticing a flicker of movement to my left, I looked up, only for the air to freeze in my lungs.

The duchessa appeared at the end of the row, wearing similar black fitness clothes to yesterday. Her lips curved into a smile as she gave me a small wave. I got to my feet, my heart thundering in my chest.

Why is she here? I thought as I dusted off my dirtied hands on the thighs of my jeans.

The duchessa approached, and the closer she got, the more I noticed a strange expression on her face. It appeared to be one of disbelief. Or perhaps awe or . . . I wasn't sure.

"Hello again," she said. She leaned in and ran her hand over the vines beside us. Her fingers padded along the leaves and grapes as though they were made of gold, as though they were most precious things in the world.

"Hello," I replied, confusion at her presence thick in my voice. The duchessa smiled wider when she looked back at me, and I saw a faint blush light up her olive-skinned cheeks. Her brown eyes were bright, and strands of her dark brown hair had escaped her high bun. I liked it. It made her look less . . . regal. Less important.

I waited nervously as she rocked on her feet, her skintight fitness clothes showing off her slim but curvy figure.

"You're probably wondering why I'm back," she ventured. I brought my eyes back up to meet hers. Her gaze dipped under my attention, and she shook her head, a self-deprecating laugh escaping her full pink lips. It only served to confuse me even more.

"Are you okay, Duchessa?"

She straightened her shoulders. "It's Caresa. Please call me Caresa, Achille. I hate being called 'Duchessa.' The title hasn't truly existed for over a century anyway, not really."

I nodded, not knowing what to say. The duchessa—no, *Caresa*—batted her hand in front of her face and took a deep breath. "You're probably wondering why I'm back?" she repeated, her eyes fixed on my face as if trying to read it. I showed no emotion. I couldn't if I wanted to. I was too busy staring at her pretty, flustered face. Her nervousness strangely brought a lightness to my chest.

I wondered why.

"You are lost again?"

She laughed softly. "No, I admit I'm not that good with directions, but thankfully I'm not so bad that I'd forget the path home after a day." She rubbed her forehead, looking as if she was anxious about something. "Look, I'm terrible at getting my words out at times. But"—she stepped closer and searched my eyes—"You're him, aren't you?" she asked, voice barely above a whisper. "Last night, when the housekeeper told me about this place . . ." She paused. "I didn't realize *this* was *it*. That *you* were *him*."

I looked around us; I had no idea who she thought I was. "I . . . I don't understand," I said, watching Caresa's blush intensify.

"I haven't been very clear, have I?" She covered her eyes with her hand in embarrassment. She lowered it again and said, "Achille, you are the maker of the Bella Collina Reserve merlot, yes?" It seemed as though she already knew the answer, but there was definitely a hint of a question in her tone.

"I . . ." I began and then stopped speaking. The king had always asked for my father's and my discretion regarding our wine. He never wanted anyone to know about this small vineyard and the Marchesi family that produced it. But as Caresa's open, expectant face froze, awaiting my response, I could not lie.

I . . . her face . . . she . . . she made me not *want* to lie.

"Yes," I whispered, heart racing fast.

Her reaction was immediate. Caresa's whole face lit up with an incredibly joyful smile. For a moment, I thought I was overcome with finally telling a virtual stranger about this vineyard, but as I stared at her dark features, feeling further and further drawn in by her impossible beauty, I knew that wasn't it . . .

. . . it was . . . *her.*

She was exquisite.

She was lovely.

She was . . .

I turned away abruptly, desperate to escape her attention and my wayward thoughts. My heart was stuttering simply by being beside her. I wasn't used to these feelings.

I wasn't used to this kind of attention from anyone, period.

"I can't believe it," Caresa murmured from behind me. My shoulders stiffened. The next thing I knew she had walked around me. I reluctantly met her eyes with my own and was taken aback by the intensity of the fascination I saw there. "Achille," she murmured. My name sounded like a prayer from her lips. "I can't believe I'm actually here, with you."

"Me? Why?"

She reared back, a furrow marring her brow. "My father is part-owner of these vineyards, and even he does not know who makes the Bella Collina Reserve. As the child of a wine distributor, specifically of the Bella Collina merlot, meeting you is . . ." She shook her head. Her gaze lowered, and then, shyly peeking up at me through her long lashes, she said, "Achille Marchesi, I have three loves in my life: psychology, horses and wine." She shrugged, and the adorable action almost destroyed me. "Especially the Bella Collina merlot. There is nothing like it for me. It is, in one word . . . " She paused, then proudly announced, "Perfection."

I wasn't sure what kind of reply that praise warranted.

Caresa waited for me to speak. When I did not react, she cast a long gaze around the vineyard. "I can't believe I'm standing in the vineyard where the merlot is made, grown and nurtured." She reached out to touch a bunch of grapes beside us. "You hand-harvest all of these?"

"Yes," I replied, watching with assessing eyes as she delicately lifted the fruit in her hand. I wanted to see if she knew what she was doing. That question was answered when she said, "These are not ready yet, are they? I can tell by the color of their skin. They are not a deep enough red?" Her eager face looked to me for confirmation. I studied the grapes in question, then felt a small smile pull on my lips. "You are right."

"I am?" she said breathlessly.

I nodded.

"Achille?" Caresa asked. "Do you do all this alone? The picking, crushing, fermenting, bottling . . . everything?"

A sudden stab of pain sliced through my chest. I cleared my throat and rasped, "I do now."

Sympathy flooded her pretty face. She did not push me for a longer answer, for which I was thankful. The truth was, I had been on my own for the past two years. With his illness, Papa hadn't been able to do much of anything except advise. He had been too ill to attempt manual labor, but he was always there beside me, instructing me, keeping me in check. I never realized how much I had relied on his advice until he was gone.

Life for me now was just so . . . silent.

"How can you be sure they are ready?" Caresa asked, pulling me back to the here and now. "The pressure to make such a sought-after wine must be so difficult to handle."

I shrugged.

"It isn't?" Her eyes were wide as she waited for my answer. Her black lashes were so long that they were like fans as she blinked, her cute nose twitching as a loose strand of hair tickled the tip.

I could scarcely look away.

"No." I bent down and took a bunch of grapes from the bucket at my feet. I plucked off a single grape and held it out. "This is ready. I know this by the shape, the weight, the color, and by the taste."

"How do you 'just know?'" she inquired, studying the grape in my hand as if it were the world's most unsolvable puzzle.

"Because these grapes are my life. My grandfather was the original winemaker of this vintage, then my father, and now me. I do not use machinery in any part of the process because everything I know is kept here." I pointed to my heart, then to my head, then to my roughened hands. "There has not been a day in my life when I have not been out here with these vines, harvesting or producing the wine. It is all I have ever known. This vineyard . . . it is my home, in every sense of the word."

Caresa's smile came slowly to her mouth. And when it did, I was trapped in her pull, fascinated by the golden skin on her cheeks. "This is your heart's passion. Your *why* in life," she said, her voice little more than a whisper.

I thought of the happiness I found out here each day, knowing there was nothing else in the world I would rather be doing. In fact, without this vineyard in my life, I wasn't sure what my purpose would be, how I would find peace and joy.

"Yes."

"It's why your wine is the best. Passion fused with knowledge always births greatness."

A sudden warmth burst in my chest at her words. *Your wine is the best . . .*

"Thank you," I said honestly. A heavy silence followed. I needed to get back to work, but I did not want to be rude by walking away. As I tried to make myself speak, to explain, I realized that I didn't really want her to leave. Shock rippled through me. I lifted my hand and ran it through my hair.

"Achille?"

I dropped my hand to my side.

Caresa's eyes went to the bucket of grapes at my feet, then back to me. "Could I . . . would it be possible, if I . . . helped?"

Taken aback, I clarified, "You want to help harvest the grapes?"

Caresa smiled and nodded. "I have always wanted to understand your wine. How it is made, the process." She took a deep inhale. "I would be honored to see you work."

I glanced down at my dirty hands and my even dirtier jeans. I allowed myself to look Caresa over. "You will not remain clean," I warned. "It is messy work. It is hard work."

"I know," she replied. "When I lived in Parma when I was young, or when visiting for the summer, I helped in our family's vineyard. I know the effort it entails." I was surprised by the quiet hard edge to her voice. She was the aristocracy. I did not know many people of the upper class, but the ones I had met or seen were not the type of people to spend their days in the fields, working from sunup to sundown.

Caresa must have taken my silence for refusal. Her arms wrapped around her waist, and the flash of hurt on her face was almost my undoing. "It's fine, really," she said and forced a smile. "I understand. It is a sacred process, and a secretive one to boot." She shook her head and moved past me. "I shouldn't have asked."

She made her way toward the end of the row of vines, and I found myself saying, "You are the duchessa. You are the lady of the house. This will soon be your land. You may do as you wish."

Caresa stopped dead in her tracks. Her back tensed. Her shoulders stiffened, then dropped, and she looked back at me, her bright eyes dulled. "I would rather you agreed not because I am the future wife of the prince, but because I am a genuine lover of wine and utterly fascinated by you and your work." My stomach rolled at the sound of the sadness in her gentle voice. She looked so small and fragile.

Then I remembered that she had not long arrived in Italy from America. Maybe she knew no one either.

I had no experience with this type of situation. I had upset her. I could see that. I never wanted to make anyone sad.

I averted my eyes to stare at the ground beneath my feet. "Then please stay."

I heard Caresa's quick inhale of breath. When I looked up she was watching me closely. I rocked on my feet. "I will show you. Not because of who you are, but because you want to know and love my wine."

Caresa didn't move for several seconds. As color filled her cheeks and a happy smile returned to her face, she walked back and stopped before me. "So where do we begin?"

Confused by the heady feeling of blood pumping fast around my body, I turned and dragged the bucket at my feet to the next section of vines. Caresa was instantly by my side. I bent down and leaned in to a bunch of grapes. As educated by my papa, I studied them, feeling their weight, gauging their color.

The feeling of her warm breath sent shivers down my spine, bringing goose bumps to my skin. My hands froze on the grapes as the warmth hit the back of my neck. I turned around; Caresa was very close, watching me over my shoulder, fascination clear in her expression. At my movement, her eyes fell from my hands on the grapes and collided with mine.

I didn't move.

Nor did she.

We just stayed still, breathing in the same air.

A gentle breeze skated over her hair, blowing the loose strands across her face. The wind broke whatever spell had been cast on us. Caresa moved back. She pushed her hair from her eyes and, red-faced, apologized. "Sorry, I was trying to see what you were doing."

I cleared my throat, ignoring the pulse slamming in my neck. "Checking the quality of the fruit," I explained. Shifting to allow her closer, I pointed to the grapes. "Please, come closer."

Caresa didn't hesitate, taking only a second to crouch beside me, concentrating on my hands. The breeze blew over her hair again, and the scent of peach and vanilla filled the air.

"You are checking the coloring and weight?" Caresa asked, unaware that I was staring at her . . . that my heart was beating too fast. Her skin was flawless, so soft and pure. Her hair was dark and shiny like the finest Perugian chocolate.

Caresa turned to face me, and I immediately refocused on the grapes. "Yes." I lifted the bunch in my fingers. "They must be heavy. It means they are full of juice and should hold the perfect amount of sweetness. The red skin must be deep in tone, with no patches of lighter flesh."

Caresa nodded, drinking in my every word. A surge of something unrecognizable took hold of me as she listened, as she learned . . . as she shared in this with me. I pulled my hand back from the grapes. "Would you like to feel them?"

Caresa's eyebrows rose, but she quickly nodded, eager to be taught. She placed her hand underneath them. "How should I do it? How will I know what I'm looking for?"

I was unsure how to explain it. I had to show her. I had to guide her.

Feeling my cheeks flood with heat, I brought my hand under hers and, with my palm and fingers, guided her to the grapes. I leaned in closer, so close that our cheeks were only a few centimeters apart. "Feel the heaviness in your fingers," I instructed. "Allow your fingertips to press lightly into the flesh to test its fullness." Caresa gently, and with an innate delicacy, did as I said.

"Like this?" she whispered, *sotto voce*, as if the very sound of our voices might disturb the grapes, currently so happy at home on the vine.

"Yes." Guiding her hand further, I slipped my fingers to a single grape and, taking hold of one of her fingers, used it to rotate the grape in a circle to check the coloring. Caresa was as methodical and patient as the task required, extra-careful not to snap the precious fruit from its stem.

"It's perfect," she murmured and turned her face toward me. She blinked, once, twice. "It is, isn't it? Perfect?"

"Yes," I rasped, unsure if my reply was referring to the grape or to her.

Caresa's breath hitched. "So it is ready to pick?"

Using the hand still on hers, I took the grape from its stem. "The last test is the taste." I placed the single grape in the palm of her hand. Taking another grape for me, I brought it to my mouth and bit into its fleshy ripeness. The burst of intense sweetness immediately told me what I needed to know.

Caresa watched my every move, then as I tipped my head toward her in encouragement, she took the grape into her mouth. Her eyes widened when the taste hit her tongue. A light groan left her throat, and she momentarily closed her eyes. When she swallowed, she opened her eyes and whispered, "Achille . . . how do you make them taste like this?"

"What did you notice?" I asked, fascinated by her first experience with the process.

Her eyebrows pulled down in thought, her cheeks hollow as she examined the aftertaste in her mouth. "Extremely sweet. Juicy and soft," she said. "Is that right?"

I felt a flutter of pride for her and could not help but smile. "Yes. This means these grapes are ready."

A happy laugh slipped from her lips as she stared at the grapes. "I see now," she said reverently. "I see why you do this by hand. Machines could not give you these moments, could they? They cannot measure what our senses are capable of telling us." Her gaze met mine. "I truly see it, Achille."

I nodded curtly, tearing my eyes from her elated face. I took the secateurs from the bucket. "Would you like to cut them?"

"Yes, please," Caresa said. As before, she let me guide her hand with my own. My arm brushed hers as she took the grapes from the vine. Pulling back, I dragged the bucket near to where she crouched. As carefully as she had performed everything else, she laid the grapes down on top.

She exhaled deeply, then with fire in her deep brown eyes, asked, "And now we do it again?"

My lip hooked up into a smirk. "I must get through three rows by the end of today."

"Then I can most certainly help with that," she said, her voice laced with excitement.

I shuffled along to the next bunch, Caresa my eager shadow. And just as before, I talked her through every step. Ever the perfect student, she readily absorbed every word and every movement. As I watched her eat another grape, assessing the taste and texture, I couldn't help but think that my father would have loved her. He wasn't a complex man. He never understood why people complicated their lives. He loved me, had loved my mother and loved what he did. But as much as that, he loved these vines.

His heart would have swelled if he could have seen Caresa, the future mistress of this land, share so passionately in his life's work.

"They're ready," Caresa said, pulling me from my musings. I took a grape from the same vine, just to make sure she was correct. As the intense flavor graced my palate, the sweetness levels at their peak, I turned to a silent, watching Caresa. "You are right."

I sat back as Caresa cut down the bunch and placed it in the bucket.

And for the next three hours, her smiles came frequently as she sorted the ripe grapes from their unripe neighbors.

With Pavarotti playing in the background courtesy of my father's ancient cassette player, we completed the three rows ahead of schedule. And for the first time in seven months, I realized how much I enjoyed not doing the harvest alone.

It was . . . nice for someone to share in these moments.

And I liked Caresa's smiles.

They were almost as sweet as the grapes.

Chapter Five

Caresa

I stood up, stretching my aching muscles. My legs shook from being crouched down for so long. Yet, despite the aches and pains, I felt good. Better than I had in a long time.

The sound of boots on the ground approached from behind me. When I turned, Achille was walking toward me. He had taken the last bucket of grapes to the barn. I had stayed behind to make sure no bunches of grapes on the row had been missed. They had not. I hadn't really thought Achille would have made that kind of mistake anyway.

His eyes were on me, and as I looked up our gazes clashed. Achille swiftly turned his attention to the ground and ran his hand over the back of his neck. I noticed he did that when he was nervous. Throughout the morning, Achille had mostly kept quiet. He wasn't one to waste his words. Everything he said was direct and offered with purpose—an instruction or explanation or, my favorite, praise that I had done something right. But there was no awkwardness in our lack of conversation. Words had not been needed. In the silence, he displayed his greatness. At times, I had been utterly taken aback by how much he knew about wine, how carefully and beautifully he cared for each precious step. It felt as if noise and idle chatter would have only soured the process.

I didn't know his age. He didn't look much older than me, maybe twenty-four or twenty-five. But what he knew about the harvest was astounding.

There was no doubt that Achille was beautiful. I thought so even more now, his bare torso glistening in the bright sunshine, his dark stubble shadowing his chiseled face. But more attractive still was the love he devoted to his work. In the few hours we had spent out here in the field, I saw more of his heart than he could have ever have expressed in words. His cheek would twitch with pride when I did something right. His nostrils would flare slightly, eyes drifting to a close, long lashes kissing the tops of his cheeks, when he savored a perfectly flavored grape. His lips would purse slightly in concentration as he felt a bunch in his rough palm, eyes cast away so he could simply *feel*. His trust in his instincts showed him the way. He was simplicity incarnate, yet simultaneously so complex. I wanted to get inside the mind of this maestro of viniculture. Wanted to hear his thoughts out loud.

Wanted to understand what true greatness felt like.

"Are . . . are you hungry?" Achille asked, dragging me back to the present.

I opened my mouth to speak, and my stomach growled. I couldn't help it. I laughed, placing my hand over my stomach. My laughter caught on the breeze and echoed around the vineyard.

Achille was staring at my mouth, his lips slightly parted. The sight quickly sobered me. I schooled my expression, and Achille seemed to snap out of whatever trance he had been in.

"I have food." He turned on his heel, heading toward the barn. I followed, wondering why my laughter had held him so captive. As I passed through the low-hanging trees toward the barn, I noticed the horses grazing in the paddock.

When I entered the barn, my eyes widened at the sight. Barrels were packed high, rows and rows stretching along the vast space. The barn seemed large from outside, but inside it was huge. To the side were a couple of fermenting vats, and beside them an old basket press. I shouldn't have been surprised to see that all his tools were made of wood. In modern-day winemaking, all tools had generally moved toward the mechanical. Presses were mostly pneumatic. This made the process quicker, easy to handle, with consistent and measurable results.

Quicker production equaled more profit.

Wooden equipment and hand-harvesting were viewed by many as unnecessarily traditional. I had never been persuaded. To me, the old-fashioned ways showed true human skill, using one's knowledge and judgment over computers and gauges. It showed that the winemaker cared for his craft, nurturing his wine like parents nurtured their children.

A poetic, revered existence, in my book.

A chair leg scraped on the stone floor behind me. I looked over my shoulder; Achille had dragged a rickety chair from a curtained-off corner of the room. He placed it before a small wood burner then took a rag and began brushing off the thick dust that had gathered on the seat.

When he had finished, Achille motioned for me to sit. He took two dishes from a wooden countertop at the side of the room, and placed them on the table beside us. My stomach groaned. "Arancini," I exclaimed. "They're my favorite."

Achille brought over two glasses of wine. One look at the deep red color, one sniff of the oaky scent, and I knew instantly what we were about to savor. "Your wine," I murmured and tentatively took a sip. My eyes closed as the heavenly taste burst in my mouth.

When I opened them again, Achille was watching intently. His hand was rigidly gripping the stem of his wine glass. I licked my lips. "It doesn't matter how much I drink it, I am still enraptured by its taste."

Achille glanced away, taking a sip of his own drink.

"What year is this?"

"2011," Achille replied, setting down his glass. He handed me a fork.

"Thank you." I groaned as I took a bite of my arancini. Shaking my head, I declared, "Why does everything just taste so much better here in Italy?" I took another bite; it tasted even better than the first. "I swear my mamma is an amazing cook. My nonna was even better. When we moved to New York they cooked just as much as they ever did in Parma, but nothing, *nothing*, ever tasted like it does here."

"It is Italy," Achille replied. "The soil, the earth. There is just something in our land that makes everything taste superior."

"Have you ever been out of Italy?"

"No, but I cannot imagine anywhere is more beautiful or magical than our home. You cannot improve on perfection."

His words caused my heart to melt. "No," I agreed. "I suppose you can't. I have traveled to many countries and places, lived most of my life in America, but I'm beginning to realize that nothing compares to Italy. I have been homesick since I arrived, but it I think it's more for my family and friends than Manhattan's skyscrapers and ever-present noise."

We ate the rest of our food in silence. Achille collected the dishes and took them to a small sink. He took two espresso cups from a high cupboard, and from his moka pot he poured two *caffè*. Just as he placed them on the table in between us, I saw a stack of newspapers on a workbench along the barn's wall. My stomach lurched. Staring up from the top paper was . . . me.

I quickly rose from my seat and picked up the faded newspaper. Chippings of wood had settled over the top—the newspapers had obviously not been read. I blew off the debris and saw myself at last year's New Year's Eve ball in Manhattan. I had a tiara on my head and wore a silver beaded Valentino dress. It was a fairytale-themed costume ball. This cleverly taken picture had made me look every inch the aristocrat.

I read the headline: "A Princess for a Prince."

I hadn't realized I had groaned out loud until Achille coughed behind me. I turned and held up the paper. "Have you read this?"

Every muscle in Achille's body seemed to tense before he silently shook his head. I checked the date—it was from last week. "Other winemakers would often bring newspapers here for us to read. My father used to read them every day when he was sick. We couldn't get out much over the past year due to his illness. I think people keep bringing them now out of habit."

I sighed and returned to my chair. Once I'd slumped down, I looked at Achille, held out the paper, and said, "Would you read it and tell me what it says? I hate reading anything about myself in the press. I avoid all articles about me or my family if at all possible. But I want to know what the Italian papers are saying. Whether it's good or bad."

I didn't know why, but a sudden tension materialized between us until it became stifling. Achille's bright blue eyes were huge, the whites stark in the low light of the windowless barn.

"Achille?" I asked, leaning forward. "Are you okay?"

He nodded, but his paling face made me think otherwise. I was about to push further when he shakily took the paper from my hands and sat on the edge of his seat. I watched, concerned, as his eyes flicked over the text. His eyebrows pulled down in concentration as he began reading the long piece. I drank my coffee and waited anxiously.

"It . . ." Achille eventually said through a thick throat. "It just talks about the prince, and how in the aristocratic circles he will now be seen as their king. It talked about how you were coming back to Italy and would be staying at this estate until the wedding."

I frowned, wondering how a journalist from Florence knew that the prince had planned to bring me here, rather than the Palazzo Savona in Florence as predicted. Achille stood up abruptly, throwing the paper in a large trash can. He headed for the doors of the barn.

He stopped dead, hands clenched at his sides. "I have completed my three rows of vines for today. I will not be crushing the grapes until tonight." All of a sudden, he was acting strangely distant. He looked at me still sitting on the chair and curtly dipped his head. "Thank you for your help today, Duchessa. I hope I've answered all of your questions about the wine, but I have much to do this afternoon and cannot be delayed any further."

With that, he swiftly left the barn, leaving me alone and speechless. *Duchessa*, I thought, hearing the faint sounds of the horses moving outside and a gate being opened and closed. He had called me Duchessa. He had addressed me as Caresa all morning . . . until just now.

What just happened? My stomach caved slightly as I replayed his words. They were a dismissal. He wanted me gone.

I got to my feet, hurt by Achille's unexplained behavior, and left the barn. I couldn't see him at first. But as I made my way past the paddock, I saw him saddling up Nico as Rosa looked on.

Feeling a little numb, I headed for the gate of his cottage to return home, when guilt assailed me. I must have hurt him somehow. Maybe he thought I was throwing my wealth and status in his face? Maybe I had bothered him this morning with too many questions?

I thought back to our time collecting the grapes. I could remember nothing but patient guidance and encouraging smiles. At no point did he seem frustrated or annoyed by my presence. Shy and timid, yes, but not inconvenienced or angry.

It was clear I had hurt him just now. I needed to apologize. I didn't know what for, but he had been kindness itself to me today and yesterday. For some reason—one I didn't let myself dwell on—I couldn't stand my assumption that Achille now thought ill of me.

Before I had time to change my mind, I hurried back to the paddock just as Achille was leading Nico from the gate. His shoulders slumped when he saw I had come back. It cut me, slayed me.

He . . . he truly didn't want me near him.

A lump clogged up my throat at his sudden coldness, and my hands fidgeted at my front. I blinked away the light sheen of tears that had built across my eyes. "I am sorry if I have hurt you somehow. That was not my attention, Achille. You have been gracious and kind to me, indulging my curiosity about your wine, giving me your time and lunch." I chased back the lump and forced my weakened voice to add, "But I'm sorry for invading your space. Nothing malicious was meant. I just . . ." I sighed and let my stupid mouth say, "I am lonely here. I don't know anyone. Zeno is away. Then, by chance, I found out about you, about this place, and I let my excitement run away with me." I winced in embarrassment at my emotional outpouring.

I ran my hand down my face. "Please accept my apology for whatever I did wrong. I won't bother you again." I gave him a tight smile. "I wish you well with this year's harvest. Though I know you don't need it. It will be faultless, as always."

Ducking my head, I spun around and hurried away. I had almost reached the idyllic cottage's gray stone path when I heard Achille call nervously, "C–Caresa?"

His husky, stuttered rasp made me stop. But what had me closing my eyes, a slither of happiness settling my distress, was my name rolling from his lips. *Caresa*, not *Duchessa* . . .

Caresa.

I drew in three breaths, then looked over my shoulder. Achille was gripping the end of Nico's reins. His dark hair was tousled from this morning's work. And his eyes, his beautiful, stunningly blue eyes, zeroed in on me—so open and honest, so raw and exposed.

I could barely breathe at the sight.

"Yes?" I whispered, the cool wind wrapping around my damp lashes.

Achille ran his hand along Nico's neck to calm him, then looked back at Rosa in the paddock. The Andalusian mare had her head propped over the fence, her black eyes focused on her master as he led her companion away.

If it was possible, she appeared . . . sad.

Achille exhaled heavily. "Would . . . would you like to join me on a ride?" His broad shoulders were angled slightly toward Nico, as though shielding himself from my expected refusal. "I have to check the rest of the vines. I . . . I thought that you might want to come. I know you love to ride, and you have already learned so much about the harvesting process."

Shock rendered me speechless; my heart beat like a whirring fan. It was the last thing I thought he might say. I looked at my jogging leggings, sneakers and long-sleeved shirt. I wanted to scream *yes*, and accept his offer. Instead I blurted, "I have no jodhpurs or riding boots to wear." I closed my eyes for a second after I had spoken.

What are you blithering about?

But to my amazement, when I brought my gaze back to Achille, an unexpected smile had formed on his lips. And it wasn't a crooked smirk, or a gentle tugging of the mouth. This smile was wide, free and true. Teeth bare and eyes bright.

And there was a suggestion of a laugh.

A single throaty chuckle of abandoned delight. A morsel of uncensored happiness that I felt all the way into the marrow of my bones.

Achille was amused by me. His shyness was momentarily forgotten, and he was . . .

. . . divine.

Achille's laugh flew away like the brief passing of a falling leaf, yet with happiness still etched on his striking Latin features, he murmured, "It is only a short ride through the fields. I am sure you will be fine."

There was a hint of a tease in his words. Unable to take offense at his dry wit, I laughed in return, lowering my head in defeat. I peeked up at him through my lashes. "On a scale of one to ten, how pretentious did I just sound?"

I did not expect him to play or respond. So I nearly fell over from shock when he scrunched up his nose, then guessed, "Mmm . . . about a hundred?"

My mouth fell open at the mock-insult. But our mutual levity broke the tension that had plagued us during the past fifteen minutes. The rediscovery of our calming peace allowed my legs to function and follow Achille through to the paddock. He tied Nico's reins to a fence post and took a halter off the tack room's outside hook to catch Rosa. While he did so, I ducked into the tack room and removed the remaining saddle from its saddle mount, and the bridle hanging beside it.

I was about to leave the tack room when I noticed a plethora of show rosettes pinned on a wooden wall. On closer inspection, I could see the titles. First place in some of Italy's biggest dressage competitions. Some were for show jumping. All were dated around thirty years ago. The latest I could find was won twenty-five years ago. First place in the national dressage and show jumping Classic in Milan.

I was more than impressed. They were highly competitive events with prestigious titles. I scanned the several newspaper clippings that were pinned to the wall; one was framed, showcasing a small black-and-white picture of a beautiful woman dressed in a smart show jacket and white jodhpurs. The camera captured her mid-jump at the Roma Regional Championships. The write-up was short, but talked of her triumphant win. Abrielle Bandini. That was her name. And she looked young, maybe no older than me.

It was dated August, twenty-five years ago.

Movement in the doorway caught my attention. Achille was watching me scan this impressive wall of achievement. Whoever the woman was, she was very much loved by whoever had made this display. A flash of something rushed across Achille's face as he saw what I was looking at. Not wanting to upset him again, I held up the saddle in my arms and said, "I'm glad you ride English saddle. I'm useless on a Western."

Achille's shoulders must have been tense; on hearing my jovial comment they dropped in relief. I followed him out of the tack room to Rosa, who was now tied up beside Nico. "My papa believed one should only ride in English saddle." Achille's lip curved at a fond memory. "He said that unless your legs felt the effects of your ride the next day, you didn't do it properly." His gaze drifted to stare at nothing. "He said that anything you did in life should be done correctly. Should be done with a full heart and pride. So we rode English saddle. It was a discipline I used to despise when I was younger and learning, but now, I could not ride any other way."

"I like the sound of your father," I said, every word the truth.

My comment seemed to summon Achille from inside of his mind. He stepped forward, arms stretched out to take the saddle and bridle from my hands. The faint lines around his eyes had relaxed at my compliment.

I hugged the saddle to my chest. "I may be a spoiled little rich duchessa, Achille, but I can saddle up a horse with the best of them." I stepped around him and said, "Just watch." I winked playfully and fought to hide my blush as Achille leaned against the wooden fence beside me, lazily watching me place the deep-purple numnah on Rosa's freshly groomed back.

"You groomed her for me?" I asked.

"While you got the tack. You took a long time," he said matter-of-factly, seeming to enjoy watching me fasten Rosa's girth, put on her martingale and then move to her bridle. This bridle was simple, the bit gentle, indicating that she was not a difficult ride. Rosa took the bit with ease, her teeth chomping against the metal as she once again got used to it in her mouth.

"It's been a while since she's been ridden," Achille explained. He stood straight and moved before Rosa. He ran his fingers down her nose. "She may be fresh at first, but she is well-schooled and responsive to the leg."

I moved beside Achille, noticing the tanned skin on his arms twitch a little at my closeness to him. The sudden wave of happiness that came with that insight should have had me backing away.

I held still.

I pushed Rosa's forelock from her eyes, untucking it from the simple leather headband of her bridle. She huffed out a breath, butting my arm with her nose. "We'll be fine, won't we, Rosa?" I said in a soothing voice. I smiled up at Achille. "I'm a good rider, Achille. I promise. She's in safe hands."

Achille stared at me for longer than normal. I wondered what was happening in that head of his when he saw me like this. When he searched so deeply into my eyes. He didn't give much away. His actions were stiff. His responses were short and clipped. And his expressions worked hard to remain neutral. Yet I had never felt so comfortable around someone I just met as I did with Achille.

My papa always said that how a man was with his family said a lot about what made up their soul. And if they were good with animals, it proved patience and gentleness, and an understanding of what it was to be pure and kind. It was funny really. My father had always wanted me with someone who bore those traits.

I wondered if Zeno possessed them too. I wondered if my father even knew.

"Are you ready?" Achille asked.

I drew down Rosa's stirrups and took her reins in my right hand. I brought my foot up to the stirrup and glanced back at Achille, who was standing silently behind me. "I might need a leg up today. It's been a while since I've had to do this."

Without saying a word, Achille cupped his hands together, bent down and hooked them around my foot. I used his strength to pull up on to the saddle and find my seat. Achille was tall, I noted idly. As I sat on Rosa, his head was almost in line with my waist. "Thank you," I said and slipped my feet into the stirrups. I tightened the girth. Once I'd adjusted my hold on the reins, I looked to my left.

Achille mounted Nico effortlessly, and something stirred in my stomach as he readied his position for the ride. Nico was strong and robust, and Achille's broad, muscled frame looked even more impressive atop the mixed-breed horse. Achille hadn't even noticed me staring at him. And I was glad he could not detect the sudden spike in my pulse and the shaking of my breath.

They would be difficult to explain.

Achille backed Nico from the fence and looked over to me.

"Ready?"

Impossibly, that already racing pulse increased in speed. I told myself it was the excitement of being back on a horse.

This self-deception was so very easy to conceal.

"Ready."

The minute I felt Rosa push forward, it triggered a feeling of coming home. Of belonging. Of contentment.

Achille led the way, his back muscles bunching with the strain of working his reins. I knew I was smiling. My cheeks ached with just how much I was smiling. My lungs were taking in long deep breaths of air, yet my chest felt light. The breeze ruffled the loose strands of my hair and the sun kissed my skin.

I felt as if I were lost in the most beautiful of dreams as we bypassed the edge of his fairytale cottage, the fall shrubbery sprouting their flowers—burnt oranges and deep greens—and the trees hanging low. I steadied my seat and let Rosa sense my calmness.

It was hard to believe I had only been in Italy a few short days. I'd expected this courting period to be more hectic, the societal pressure on me much greater. And I wasn't naïve. I knew the madness was yet to come. This brief reprieve was simply the prelude to my future married life, of my expected royal duty for the pretender crown. For now, I let this mysterious, fascinating winemaker lead me through his award-winning vines. Doing the thing I loved most, in the most serene of surroundings.

This isn't so bad, I thought. In fact, this simple embracing of passions with a beautiful like-minded soul . . . it was like a dream come true.

So I intended to cherish every moment, for as long as I could.

With Rosa, Nico and Achille, and the scent of sweet freedom in the air.

Chapter Six

Achille

Nico's ears were flicking in all directions as we passed through the entrance to the vineyard. His heavy hooves padded like distant thunder on the soil. But that wasn't what was soothing my ever-present grief right then. That was down to a secondary set of hooves pressing into the same ground, and the other rider accompanying me on this ride.

I glanced behind me, and my breathing stuttered when I saw Caresa casting her big brown eyes over my land and the rolling hills of Umbria beyond. I allowed myself to look down to her body. She hadn't been lying or even exaggerating. Even from this light trot out, I could see that she could ride, exceptionally well, I would guess. Her seat was solid and her legs at the perfect angle, her heels pressing low in the stirrups. Her back was straight, and her hands held the reins in a way that only came with years of practice.

And it was even more obvious that she was proficient in dressage. Her entire posture was elegant in a delicate way. Even Rosa, who had not been ridden for more than a year—and even then it was simply around the paddock—was calm. She had submitted naturally to Caresa's control, trusting the rider to keep her in check.

87

Caresa must have felt the heavy weight of my stare, as her wandering eyes snapped back to clash with mine. I needed to say something. I needed to speak, so I simply asked, "Good?"

Caresa's responding smile was as bright at the afternoon sun. "More than good," she replied. I measured her height to Rosa's build and frame. They were a perfect match. Rosa was a good size, fifteen-three hands, strong but not too heavy. And I'd guess that Caresa was five foot five to five foot six, slim and athletic, perfectly proportioned to her Italian curves. My skin prickled as I allowed myself to notice that about her.

I steered Nico right at the end of the first row. A wider track stretched out over acres and acres before us. It was the main road of my land. Nico's hooves padded harder, wanting the chance to stretch his legs on the open field.

Caresa trotted beside me; her rising trot was impressive. Excitement flared in her eyes. She looked at the field ahead and the level track, which was straight and well worn. A knowing smirk tugged on her mouth. "So, Achille?" she said, an air of levity to her soft voice. "How good a rider are *you*?" My eyes narrowed as she tipped her head to the side, awaiting my answer.

"Good," I said, feeling the infectious allure of her playfulness seep into my bones. "Very good."

She nodded slowly and pursed her lips. She tightened the grip on her reins. "Then let's see if you can keep up."

The final word of her sentence had barely left her mouth before her legs squeezed Rosa, and my eager Andalusian leaped into a quick trot, immediately followed by a canter. It took me a moment to give chase, but all I needed to do was allow Nico his head to set a good pace. Seeing Rosa now at a full gallop was all the encouragement he needed.

I dug in my heels and leaned forward, embracing the blood surging faster and faster through my veins. Nico was well-ridden and fit, so it took us no time to shorten Caresa's lead. She glanced over her shoulder and grinned. In that moment, the beauty of her face caused an uncharacteristic swaying in my always-perfect seat. Caresa laughed loudly as I wobbled. Now facing north, I leaned further forward, urging Nico to gather speed.

The echo of her joy darted past me, the high-pitched notes sailing back toward the barn. The challenge was set. Raising my reins further up Nico's neck, I pushed him to his maximum speed, seeing the end of the track up ahead. Caresa verbally spurred Rosa on; I did the same with Nico.

It wasn't long before Nico's fitness and longer stride pulled us alongside Caresa and Rosa. Caresa looked at me, a mask of competitive determination etched on her face. We hit the end of the track at the same time, Caresa pulling Rosa to a slow canter to the left, and me pulling Nico to the right. I wound Nico down to a canter, then a steady trot, before bringing him to a walk. He was breathing heavily, but his ears were pointing forward, his spirits raised by the hard exercise.

I steered him around. Caresa was bringing Rosa toward us in a slow trot. When she reached us, her giggle was loud and light. "Achille

Marchesi, that was the most fun I've had in a long time!"

We continued on next to each other in a slow walk, allowing the horses to gather their breath. A light sheen of sweat blanketed Rosa's coat. Caresa must have seen what I was looking at because she said, "When was the last time she was ridden?"

"Over a year ago, but it was just on a lead rein. Her last real ride that pushed her was over two years ago. I tried to take her out myself, but she struggled under my weight. I lunge her out in the paddock, but you'll know that's never the same as having a rider schooling her."

Caresa reached down to pat Rosa's neck. When she straightened, she assessed me with narrowed eyes. "You're a very good rider, Achille. Excellent, in fact."

"You are too."

"How old are you?"

"Twenty-four," I replied, seeing Caresa's lips hook up at the corners.

I pointed to the farthest set of vines. "We can start there. I planted these vines at a later date than the ones we have been harvesting. I do it days apart or in accordance to the soil's pH, quality and amount of sun exposure the area gets. I must time it perfectly so that when I harvest I can collect the grapes when they are at their perfect ripeness." I shrugged. "It's not always an exact science, so if I finish the picking early some days, I ride out and make sure none of the rows need any extra attention. Or if I need to change my schedule and harvest these first." I studied a few bunches of grapes, judging by their coloring and size that my estimation of their readiness was on track.

"I never knew so much attention to detail was involved. I knew the traditional method was much more intensive, of course, but I think I have been spoiled by seeing only mechanical tools used in the fields." She shook her head. "Your way is so much more inspiring, Achille. Truly."

"Thank you."

Minutes of companionable silence passed. Caresa allowed me to check the row uninterrupted. As we made our way to the next, she said, "That's why you ride then?" She pointed to the soil. "So everything stays as pure as possible?"

"Yes," I replied, reaching down to run my fingers through Nico's mane. "A winemaker is not a good winemaker unless he respects the soil that yields his fruit. Tractors can cause too much compaction of the soil. With horses, there are no chemicals seeping into the ground or clogging the air. The Bella Collina soil is impressive, probably because of its distance from any sources of pollution." I took in a breath of the clean fresh air I was talking about. "But this path, this small acreage of mine, there is something even more special here. The soil is different somehow. It's incomparable to anything nearby. It is sacred, and, as such, deserving of a winemaker who nurtures and cherishes the gift it gives. It would be sacrilegious to reward it with the introduction of gas and oil. A horse's hoof is gentle and kind. It doesn't punish, it . . . understands."

I didn't realize Caresa had drawn to a stop until I noticed that the rhythmic sound of Rosa's hooves on the ground had faded to silence. "Caresa?" I called, concerned. I found her motionless, staring at me with an intense expression on her face. I pulled on Nico's reins and walked carefully to where she sat. "Caresa? Are you well?"

"You care so much," she whispered, so quietly I almost didn't catch her words. She blinked twice. "All of this, what you have created, what you achieve each season . . . it's . . . breathtaking. More than inspiring, your grace and devotion is . . . majestic." She shook her head as if she was searching for the right words. She finally settled on, "You should be very proud." She paused, tilted her head to the side and, with a heartbreakingly honest expression, added, "Your father . . . he must have been so very proud of you. And he must be still, smiling down from heaven at the man you have become."

I was glad the wind chose that moment to swirl around us, because then I could blame the sudden wetness on my lashes on the breeze. I could blame the blurring of my vision on the cool waves of wind washing over my face.

"I just had to say that to you," Caresa said. My head was turned to the side, evading her watchful gaze. I kept my focus on the smudge of dirt on the back of my hand as I gripped the reins tightly.

She spoke again. "My papa always told me that when someone deserved praise, they should be given it. That when something floored you so incredibly, you should explain why." She held her breath for a moment. "And you deserved to hear that, Achille. That and much, much more. I couldn't let another second go by without saying it aloud."

I didn't know how badly I had needed to hear such a sentiment until that moment. Hadn't realized how devoid of kindness or affection my life had been until her compliment burrowed its way deeply into my heart.

Hadn't realized how lonely I was until I had someone walking beside me, laughing with me under the sun.

Seconds passed before I breathed easily again. Until I could meet her eyes. Caresa gave me a small smile. I turned Nico and said, "We must check the rest of the vines."

We walked slower this time, as though the sun was not beginning to lower in the sky. I tipped my head up, noticing gray clouds moving in. The air smelled fresher, the wind blew colder. No doubt a downpour would hit within the next few hours.

I didn't mind. The rain always created better-flavored grapes.

Caresa brought Rosa beside us. We silently searched row after row. When we arrived back on the track to go to the next section, she asked, "Achille?"

"Yes?"

"Who was that woman in the framed picture in the tack room?" I tensed a little at her question. Growing up, there had only been my father and me. I had always been quiet, reserved, unused to talking much about myself. My father knew that, but never pushed me. He could talk enough for us both.

Caresa's question made me see that, in my life, I had barely spoken to anyone outside of this land.

"My mother," I answered, seeing her face from that picture so clearly in my mind.

Caresa sighed. "She is so beautiful."

"Was."

Caresa stopped breathing for a moment, then said, "Oh, Achille, I am so sorry."

"I didn't know her." I looked at Caresa from the corner of my eye. She was watching me intently. "She died at my birth. She hemorrhaged. It was a home birth here on this estate, so the paramedics couldn't get to her in time to save her."

"That is so sad," Caresa said. The sound of a tractor intruded from the near distance. The other winemakers of the mass-produced Savona wines used mechanics in their harvest. As far as I knew, it was only me who did not.

"He must have missed her terribly," Caresa said, muting the tractor in my ears. I turned to face her. "Your father," she explained. "He kept all of her rosettes and newspaper write-ups in the tack room." Her expressive brown eyes had drifted from bright to sad. "He must have loved her a great deal."

I pictured my father every night before his death. For the last few weeks, when we knew his time was near, he held my mother's picture in his arms as he lay in bed. With each passing day, he clutched it tighter; he knew the time to meet her once again was nigh.

My father had held no fear of death. Because . . . "He would be whole again," I verbalized, not meaning to finish my thought aloud.

My cheeks blazed as Caresa studied me. "What?"

I shook my head, wanting to forget it, but Caresa surprised me by reaching across and laying her hand on my forearm. The moment her fingers touched my bare skin, warmth rose up my arm. Her fingers were small and slim, and I couldn't take my eyes off her nails. They were perfectly shaped and painted a light lavender color.

I looked up; when I did, I felt Caresa's thumb brush back and forth on my arm. It was only the once, and it was as light as a feather, but I liked this soft caress.

She stilled. It had been an absent-minded action, but one that caused my skin to bump in the wake of her touch.

Caresa took back her hand. Clearing her throat, she asked, "Please continue. I would like to hear about your father. About whatever it was you were going to say. You said something about him being whole again?"

Browning leaves from a low-hanging branch brushed my cheek as we passed. I took a deep breath. "Yes."

Caresa waited patiently for me to continue. I shifted nervously on my saddle. Nico must have felt it; his head flicked up and he huffed out a long breath. Caresa laughed gently at my gelding's quick-changing mood.

I couldn't help but smile in reply.

"You don't have to tell me if it makes you uncomfortable," Caresa said. "You've only just met me. I shouldn't be prying."

I shook my head. "No, that's not it. It's just . . ." I paused, trying to phrase my words correctly.

"What?"

I shrugged. "I don't know. It's almost silly, I guess. My father . . . he

95

was a hopeless romantic. Yet he only ever truly loved my mother. He never remarried, never looked at another woman in all the years he lived after her death." I glanced out across the fields of green. "He had unique beliefs about love and matters of the heart. Maybe unrealistic. And I don't . . . I couldn't bear . . ."

"To have his memory ridiculed?" she completed when I couldn't finish my sentence.

I nodded. "He was my father. He . . . he was everything I ever had."

"I would never ridicule him, Achille. It would be the last thing I would ever consider."

I searched her eyes then. Actually peered into their darkest depths. And all I saw was the truth shining back at me. Acceptance and understanding.

And maybe . . . affection?

I steered us right, around the perimeter track. I could see my cottage in the distance, the autumn colors creating a masterpiece of my home—my father's home. "Have you heard of Plato?" I said.

"The Greek philosopher?"

"Yes."

Caresa looked confused, but she didn't push me. My stomach lightened. She wasn't what I thought she'd be. Well, I had never given her much thought before she turned up at my vineyard, but I had assumed she'd be like the prince. Arrogant and rude to anyone but those on his level of social standing.

She was not like that at all.

"My father liked to read," I went on, feeling my lips turn up at the memories circling my mind. "He read all the time, anything he could get his hands on. He used to read me Tolkien as a child. That was my favorite." Caresa absently reached down to pat Rosa's neck. "He liked pretty much everything, but his favorite by far was philosophy." I released a nervous laugh. "Strange for a simple winemaker, I know."

"Not at all," Caresa said vehemently. Her strong response surprised me. "I see every reason to believe why he would embrace philosophy. Philosophy contemplates the world in every facet—its creation, its beauty, its flaws, its meaning. A winemaker takes the seeds from a simple fruit, uses the earth to nurture it, then gives it new life in the most beautiful way. I can see exactly why your father loved philosophy. He lived it, as do you. I don't think many people can say that about their life's work."

I stared at Caresa. I couldn't look away. Her words were a balm to a wound I never knew I had. She didn't regard what we did here on this land as lowly, like some. She saw its value.

She saw mine.

"My father was obsessed with Aristotle. But his favorite was Plato. He read Plato's *Symposium* to me as a child." My throat grew thick at the memory. "He . . . he would especially read me the parts about love." My face and neck seemed to ignite with fire. I had never talked to anyone about love before. Never mind the duchessa.

"Love?" Caresa asked. "What does Plato say about love? I'm afraid my recollections of philosophy are limited."

I loosened Nico's reins, allowing his head more freedom as we

97

strolled down the long, lazy track. "My father liked Plato so much because he proposed the theory of 'split-aparts'. It's how he saw my mother and himself, their life together. It's why he loved so hard for so long, even long after she was dead. She made him whole."

"I'm sorry, I still don't understand. What is the theory of 'split-aparts'?"

"This is where it becomes fantasy, I think. Plato wrote that once upon a time—according to Greek mythology—humans were created as one whole being with four arms, four legs, and a shared head with two faces. It was written that they began to challenge the gods, who feared that humans may one day become successful and overthrow them. Zeus sent down a thunderbolt, splitting them into two parts—two parts of one whole. The two parts were sent to different areas of the world."

I glanced at Caresa to check if she was still listening. Her eyes were locked on me, her pupils wide. "Then what?" she asked softly. "What happened to them?" I thought, in that moment, she seemed as taken by the concept of the split-aparts as my father had been.

"They were broken, in pain, never feeling complete without their other half. Zeus, in an attempt to keep power, had condemned the split-aparts to spend their lives searching for their counterparts. They could not challenge his power when they had only half a soul."

"And your father . . ." Caresa trailed off.

"He believed that the story was really just fiction, for the sake of ancient myths, but the theory was not. He said that when we're born, we also have the other half of us, our split-apart, waiting for us out

98

there in the world. Not everyone will find theirs. Finding them can also go very badly. Some who do find their missing half become so consumed by the other person, so addicted to them, that the blessing becomes their curse—their love is too consuming, obsessive, unhealthy. But for others, it is pure destiny. It is meant to be. It is perfect and benevolent. He said that it explained the circumstance of instant love. And of the loves that defy the odds and last a lifetime."

"Like that of him and your mother," she said softly. Her eyes were glistening, and the apples of her cheeks were pink.

"Yes." I sighed. "He said that once you find that person, your split-apart, you are blanketed by such belonging, such desire, that you will never want to be without it . . . as Plato said, *'and they don't want to be separated from one another, not even for a moment.'*"

We followed the direction of the track to a part of the dirt road bordered by tall, imposing cypress trees. We were almost back at my home. As I saw the chimney smoke from my wood burner rising into the darkening sky, I found myself wishing this ride could last just a little bit longer.

"I . . ." I met Caresa's gaze. She blinked away the shine from her eyes and said, "I think that is the most poetic and heartrending view on soul mates I have ever heard."

My heart pounded. My hands grew damp, and shivers darted down my spine. "You do?" When my father had told this to his friends over the years, most had ridiculed him as over-sentimental.

Secretly, I had always thought my father had been right. I saw the undying love he had for my mother in his eyes every day. She had

99

been his everything.

Caresa's hand went to her chest, right above where her heart lay. "To have someone feel that way about you. To have someone love you so much for so long." She shook her head. "How could anyone ever wish for more?"

"The prince may feel that way about you." I didn't know why I said it. But at the mention of the prince, Caresa's expression hardened and she cast her eyes away. The words infused my mouth with a bitter taste.

"We shall see," Caresa answered after a beat, but even I, a man who had no experience with women, or even people, could hear the doubt lacing her words. She believed the prince was not her split-apart.

He would never make her spirit whole.

We turned the final corner onto a narrower track that led home. Just as we reached the gate, Caresa said, "How did your father live all those years without her?"

This time it was my turn to find water in my eyes. "He said a part of her soul lived within me. He saw her every day through me. I looked like her and had her personality. And he knew he would meet her again in the afterlife. He said that years on earth were nothing to wait through. Not when soul mates' bound eternities were promised after this life. Until then, he was content to be a devoted loving father to me . . . to his vines."

A lone tear had escaped onto Caresa's smooth, tanned cheek. I wanted to reach out and wipe it away. Caresa chased it away with her hand. "It gives us all hope, does it not?" she whispered. "That we may even have a mere scrap of the same?"

"My father said you would know when you found it. It may not be apparent at first, but eventually, an overwhelming sense of peace would settle in your heart, and you would just know . . . know that you were bonded for life."

"Abrielle," she whispered my mother's name, tipping her head up to the sky as though my mother could perhaps hear her in paradise. She must have read some of the articles my father had placed on the tack room wall. She dropped her head. "She was a national champion in dressage?"

"Yes. She rode until she fell pregnant . . . then she never rode again. She set her dressage routines to opera, symphonies or choral music."

"So do I. When the competition calls for it," Caresa remarked fondly. When I looked at her this time, it took us longer to break our locked stares.

We arrived at the paddock and drew our horses to a stop. I pointed to the small practice arena where my horses now grazed most days. "My father built this for my mother. He would tend the vines and she would ride. After her death, he taught himself dressage in her honor. He even trained Rosa to a high standard before he got ill. It helped him keep her memory alive, I think."

Caresa smiled as she looked at the arena. I dismounted from Nico and took the reins over his head, ready to lead him away, when she said, "Achille?" I looked at her over Nico's back. "Do you have the music you play in the fields nearby?"

My eyebrows pulled down in confusion, but I nodded.

101

"I don't suppose you have "Sogno" by Andrea Bocelli, by any chance?"

"Yes."

Caresa squeezed her legs and steered Rosa through the gate to the paddock. She turned to me. "Could you get it for me, please?"

I didn't question her further. I tied Nico's reins to the fence and ducked inside the barn. My old cassette player was on the counter where I always left it. I took the Andrea Bocelli cassette from its case and inserted it.

When I went outside and saw Caresa in the arena, I stopped dead. Caresa was schooling Rosa, warming her up.

She was doing dressage.

Only she was not only doing it, it was a flawless execution as she urged Rosa into a smooth extended trot. Caresa was sitting perfectly in her seat, even more so when she turned Rosa and brought her into a piaffe—an elegant and complex diagonal movement—directly across the paddock. The mare was slightly rusty in her movements, but I could see that she had retained some memories of my father's training.

Caresa saw me watching and came over to the edge of the fence. "Press play when I give you the signal."

I sat on a stone bench just behind the fence and watched her move to the center. She closed her eyes, leaning forward to run her hand over Rosa's neck. It looked like Caresa was whispering something to her. When she straightened, she looked my way and lowered her head. I pressed play. The music began.

102

Then I sat, mesmerized, as Caresa began an obviously well-practiced routine to the slow tempo of Andrea Bocelli's voice. Her movements were fluid and poised, like a prima ballerina on stage. Rosa responded to every subtle command Caresa gave, the Andalusian doing what her breed did best—dancing with breathless grace.

She was almost as beautiful as the angelic rider on her back.

Even in fitness clothes with her dark hair pulled back off her face, Caresa's beauty was a shining light, a beacon. Her smile was soft on her lush lips as she executed each move with practiced ease. Her skin was flushed from the exercise. Or maybe it was from doing something she loved.

As the music faded out, Caresa brought Rosa back to the center of the arena. My jaw dropped when Caresa worked her legs and Rosa dipped to bow. I saw the burst of joy take Caresa hold as Rosa completed the difficult move.

When Rosa righted her stance, Caresa directed an elegant bow my way. The only things I was aware of were her happiness, my awe and the singing birds nearby.

Caresa dismounted and removed Rosa's tack. After Rosa had been turned out to graze, Caresa returned, carrying the saddle in her hands and the bridle over her shoulder.

When Caresa approached me, I had absolutely no words.

"She is an excellent horse," Caresa commented. "Your father has trained her well. She is a natural at dressage, but then most Andalusians are."

I nodded. I wanted to tell Caresa that only a rider of her caliber could get such a performance from a fresh horse. But I didn't. Something inside me suddenly felt different, stealing my confidence.

I didn't know what it was . . . it made me feel both empty and filled at the same time.

A roll of thunder sounded in the distance. Caresa looked at the approaching gray clouds. "There's a storm coming. I had better go." I still didn't say anything as she took the tack into the tack room then, with a delicate wave goodbye, headed for the path toward the main house.

A flash of lightning illuminated the sky. "Caresa?" She turned. "You . . . you are welcome to come back tomorrow . . . if you wish, if you don't have any engagements to attend. To harvest, and maybe school Rosa, if you want? She . . . she has no one else to ride her." I ducked my head, unable to look her in the eye. My heart was beating incredibly hard, so hard I rubbed my hand across my chest, searching for relief.

"I would like that," she replied quietly. I didn't look at her again. I didn't watch her leave. Instead I removed Nico's tack and put the horses in their stables. I gave them fresh water and a hay net each, and then the heavens opened.

Taking the cassette player, I was about to go and crush the grapes in the barn. But when I looked over at the tack room, I changed my plan. I entered the small room, walked to the locked closet at the back and unlocked the door. A spray of dust and the distinct scent of stale leather assaulted my senses. I flicked on the light, my mother's old horse equipment suddenly revealed.

I took the pieces out, one by one, assessing what I could salvage and what had perished beyond recall. Then I lit a fire and sat down beside it, saddle soap and wax at my feet.

Against the climbing orange flames of the burner and the pounding rain hitting the roof above, I began the hard task of restoring the tools of a lost dream, of bringing them back to life.

As the cassette player at my feet flooded the room with "Sogno," I thought of Plato and vines. Of split-aparts and soul mates anew . . .

. . . and a single, solitary tear rolling down flushed and flawless skin.

Chapter Seven

Caresa

It was two days before I could get back to Achille. Maria had returned from Assisi early, and we had nothing but meetings to occupy each day. I had now chosen the silverware, the color scheme and the menu for the wedding.

The hours had dragged. Each minute that I spent in the great room, tasting the exquisite food and running my hands over plush velvets and silks, my mind had been back with Achille in his vineyard. I wondered how far he had got with the harvest.

I wondered how many times he had ridden out around his land. I wondered if he had missed me being there.

The very thought should not have ever crossed my mind, yet it was the single most occupying question I had.

"We're done for the day," Maria said. "The luncheon is tomorrow at noon. Some of the women from the biggest families are coming from Florence. There should be about twenty-five in total." Maria stood. "Your outfit is in your closet."

"Thank you," I said and got to my feet. I walked Maria to the door. "Any word on when Zeno will be back? I've had no word from him since my arrival."

Maria tried to hide the sympathy in her eyes. No, not sympathy, *pity*. Her hand gently landed on my arm. "He will be back for the Bella Collina grape-crushing festival, which is also the day the International Wine Awards will notify the winners. Then, that night, it will be his coronation dinner. The most important families from around the country will attend." Maria released my arm. "We then have the masked ball to prepare for at the beginning of December, and the Christmas festivities later that month." She gave me a tight smile. "Then your wedding. My advice would be to get your sleep now, Duchessa, while you still can."

Maria left, and I shut the grand doors behind her. I pressed my back against the wood and closed my eyes. The grandfather clock began to chime three o'clock. My eyes opened and drifted to the oil painting of Achille's land. Before I had even had time to contemplate my decision, I was darting up the stairs to my rooms, where I swiftly changed into my jodhpurs, boots and long-sleeved riding shirt I had brought with me from New York. Clutching my riding hat and crop in my hands, I decided to exit through my balcony's double doors. The staff here never questioned anything I did, but for some reason I found myself wanting to keep my whereabouts from prying eyes.

The sky was overcast, and the sun was partially hidden by the clouds. I picked up my pace as I passed through a shortcut I had found. My walk was brisk, and in only half the time it usually took, I arrived at Achille's home. I had been away only two days, yet when my eyes beheld the gray stone cottage and the majestic garden, the same sense of wonderment seized me.

When I arrived at the barn, there was no opera music playing, no Verdi blasting like a siren to signal where Achille worked. I searched the vines, yet I could not see him anywhere. Eventually I saw Rosa alone in the paddock; he must have been out for a ride.

I decided to take the opportunity to school Rosa. I turned for the tack room, and then I heard the sound of galloping hooves beyond the trees. As I ducked through the branches, my feet instinctively carrying me forward, I didn't realize there was a smile on my face until my cheeks ached in a cool snap of the wind. The trees were on a slightly raised hill, and the elevation awarded me a perfect view of Achille racing Nico toward home.

Like every other day, Achille was shirtless, his uniform of faded work jeans cladding his legs. But what held me captive was the happy expression on his face as the wind whipped through his black hair. Every well-toned muscle was flexing as he controlled the reins. So much so that the sensation of butterflies swooping in my stomach stole my breath and parted my lips. The grip on my riding hat's chinstrap became impossibly tight, and I felt heat rise to my cheeks.

Achille drew Nico back to a canter, then to a slow sitting trot. As he turned right toward the closed gate to the residential part of his property, his eyes collided with mine, and he jolted in his saddle.

He must have thought I had decided not to return.

I waited beside the path on the inside of the gate for him. He came toward me and dismounted, dropping only inches from where I stood. I shifted on my legs when they actually weakened at his close proximity. His scent assaulted me, all fresh air and an earthy musk.

"You came back?" he said, his voice cracking. His handsome face was drawn into a serious expression. My heart stuttered.

He was beautiful. Achille was absolutely, breathtakingly *beautiful*.

I must have been staring at him too closely or for too long, because his eyebrows rose and he began rocking awkwardly on his feet. I pushed my hair back from my face in an attempt to break the sudden tension. Yet my hand shook as it ran through my shoulder-length strands.

I didn't know if he meant to do it. By the lost expression on his face afterwards I assumed he did not. When I dropped my hand, Achille reached out with his and caught a strand of my hair between his finger and thumb. His full lips parted and a slow breath escaped. "Your hair is down," he said with such reverence that I was in no doubt that he liked it better than my jogging bun.

I stood motionless, fighting my body's natural pull to his—*like magnets*, I thought. This close, my body was drawn, striving to get closer. I . . . I had no idea what to do with this startling truth.

Achille must have realized what he was doing. He dropped my hair like it was a naked flame. He took a step back, his tanned face flushed. He turned and led Nico toward the paddock. I held back for a few seconds to steel my frayed nerves. I stared at the grass beneath my feet. But when I looked up and saw Achille's tense, naked back highlighted so perfectly in the afternoon sunlight, my heart raced anew.

You can't do this, Caresa, I told myself—no, *commanded* myself. At that very moment, Achille glanced over his shoulder. As his gaze locked on mine, my instruction to myself fled with the last of my good sense.

His nostrils flared and his biceps tensed, I allowed myself a moment to admire him—guilt-free and uncensored. I could see he was doing exactly the same with me.

It took an impatient whinny from Rosa to release us from the spell.

Deciding to act like the grown-up woman I was, I pulled myself together and went to the paddock. I leaned against the fence as Achille went to release Nico. Before he did, he asked, "Did you come to ride Rosa?"

"I did," I replied. "But if it's too late, I understand. I have been kept away the last couple of days with meetings. This was the first chance I got to escape."

It was slight, but I saw Achille's expression soften. I realized I must have answered his unspoken question: why had I not returned sooner?

"It's not too late," he said softly, steering Nico away from the paddock's gate and toward his stable instead. He led the gelding inside, then carried his tack toward the tack room. I followed to retrieve Rosa's.

I moved toward the saddle and bridle I had used on Rosa a couple of days before. Then, to the left, I saw a set I hadn't seen before. The light was dim in the dark room, so I moved closer. My hand flew to my mouth. On a wooden plinth were an exquisite dressage saddle and bridle. They were old, but their condition was immaculate.

I kneeled down to examine them further and spotted the Savona royal crest embossed onto the saddle's skirt. I sensed him close by. I didn't have to look around to know he was there.

"Achille, these are stunning."

I heard him take a deep breath. Then I felt his body heat as he came closer. It took him several long seconds to say, "They were my mother's."

My heart melted at the gentle edge to his deep rasp. When he said the word "mother's" it was more pronounced than the rest, as if he was unused to saying that word aloud. I supposed he was. He had never known her.

Not even a little bit.

"This was her championship tack?"

"Yes. My father kept it all these years. He took care of it every week for as long as I can remember—soaping, waxing and oiling the leather. I have not touched it since his death . . . but then . . . when you . . . the other day . . ." He stumbled over his words, and I looked up. His arms were crossed over his chest, his tense posture exuding discomfort.

"It's beautiful." As I looked back at the tack, his previous words finally sank into my brain. *I have not touched it since his death . . . but then . . . when you . . . the other day . . .*

A sudden pulse of emotion swept over me like a cresting wave. My fingers trembled as they ran over the cantle of the saddle. He had not touched it in several months . . . until now.

Until me.

"I . . . I thought that if you liked dressage, you might want to use this." He shrugged one shoulder awkwardly. "Or not. You don't have to, if you don't want to, I—"

"I'd love to," I interjected, cutting off his spiraling nervousness. Moving just inches from him, I looked straight into his bright sea-colored eyes and laid my hand on his. "I would be honored."

Achille exhaled a deep, relieved sigh. We stayed that way for what felt like an eternity, simply sharing the same air, embracing our newfound peace. Then he stepped back and disappeared into a closet. When he came back out, he was carrying a pair of tall leather dressage boots. As with the tack, they had been polished to perfection.

"I didn't know what size you were or if you had boots already . . ." He trailed off as we both looked at the boots on my feet.

His shoulders sagged, so I blurted, "I'm a European 37."

Achille handed me the boots, and I tipped them upside down. The size imprint had worn off the sole.

"You can try them if you want?"

I walked to the chair, took a seat and placed the boots beside me. I tried to pull my boots off, but couldn't get them past my heels. I was out of breath at the effort. I heard a burst of quiet laughter and lifted my eyes to see Achille watching me with unconcealed amusement on his face. His arms were crossed in front of his chest again.

In a rare display of humor, he said, "Do you normally have a servant to take them off for you?"

My mouth dropped at his quip. That only seemed to make him laugh more. My chest seized at the sight of him loosening up, and shivers trickled over my skin at his low-pitched chuckle.

"For your information, Signor Marchesi, I usually have a boot jack. I don't suppose you have one of those lying around, do you?"

He shook his head. "No. But I have these." Achille held his hands in the air and dropped down to his knees before me. I stared at him, unblinking. Achille raised a knee and tapped his thigh. "Give me a foot."

I prayed he didn't feel the slight trembling of my leg as I placed it on his thigh. The muscle was so hard and defined I could feel the ridges through the leather of my boot. Achille's hands wrapped around the toe and heel of my boot. He pulled gently. The boot slipped off, and surprising me, he cupped my foot and ran his hands over the arch. No sooner had he touched me than he placed my foot on the floor. He drew up my other foot and repeated the process. I practically melted into the seat of the chair.

He had only touched my feet, and over my socks at that, yet his hands on me were almost my undoing. Everything he did, he did with such incredible intensity it was addictive. He didn't speak much, but his actions displayed the kind of man he was.

Honest and pure.

Achille didn't seem to have noticed my internal musings. He held up one of his mother's boots and slipped it onto my foot. The leather was butter-soft as it slid over my calf. It was tight, but Achille pushed harder until it sat perfectly around my foot. I smiled as I looked down at my calf. As with the saddle, the royal Savona crest was embossed into the leather at the top of the boot.

Achille caught my smile and awarded me one in return. When both boots were on, Achille got to his feet as I rolled my toes, testing for feel.

"My feet have fallen asleep. They do that when I wear my riding boots—too tight a fit," I said when I pressed my sole to the hard ground of the tack room. "I'm not sure I can get up!"

One of Achille's hands was suddenly in front of my face, palm up. "I'll help you," he offered. I slipped my hand into his. Achille gently pulled me to stand, but the minute I was upright, the numbness increased tenfold, causing me to lose my footing.

I yelped as I stumbled. A hard wall of flesh broke my fall, two strong arms wrapping around my back to keep me steady. My palms reached out, trying to find purchase on something, only to land on Achille's firm chest.

I knew I should have removed them immediately. The minute I felt the warm skin under my own, I should have backed away or insisted I sit back down.

But I didn't.

Instead, I allowed the pads of my fingers to drink in the heat from Achille's chest. I gave them permission to move, a painstakingly slow caress over his pectorals and down to the top of his defined abdominal muscles.

The more they explored the hard ridges, the tighter Achille's arms became on my back.

He breathed.

I breathed.

The heat between us soared.

Yet neither of us moved away.

There was no urgency to separate, only an unspoken eagerness to stay close.

Magnets.

My head moved closer to his chest, my lips barely brushing over his burning skin. His fresh, earthy scent invaded my senses, taking me hostage. Achille's hands on my back drew me closer, his hold an inescapable vise. He exhaled, the warm air sailing down the back of my neck and over the length of my spine. My head tipped up, as if starved of seeing Achille's eyes. The tip of my nose edged along the bottom of his neck and up to the rough stubble of his jaw.

I felt his pounding heart pressing so closely against my own. They sang the same symphony, exactly, precisely, mirror images of the same beat.

Achille's hands drew up, his fingers wrapping loosely into the strands of my hair. My lips traveled past his chin, to the corner of his mouth. I didn't dare look up. I was not sure my heart could take the reaction that sea of blue would inspire.

The taste of coffee and mint kissed my cupid's bow as I skirted the edges of my lips over his, the promise of our joining mouths hanging on a precipice.

I closed my eyes, needing to feel his lips against my own more than I needed to breathe, when suddenly a voice called out loudly from outside, "Achille?"

The deep call of his name was all it took for Achille to pull away.

His arms released me from their protection, and he staggered back. His eyes were wide, like a deer caught in headlights. His chest rose and fell, betraying his panic.

"Achille?" the man's voice sounded again, only closer to us this time. Achille raced from the tack room, leaving me alone.

I heard Achille greet the man and lead him away, and I slumped back down to the seat and placed my hands on my head. "What the hell are you doing?" I whispered aloud, closing my eyes, but swiftly opening them again when all I saw in the darkness was Achille's lips a mere hairsbreadth from my own, his hands pressing me close against his torso and the taste of his skin on my tongue.

I didn't know how long I sat on the seat, warring with my conscience. But I needed to move. I needed to do something to occupy my mind. I took the new tack Achille had given me over to Rosa in the paddock, and in no time at all, had her saddled up. I schooled her for an hour, squeezing the last rays of daylight from the sun. And I rode her hard. When I removed my hat, my hair was damp from exertion; my legs and arms ached from taming Rosa's strength.

I set Rosa in her stable and, after feeding both horses and giving them fresh buckets of water, decided to find the man I had nearly kissed.

The melodic sound of "Spring" from Vivaldi's Four Seasons came drifting from the barn. I stopped at the door, peering inside. Achille was by the basket press, working hard, yet with the same thoroughness and gentleness I had seen from him in the days since we met.

As if he was beginning to be as aware of me as I was him, he lifted his head. A scarlet blush blossomed on his cheeks when he saw me hovering by the entrance. He turned his head from me, recommencing his work without a word. But it was only seconds later when he stood back from the wooden press, arms by his side and shoulders down.

It shattered my heart.

"Achille," I said quietly, edging into the room.

Achille walked to a small box that must have been delivered by the man who interrupted us in the tack room. He took the top sheet of paper from the open box and ran his eyes over the page.

Taking a pen from his pocket, he clumsily drew a tick at the bottom of the paper and placed it back down. He held the pen tightly in his fist rather than with his fingers; I could see it shaking. It was obvious by the way he averted his eyes from me that he did not want to talk of what had happened between us.

"The tack was beautiful," I said, trying to get him to at least acknowledge my presence. "Thank you for letting me use it."

Achille briefly glanced my way, then nodded. He moved back to the press. Out of natural curiosity, I looked down to see what had been delivered. I recognized the familiar grayscale drawing of Bella Collina and the cursive script of the well-known title.

"The labels for this year's vintage?" My own question was answered when I saw this year's date written on the bottom of the sample label.

"Yes," Achille said, without turning around.

I picked up the sheet and scanned the text. Achille had ticked the box that approved the sample. His tick was a messy scrawl, barely legible. I remembered his shaking hand and instantly felt guilty. I had completely thrown him off guard. So much so that he couldn't even write.

I looked at the text again. Two. I counted two misspellings on the label. An *l* was missing from "Bella" and the *r* from "Merlot".

"Achille?" I said. "Have you signed off on the labels?"

He stopped what he was doing and came closer. He wore a wary, almost fearful look on his face. I studied him as his blue gaze ran over the label. His dark eyebrows were furrowed and his lips were pursed.

I pointed to the mistakes. "There are two letters missing, here and here."

Achille blinked and blinked again, then handed me the pen from his back pocket. "Could you circle them, please?" His hand was still trembling. Obviously I had completely shaken him.

It had even affected his work. Work that was his entire life, details that I knew he would never have overlooked had he not been distracted.

I took the pen from his hand. "Did you not see them?" I asked, trying to make conversation. "It was a silly mistake for the printers to make. They should have been more careful."

Achille didn't reply. I circled the mistakes, writing a note along the bottom of the sample to explain to the printers what was wrong. I lifted my head to see Achille standing by the countertop, gripping the edge tightly.

His back appeared to be trembling, and his head was downcast.

"Achille?" I inquired tentatively, only to rear back when Achille spun to face me wearing an expression so severe it turned my blood cold.

"I need you to go," he said, no inflection of emotion in his flat voice.

"What?" I whispered, feeling the color drain from my face.

Achille glanced out of the barn doors to the darkened sky. "I need you to leave. I need you to go and never come back."

Slices of pain rippled through my chest. I wondered if I was physically feeling the effects of a heart breaking, of the fissures cracking through the flesh. "Why? What did I do . . . ?"

"You are marrying the prince. I am a winemaker in the middle of the harvest for this estate's most important vintage. I . . . you distract me. You . . . should not be here. I can't think . . ."

"Achille—" I tried to protest, but he raised a hand to cut me off.

"Just . . . please, go." This time his voice brooked no argument. Once again, I had no idea what I had done to hurt him, to cause him to be *this* upset. And I hated myself for caring. I should be heeding Achille's words, thinking of Zeno. Instead, all I wanted to do was reach out and press my lips to his, just to see how it would feel.

"Please," he whispered—no, *begged* me. Tears filled my eyes as I watched him curl in on himself, as if some devastating internal pain was causing him to retreat from the world.

I didn't want to see him hurt. So when he looked into my eyes, and all I saw in their blue depths was unconcealed sadness, I did as he asked. I left the barn without a second glance. I didn't look back as I ran home, Abrielle Bandini's prized dressage boots still on my feet.

Even when I came through my balcony doors and arrived at my rooms, I didn't turn to look at Achille's house in the distance. I sat on the end of my bed and let myself slowly absorb the truth.

Over the past week, I had found myself increasingly drawn to the shy winemaker of the Bella Collina merlot. I rubbed at my chest, noticing for the first time that when I was not in his addictive presence, a dull ache would flare in my heart and would not calm down until I was back by his side.

I prayed this new development would fade as quickly as it appeared. Because Achille never wanted me to return. Not to ride Rosa, not to help him harvest the wine or laugh with him amongst the vines.

And that *had* to be okay with me.

Because I was the Duchessa di Parma, soon to marry the prince.

I just had to remind my heart of the fact.

Simple.

Chapter Eight

Caresa

"I would like to thank you all for coming here today." I met each of the society ladies' eyes as I held my glass of champagne in the air. "I know I met many of you when I was a child, and I look forward to remaking your acquaintance now that I am full grown and not in diapers." My joke was met with polite laughter. Raising my glass higher, I said, "To Italy!"

The ladies repeated my toast, and then the bell rang out in the opulent dining room signaling the beginning of our luncheon. Our antipasti were placed before us. As I lifted my fork to eat my *affettati misti*, I could feel the heavy stares of the aristocratic ladies on me.

"So, Duchessa," one of the ladies asked. I looked up to find Baronessa Russo regarding me closely. She was in her mid-twenties, with long blond hair and bright blue eyes. Her light features showed her heritage—she was from a town near the Austrian border. "Is the prince at home?"

My stomach flipped as the table grew quiet. I forced a smile. "No, he has been busy at the vineyards in Turin. This month sees him occupied with the harvests of Savona wines; he will return for the grape-crushing festival."

121

Baronessa Russo tilted her head. I thought I saw a hint of triumph in her eyes. "That's strange," she said. "I was recently in Florence and met the prince for a private dinner at the palazzo . . ." She pulled her features into a dramatically thoughtful expression. ". . . Oh, perhaps two days ago?"

I understood the underlying message—she had been with him for more than just dinner.

I did not let my smile slip. Instead, I nodded. "He goes back and forth to where he is needed most. Florence is his home. It's his business base."

"Yet you stay here?" Contessa Bianchi asked curiously. I remembered her face from the photographs Maria had made me memorize before the luncheon.

"I prefer it," I said smoothly. "I love the Umbrian countryside. It is peaceful." I chuckled. "Peace is welcome. I know my life will only become more hectic toward our wedding."

Of course it was a lie. Every lady here knew it was a lie, but good women of society were adept at falsifying truths and ignoring the glaring subtext of anything said aloud.

"A wedding date, yet no engagement ring," Baronessa Russo observed, holding out her champagne glass for a member of the staff to refill.

"I'm sure it's coming," the woman beside me said. "The prince is a busy man with a hugely successful enterprise. I'm sure when he returns he will spoil the duchessa rotten." Some of the tension released from my shoulders when all but the baronessa nodded in agreement. Most of them wore their obvious envy of my marriage to the prince clearly on their faces.

I felt like telling them there was nothing to envy.

As the servers began to clear the table of the first course, I leaned closer to the woman who had defended me. I studied her face, searching my mind for her name—Contessa Florentino. "Thank you, Contessa," I whispered so no one else could hear.

The pretty petite brunette with large green eyes waved her hand in dismissal. "Not a problem." She leaned closer still, turning her head away from the rest of the table. "I'm afraid this luncheon is more like a den of snakes for you, Duchessa. I don't know how much you know of the prince, but many of these women know him *very* well. Thankfully, I'm not one of them." The contessa never broke my gaze. She was direct and ballsy. I liked that in an acquaintance. Often in Italian society, or even among those in Manhattan, people rarely spoke the truth to one's face. They preferred to do it behind your back, because apparently it is more *ladylike*.

Societal politics was a peculiar game to play.

I took a sip of my champagne. "I am well aware of Zeno's reputation, Contessa. But thank you for being so forthcoming. It is more than welcome."

She smiled. "Call me Pia."

"Then call me Caresa."

I clinked my glass against hers. "I'm guessing the baronessa is one of Zeno's conquests?"

Pia nodded. "I live in Florence, Caresa. And I hate to be the bearer of bad news, but she is just one of many."

"I thought as much. She has been weighing me up since she arrived."

"At least you're not crying into your pasta over the news that your fiancé is a cad. Then again, one would have to be naïve to believe that these elaborate marriages we enter into are for love, no?"

"I knew I'd like you," I said to Pia and laughed when she threw back her head.

The other ladies were watching us, deeply intrigued. "Pia was just telling a funny story about my fiancé," I said. The women seemed satisfied by my vague explanation.

"We all have stories, Duchessa," Baronessa Russo said under her breath. The awkward tension from the women in her vicinity was palpable.

"I suspect you do," I quipped back, letting her know I had heard. Her embarrassed, flushed cheeks were but a small victory.

"How are you enjoying life in the country?" Pia asked, loud enough for the whole table to hear.

"It is beautiful. The estate is no doubt the most magical place I have ever seen."

"What do you do here for fun?" Contessa Bianchi asked.

My mind traveled to Achille. Unable to refrain from speaking the truth, I said, "Ride. Mainly dressage. I like to walk. Jog. I spend a great deal of my time doing that. And of course, I watch the harvest."

"The king owned a dressage team, did you know that? They were frequently the national champions. King Santo was horse-mad," Pia informed us; my interest was piqued.

"How quaint. But I'm not sure watching the harvest constitutes fun, Duchessa," Baronessa Russo said, pulling my attention from Pia.

"On the contrary," I replied. "This is the jewel in Savona Wines' crown. My family is tied into the business, as well you all know. I have been a part of this industry my whole life." I hid a smile as I added, "Zeno has been extremely happy with my interest. He will soon have a wife who understands his *entire* world—both his status and his business. I can share in all his victories."

A collective sigh came from all but Baronessa Russo and Pia. Baronessa Russo because she had meant what she said as a slight. And Pia because she knew the game I played.

"Did you work with your father in Manhattan, Duchessa? With Savona Wines?" Viscontessa Lori asked.

I shook my head. "No, I was at college. I had just finished my master's degree when I came here."

"In what?" Pia asked.

"Educational psychology. I would have loved to have pursued a career in education. Working with children and adults to overcome learning difficulties."

"There are many charities under the king's name that promote work such as that. I'm sure now he has passed, the chairs of those charities would appreciate the future queen taking his place," Viscontessa Lori told me. Excitement lit up my heart. I hadn't known about that side of the king's business.

"Thank you, Viscontessa," I said sincerely. "I will look into the possibilities immediately."

The entrée of *tortelli di zucca* was placed before us, and I inhaled the scent of the Bella Collina olive oil drizzled over the fresh pumpkin-filled pasta, curls of *Parmigiano-Reggiano* lying gently on top. "A treat from my home," I said, pointing to the dish. "I know we are in Umbria, but I wanted to bring a little of Parma to the table. Please, eat."

I ate my meal, listening to the ladies talk about the charities they were involved in or about their husbands and betrotheds. Contessa Bianchi had the table enraptured with a tale of a "commoner" she had once had a fling with.

"Caresa?" Pia said in a low voice.

"Yes?"

"Do you know methods of helping those who struggle to read or write? Those with learning difficulties?"

Her comment took me by surprise. "Yes," I replied. "I worked for many charities and schools during my studies, and assisted some of the best educational psychologists in Manhattan. I didn't get as far as I would have liked in the field, but I am proficient."

Pia glanced around to check no one was listening. She looked into my eyes. "My nephew." She cleared her throat. "He doesn't always do well in school. My sister married well, and her husband is ashamed that their son struggles to read and write. I love my nephew—when I talk to him he is bright and knowledgeable. But academically, he is weak. Very weak. He struggles with such simple tasks as holding a pen. He can barely write, and worse, he confided to my sister and me that when he reads, the words jump around the page. He can never focus enough to make out a single sentence."

My heart broke for Pia and her sister. "It sounds like he is dyslexic and maybe has dyspraxia. It is scary for the person at first, as they see everyone else doing these things with ease, but there are methods to help overcome the challenges."

Pia's eyes filled with tears. "Really?" I nodded. "His father, he won't help. He won't have his reputation damaged by his son being regarded as slow. He is threatening to send him away to a Swiss boarding school."

I covered Pia's hand. "If you want my help, Pia, it's yours. No one need know."

"You would do that?"

"Of course," I assured her. She squeezed my fingers in appreciation. She didn't speak for a while after that. I could see she was still teary.

As the dessert of limoncello gelato was placed before us, Pia said, "It was just little things at first. He would make up the stories for the books he was assigned to read as homework for school. He would get angry when we questioned him on silly mistakes in his class work. It wasn't until my sister gave him a book she knew by heart and asked him to read it and tell her about it that she realized he was fabricating stories about what he was supposed to be reading. He broke down after that and explained his troubles. It's . . ." Pia sighed. "It's been quite a challenge. But the worst part is seeing the frustration he bears. He is a kind, shy boy, but can explode with bouts of aggression when his pride is threatened."

I knew Pia kept talking to me. Somewhere in the back of my mind I heard her voice telling me more of her nephew's plight. But I couldn't make out what she had said. Because I was too busy feeling my face pale as a cold realization began to hit.

The newspaper story . . . the labels . . . the illegible tick . . . the holding of the pen . . . the shaking . . . asking me to circle the mistakes . . . asking me to leave . . . the pain and fear in his beautiful eyes . . .

He struggled to read and write. Or . . . maybe he couldn't read or write at all.

Achille, I thought, a stab of sympathy hitting me like a knife in my stomach. *How did I not see it? Caresa, you stupid, stupid girl.*

"Caresa?" Pia's questioning voice called me from my inner turmoil. I faked a smile and, somehow, for the next two hours, managed to make small talk as the ladies and I made our way to the grand reception room for drinks. I was sure I agreed to more dinner and charity functions than I could truly commit to, but I couldn't remember a single one.

Pia was the last to leave, taking with her my promise to see her nephew very soon. The minute she left, I told Maria I needed to lie down—a sudden headache, I explained. I just needed to rest after such a long function.

I didn't even bother changing from my white cap-sleeved Roland Mouret dress or my matching Prada heels. I didn't take off the Harry Winston diamond chandelier earrings that hung in my ears, or tie back my hair that had been curled into 1940s pin curls and left in flowing waves to my shoulders. Instead, the minute my bedroom door was locked, I fled through my balcony exit and hurried toward Achille's home.

The pace of my furiously beating heart kept time with my rushing feet. A crack of thunder roared above and spots of fat raindrops came sailing down from the sky. I ran into the barn to find Achille standing in the center of the floor, placing a bucket of freshly picked grapes beside the crushing barrel.

He started when I came rushing in, as a curtain of torrential rain dropped from the dark clouds outside. His blue eyes were surprised at my intrusion, but then heat exploded in my stomach as Achille, completely frozen to the spot, raked his gaze over me in my dress. And there was nothing innocent or timid about the sudden flare of passion in his eyes. The need and want was there, as plain as day. The muscles on his bare torso bunched and tensed; his hands clenched at his sides. Spatters of dirt and grape juice lay on his bronzed skin, his black hair unkempt and in disarray.

I imagined the picture we made. Me, a duchessa, styled and dressed to the nines and him, a winemaker, dirtied and roughened from an honest day's work.

I averted my gaze when I could no longer take the hunger in his eyes. I strived to find my composure, to find the courage to speak. But when my eyes landed on the trash can in the corner of the room, on the wrinkled newspaper that was still its only occupant, I rushed forward. I took out the paper and read the article, no longer caring if the story about me was good or bad. I just had to know. I read every word, and with every sentence, my heart broke a little more.

How long had he kept up this charade? How long had he kept this secret? Then my soul cracked completely. He had been without his father for months. A man who would have helped him. A man who read to him when Achille couldn't read for himself.

Achille . . . he was so alone.

So completely lost.

I felt him behind me. Still on the same spot across the room. I looked up; his distraught eyes were focused on the paper in my hands. "Achille," I whispered, feeling tears build in my eyes. "It made no mention of my staying here in Umbria. Or anything about the prince, like you said. It was a piece about my life in New York, about my family and the business."

Achille's skin became ashen. He looked away at the sheet of rain dancing beyond the open barn door.

"The labels." I dropped the newspaper on the floor. "The missed mistakes, the incorrect sample . . . you didn't know, did you?"

"Don't," Achille bit out when I was a mere three feet from him. "Don't talk of things you don't know, Duchessa."

"Achille—"

I expected him to shout, to display the aggression I knew he harbored so deeply inside, the aggression he had shown me twice before. The aggression born from frustration.

But instead Achille tiredly hung his head, his body losing its will to fight. "Please . . . don't . . ." He took a deep breath. "Not you . . . not from you . . ."

My bottom lip shook at the defeat in his voice, in his stature. My soul screamed in sympathy for the torment afflicting his. Because this reaction, this lack of willingness to argue, told me everything I needed to know.

He truly couldn't read or write. He could make the world's finest wine, could be such a kind and gentle man, yet he could not read the labels of the award-winning merlot he made with his talented bare hands.

It was the cruelest of God's jokes.

"Don't pity me." My breath paused at the softly spoken request. "I don't want your pity."

"I don't pity you," I said, my voice shaking with the tension of the moment. "I am angry for you. I am so angry that you were never given the help you should have been."

Achille flinched, as if my words had physically wounded him. An expression of pain disfigured his beautiful features.

Achille avoided my eyes, instead searching the barn. His hands shook at his sides, but not with anger. There was no anger left in this hollowed-out space. I could feel only Achille's despondency, his lack of understanding about what to do now that his greatest secret had been exposed to the harsh light of day.

I saw the empty buckets spread around his feet, only one still full. I saw the rest of the grapes in the barrel ready to be crushed. Achille's eyes shone like the most beautiful stained glass as helplessness gathered in their depths.

I had never wanted to hurt him, to shame him. I only wanted to help. My pained soul wanted nothing more than to see him healed of this injustice.

I needed to make him feel comfortable.

I needed this lost boy found.

The old cassette player was sitting on the countertop. Skirting around the motionless Achille, I pressed play . . . and my eyes closed as a wave of emotion washed over me. The opening bars of "Sogno", my dressage music, graced the humid stormy air with their perfect sound.

Achille had been listening to this music today. The old speakers of the player were still warm. He had been listening to this song. As Andrea Bocelli sang of sleep and of dreams, I turned and saw a bead of sweat travel the length of Achille's back. His skin shivered in its wake and his muscles danced.

I approached him slowly, like one would approach a wild animal. I stood before him, and his nostrils flared. His eyes were still focused outside. "Were you about to crush the grapes?"

My diversion tactic worked; Achille's eyebrows pulled down in confusion and his eyes fell to mine. "Yes," he said.

"Then let's crush them." I bent down to take off my shoes. Achille watched me as I kicked my heels aside. He looked dubiously at my dress, but I didn't let that stop me. It was only fabric, and replaceable. Achille was a fellow human in pain. There was no comparison.

"Do we wash our feet?" I asked, looking around the barn for cleaning supplies. Achille took a while to move. He led me to a metal trough filled with an astringent-smelling solution. As I stepped into the cold liquid, Achille bent down to rid himself of his boots and roll his jeans up to his knees.

I stepped out of the bucket. Achille washed his own feet, then he poured the final buckets of grapes into the barrel. Lifting the hem of my dress, I hitched the material up to my thighs and tried to climb in, but the sides were too high. Just as I was about to ask for Achille's help, he slipped his hands around my waist, and as if I weighed no more than a feather, he placed me in the barrel. The top layer of grapes exploded under me, the juices slipping between my toes and flowing over my feet and ankles.

Achille watched me in fascination. The final note of "Sogno" sounded from the cassette player. A clicking noise sounded though the speakers, and then another song began to play.

"Are you getting in?" I asked.

I was rewarded with a timid smile. Then Achille stepped in, his tall, broad frame crowding me in the barrel. I yelped as I was thrown off balance by a shift in the mass of grapes beneath us. Achille reached out and steadied me. His hands wrapped around my own, causing the hem of my dress to fall back to my knees. His gaze drifted downward, and mine followed. The bottom of my dress was covered in red juice.

"You are ruining your dress."

"Yes, I suspect I am," I replied. A husky sliver of a laugh escaped his lips. It was the most heavenly sound. "So," I asked, ignoring his concern for my attire. "How do we do this?"

"We stomp." He began lifting his feet, slowly crushing the grapes under them. Holding onto him more tightly, I copied his movements, the sticky juice flowing faster the more we stomped.

"It feels bizarre," I said, looking down at the grape juice rising up the sides of the barrel. "The juice is sticky, the grape flesh soft, but the stems are hard. They keep stabbing the soles of my feet."

"We leave the stems on to strengthen the tannins and deepen the color of the wine." The more Achille talked of the wine, the more his confidence returned to his voice. Wine, he knew. He could never be caught off guard when it came to his beloved merlot. It followed a system at which he excelled. A routine that he knew as well as he knew himself. There was no threat, no feeling of inferiority.

"How long do we do this?" I asked as we circled the barrel, ensuring each grape was paid equal attention.

"As long as it takes," he replied. "I can be here for an hour on my own. With you, it will be less." As the minutes passed and the juice rose, the splashes came higher, reaching my chest and his stomach.

"I believe your dress is beyond saving," Achille said, a slight breathiness to his deep voice. I checked out my dress, and, sure enough, it was now sodden with red grape juice up to my waist. The once-white material had become transparent due to the wetness of the juice.

As I flicked my head up in embarrassment, a drop of grape juice splashed from the barrel to spray the side of my neck. And then everything happened at once. I cried out in surprise. Achille's hands released mine, moving to my waist. And he lowered his mouth to my neck, his soft lips stilling on my skin as they kissed away the sweet, rolling drop of juice.

I felt as though I was in a dream, a surreal out-of-body experience where Achille's mouth was on me. I could feel his breath ghosting down my skin and his hard chest pressed flush against mine. I wanted this dream to be real. I wanted to be in Achille's warm embrace. I wanted him to want me enough to drop his guard and let me in.

I wanted him to want me, period.

Then when a low groan sailed into my ears, and I felt the soft swipe of a tongue lapping at the spilled juice, I knew I wasn't lost in a fantasy. I was here. In the barn . . . wrapped tightly in Achille's arms.

His mouth *was* on my neck.

He was against me, body against body . . . feeling exactly like I knew it would: perfect, like we had always *been*.

Achille's lips suddenly stilled against my skin. His hands tightened on my waist, then he slowly withdrew his head, stopping just inches in front of my face. His pupils were dilated, the black nearly eclipsing the blue, as his wary, shocked eyes fixed upon my face. Heat filled his cheeks, and his mouth worked as if he wanted to speak but could find no words to say. His breathing was heavy; mine had stopped altogether.

I stared.

He stared.

The air between us crackled with tension.

I wasn't sure who moved first. Like the last time we had been this close, something pulled us together, an unexplainable attraction that seized our minds and our hearts and our souls. One moment I was

135

transfixed by his eyes, the next, Achille's mouth was fused with my own, his soft lips against mine, his large hands in my hair.

My hands landed on his back, my fingers clawing at his naked skin, trying to pull him even closer. I needed him closer than he was, needed to feel him against me, within me, taking me. It was irrational and wrong, but I couldn't persuade myself to stop.

My fingernails scraped along the flesh of his back, and Achille hissed into my mouth, followed by a deep groan. His hands tightened in my hair, and he plunged his tongue forward to meet mine. The taste of him exploded on my taste buds—fruity and sweet with just the faintest hint of wine.

This time it was me who moaned, heat surging through my veins and muscles and bones. I felt on fire, dancing on the precipice of something I wasn't sure I could come back from. But, like anything addictive, I took and I took until my lips were bruised and my desire was raw.

I broke away to recapture my lost breath. Achille's lips didn't stop, traveling over my cheeks, down my neck and along the top of my chest. My head tipped back, eyes rolling shut as he seared me with his touch, setting fire to my blood.

My hands traveled to his arms, then up into his hair. Achille's nose ran up my neck until his forehead pressed against my own. "Caresa," he murmured in a slow, graveled tone. "I feel you inside me. Here and here and here." His hands moved to his head, his mouth, his heart.

I should have stopped it. I knew I should have stopped it. But I moved closer, pressing my breasts to his chest, breathless as he hissed and let out a groan.

And that was all it took.

That was all it took to break the shy, retiring winemaker into a soul untamed. Achille reached down and took hold of the bottom of my thighs, lifting me until my legs wrapped around his waist. My already ruined dress split at the back, but I didn't care. All I cared about was the man whose neck my arms were wrapped around, the warm skin searing its blazing heat through mine, and the lips that were joined against my own—wanting me, needing me, taking me—just like I craved.

I closed my eyes as we urgently explored each other's mouths, as if time were a fragile hourglass, the sand taunting us, stealing away this moment, reminding us that our hearts could not entwine.

Achille stepped out of the crushing barrel and carried me into the heavy sheet of rain outside. The water was a cooling balm as it fell from the stormy sky above, drenching us, yet our lips still did not part.

We could not be separated . . .

. . . not even for a moment.

Achille's feet sloshed on the flooding ground, and the remaining sounds of Andrea Bocelli's hypnotizing voice sailed away into the distance as he carried me into his house.

I pulled my head back with a gasp, blinking as my mascara rolled down my cheeks. Achille's lips were reddened from my smeared lipstick, his eyes dancing with light. He clearly didn't care what I looked like. In that second, I couldn't care either. Our movements were rough and raw and fumbled . . . we were tangled, chaotic perfection, a frantic, flawless mess.

The fire was roaring, basking the small living room in burnt orange and yellow and red. The wood crackled and split, and its earthy smell filled every inch of the air.

Achille's eyes met my own, and for a brief, suspended moment we simply stared at each other. I drank in his beauty as he did my own. No words were spoken, yet we communicated with ease.

His parted lips told me he wanted me. His flushed cheeks told me he hungered for me. But his open, honest gaze told me he needed me more than air.

"Yes," I whispered. It was all that needed to be said.

Achille took me from the living room, down a small hallway and into a bedroom. The entire time, I ran my hands through his thick, black, wet hair and over his stubbled cheeks and tensed neck. I had to touch him.

I could not let him go, not even for a single second.

He was a drug I could not forego. I lusted for the hit of his taste, the high from the heat of his body.

Achille stopped before a simple wooden-framed full-size bed. The room was sparse but for the bed and a nightstand. An oil-burning lamp sat in the window, a curiously old-fashioned light, yet perfectly suited to this cottage. The warm glow cast a golden sunset hue over the room, the slightly open window allowing the pitter-patter of rain to be our serenade.

I could hear his heart pounding next to mine. Then, in a move that made my legs tremble and an intense lightness fill my chest, Achille ran the back of his finger so painstakingly slowly down my cheek that it brought tears to my eyes. He was cherishing me . . . memorizing me. He was worshiping me as though I were the answer to his prayers.

In that moment, he felt like the answer to all of mine.

His hands drifted from the tops of my shoulders to the nape of my neck. He unzipped my dress. Cool air kissed my damp skin as the ruined material slid delicately from my body. I did not move my eyes from Achille's the whole time. So, when my dress slipped to the floor, pooling at my feet, and my white lace bra and panties were exposed to his naked gaze, I witnessed it all—the burning desire filling every part of his beautiful face, his clenching jaw and flushed skin as he dropped his eyes to study my bared body.

A moan slipped through my lips, my eyelashes fluttering to a close, as his fingers wandered along the crests of my breasts. The feel of him touching me so closely, of having Achille Marchesi caressing me just as reverently as he nurtured his wine, was the headiest of sensations.

I opened my eyes, lids heavy, as warmth built at my core. Achille reached down to unfasten the front clasp of my bra. With a soft tug, the bra joined the dress at my feet.

My nipples ached as my damp skin was exposed to the warming air. Achille cupped my flesh in his hands, and a hiss ripped from his throat. I moaned at the feel of him touching me so intimately. He stepped closer and pressed the bare skin of his chest against me.

The sensation was almost too much to bear. Every cell in my body roared to life, a mighty ache in my chest pulling me further and further against Achille, yet yearning to get closer still. He molded me to him like a second skin. His hands on my back trapped me in their grip, his cheek running along my cheek, his earthy musk warming my skin.

Our lips fell back together, and all the tenderness ebbed away, along with any worries I had that this act between us was wrong.

His tongue slipped along mine. Our hands roved and branded, clawing at one another with a desperate urgency; no more patience remained. My hands moved down his hard abdominals, feeling them flex and twitch, before landing on the waistband of his jeans. My fingers trembled as they unsnapped the button and pulled down the zipper, brushing down over his hardness.

Achille groaned as my hand reached inside, shaking like a leaf with anticipation. I returned the pained sound when my hand met his flesh, no underwear blocking my way.

He was hard and large and so warm to the touch. My free hand tugged on the falling waistband of his jeans and helped drop them from his tapered muscled hips. Achille's tall, broad frame dominated me, towering over me, making me shake where I stood.

As I gave him one gentle stroke, it unleashed something wild within him. His hands fell to the sides of my panties and, with one pull, tore them from their seams. The delicate French lace fluttered like gossamer feathers to the floor.

And that's how we took pause. Exposed, vulnerable—two hearts and souls and bodies unveiled. Achille's breathing echoed in my ear, roughened like a harsh wind rustling through fallen autumn leaves.

Achille, with an easy strength, lifted me from the clothes at my feet, and into his muscled arms. I held on tightly, never wanting this feeling to end. Never wanting to leave the security of his embrace, and never wanting to be parted from this man who was burrowing his goodness into my blood and my bones.

He turned and lowered me down until my back landed on the soft mattress below. As the weight of my body hit the faded patchwork comforter, his scent from the fabric engulfed me. This was the bed where he slept each night, where he dreamed and despaired, resting his tired body and gentle soul.

Achille moved back as he freed himself from the jeans at his ankles, standing in the oil lamp's glow. And I couldn't breathe at the sight. His body was toned to perfection, not over-muscled, but athletic and strong, with the most stunning golden olive skin just begging for my touch. He looked down at me, naked and exposed on his bed, with nothing but fire and desire in his eyes.

For me.

Only for me.

"Caresa . . ." Achille murmured, edging forward. For the first time since we had given in to our lust, I saw nervousness etch across his beautiful face. He froze; fear had robbed him of his courage.

I held out my arms, guiding him to me, coaxing him near. "I have to have this," I said softly, a slight tremor to my voice. "I have to have you, Achille."

"Caresa," Achille moaned again, but this time came forward, his hands landing on either side of my body.

The minute he was over me, his arms caging my head and his body covering mine, we locked eyes—blue searing brown. He pushed a damp curl from my face, a gentle, contented smile upon his lips. An all-encompassing emotion swept through me, a realization of peace found in another's embrace.

Achille laid the sweetest of sweet kisses to the center of my forehead and whispered, "Beautiful . . . beautiful . . ." The ravenous heat of the previous moment was, in a second, turned on its head. Gone was the hungry, desperate need, and in its place a calm serenity shared in the vulnerability of the other.

Before Achille could see the tear escaping from the corner of my eye, I threaded my hands through his hair and brought his lips to mine. He melted against me like ice under the Umbrian sun. This kiss was slow and deep and true.

It was a tattoo on my heart.

Achille's hand skirted down my waist, landing on my thigh, pushing it to the side. He slipped his hips between my legs, placing his body flush against mine. Stomach to stomach, chest to breast, kiss to lips.

I felt his hardness against my core and spilled my moan into his mouth. He rolled his hips, touching me where I needed it most. "Caresa," he rasped against my mouth, his skin scalding the palms of my roaming hands.

I reached down between us as our temperatures soared, stroking him in my hand. He followed my lead, running his fingers along my most sensitive part. My back arched and my skin prickled.

Achille peppered kisses along my jaw and over my cheek, until I hit a sudden peak. I screamed out his name, pressing against his fingers until every last morsel of pleasure had been wrung from my body.

But I wanted more.

I needed more.

Guiding Achille's hand away with my own, I shifted until he was moving toward my entrance, exactly where he belonged. He stared into my eyes, his jaw clenching as I took him in my hand once again. His olive skin glistened under the strain of maintaining his composure.

"I want you so badly," I whispered. Achille's eyes closed, and he pushed forward. My head tipped back as his length filled me, until I was consumed by his scent, devoured by his touch. I could not see where he ended and I began. I felt him within me, both physically and spiritually, the connection simultaneously wondrous and terrifying.

Achille tensed as he filled me to the hilt, his breathing ragged and raw. His arms tensed as he held me close. I looked up at his face, and I melted. His eyes were studying me as if I were a dream, as if at any moment I could disappear, to leave him all alone once more. His lips were red and slightly open, and his soft skin was flushed and warm. I lifted my hand and pressed it against his cheek. Achille curled into my touch just as surely as a sunflower follows the warmth of the sun across the sky.

His mouth found the center of my palm and pressed on it a single kiss. I wasn't sure why, but that pure, sweet gesture shattered my heart. It was as though it was a silent thank-you; for what, I could only guess.

Then, as if he could not wait any longer, he rolled his hips, moving inside me. My hand, still burning from his kiss, became wrapped in his hand, his fingers threading tightly through my own. His lips sought out mine. In seconds there was nothing unconnected between us. We were two halves of one whole, clinging and clutching, desperate for each other.

Achille increased his speed, the hard muscles of his chest brushing against my breasts, shivers of pleasure darting straight to my core. "Achille," I murmured over and over as the feeling of him inside me became too much, yet not enough.

He moved faster and faster, low raspy groans slipping from his lips. The heat between us rose until condensation built on the window and our skin was slick with sweat.

When I wasn't sure I could take any more, a tension so great, so earth-shatteringly beautiful, began surging at my core and flooding through my veins. "Achille," I cried, my fingernails pressing into the flesh on his back.

I knew Achille was as close as I when his movements became stronger and more jagged, his head tucking into my neck. My eyes closed and I smiled, feeling him take such comfort in me, such absolute happiness.

And then it hit. Pleasure, like nothing I'd ever felt before, engulfed me like a flame, taking every part of my body hostage as it burned through all my senses, only to restore them with bliss and light and life.

Achille groaned. His body stilled above me and he filled me with his warmth. The muscles in his back bunched and jerked, then slowly calmed along with his rapidly beating heart.

I ghosted my fingertips over his back, more than content to stay exactly like this—joined in every possible way, calm in the peace after the storm.

Achille's warm breath dusted over my neck, until he carefully lifted his head. I had thought him beautiful since the day I had first seen him working in his vineyard, torso bare with jean-clad legs. But as his sated face met mine, awe and reverence so clear in his expression, I knew I had been mistaken. Because nothing could ever beat this moment.

The moment I realized this had not just been about making love. But that something bigger, deeper pulsed between us. And then my heart broke, because whatever dormant spark had just ignited within us, it must not be given chance to flourish.

Tears filled my eyes. This could never be. We were from two completely different worlds. We weren't written in the stars.

"I know." Achille spoke in a pained and graveled voice. I turned my head and allowed myself to look into his eyes. His chest expanded as he took in a heavy breath. "I know." He slid to the side and wrapped me in his arms, cradling my face into the crook of his shoulder and neck. "There can never be more than this—"

"Achille," I whispered painfully, hearing the sadness and resignation in his tone.

"You are not part of this world, and I am not part of yours." I didn't have anything else to say. It was the truth, and no frivolous sentiments or empty promises would ever change things.

So I relaxed into his chest, savoring each second that we had left. Achille's hands ran lazily through my hair, and I stared through the window at the falling rain.

The oil lamp flickered in the breeze, the golden reflections dancing over the white-painted walls. My eyes became lost in the trance, so much so that I nearly missed Achille take a long breath, then softly say, "They said I was slow."

My gut clenched. I stilled, every muscle in my body going rigid.

"They said that I was dumb and nothing would ever change that."

I winced. My chest cracked in two at the embarrassment in his voice. I didn't speak. I didn't want to push him or say anything that would stop him from opening up.

He no longer had his father. No one to share in his pain.

I would be that person for him tonight. He needed this from me. I couldn't give him my heart, so this would have to be enough.

When the sun rose, this would all be a distant dream.

So I prayed to God and begged him to keep the darkness at bay as long as he could. To keep our stars shining and the rain crashing down . . . so I would have time to say goodbye.

Chapter Nine

Achille

Caresa had become a statue in my arms. I was racked with nerves as I bared my shame. My father had always told me that I wasn't dumb, that my weakness in academics did not define me or how intelligent I was. But I was sure he had only said that to make me feel better.

I wasn't like everyone else. The teachers, even the king, had made sure I knew that. *He is not meant for academia, but instead for the fields*, King Santo had said to my father.

I always found it strange that I could use my hands to make the wine, yet the minute I tried to hold a pencil or pen, my fingers would fail.

I couldn't even write my name.

"When I . . . when I look at the words on a page, they never make sense. The lines blur and the letters jump around." My breath caught in my throat. "My eyes don't see what other people see when they read. My brain doesn't function the same way as everyone else's." I laughed a humorless laugh. "I talk of Plato and Tolkien's books, yet I haven't managed more than a few pages in my entire life. My eyes get tired from trying to decipher each word, and I get so frustrated that I have to walk away." I sighed, my stomach sinking. "Maybe I am just dumb after all. Maybe the teachers and King Santo were right—academia isn't for me."

Caresa's head snapped up at my words. Her skin was still flushed from when we had made love. But her soft expression had changed into one so severe it took me by surprise. "They were wrong," she said. "They were all *so* wrong it incenses me." I blinked at her in surprise. Caresa shuffled from under my arms, flipped onto her stomach and rested her folded arms on my torso. "Achille, you are not dumb. One only has to be in your presence for a few minutes to see that you are one of the brightest, most talented people walking this earth." She closed her eyes, calming herself down. I didn't take my eyes off her, her compliment seeping down deep into my bones.

She opened her eyes. "I am not fully qualified. I have no official papers to diagnose you. But I think you are dyslexic and maybe dyspraxic. The two commonly go hand in hand." Her eyes narrowed. "So let's get one thing straight. You are not dumb. Your vocabulary is extensive, your understanding of any given topic is vast and sound. You are not dumb, Achille, and you are selling yourself short by allowing that falsehood to take root."

"What is dys . . . dysle . . ." I shook my head, not able to remember the names.

"Dyslexia is when your brain struggles to make connections to words. It is not uncommon and can be aided tremendously with specialized, personal programs. Dyspraxia has many forms. It is when some of your motor skills are not as strong as others. It may be why you struggle holding a pen yet you are able to easily hold reins and make wine. There is no blueprint. Everyone is different. Some tasks you think will be difficult come easily; other simple tasks may feel like the most impossible thing in the world."

"I find bottling the wine difficult too. Nothing else, but I struggle when it comes to bottling," I admitted shyly. "The small pieces that are used in the process are hard for me to control." Caresa nodded as if it made perfect sense. Nothing about this had ever made sense to me, yet she understood my problem in mere seconds.

"It is a case of crossed wires. Picture it as the brain's usually clear path being blocked with fallen branches. We simply have to find another route, but that route *can* be found, no matter how hopeless it seems." She gritted her teeth, looking so adorably fierce. "I will not allow you to think of yourself as unworthy or subpar. You are not. I won't accept that, and you should not accept that of yourself either."

She abruptly stopped. Not even my father had fought for me that hard. Caresa slid her hand into mine and linked our fingers together. She appeared fascinated at the joining. She squeezed them once, twice, then said, "Let me help you."

I froze.

The offer terrified me. Caresa seemed somehow fooled by me; she thought I was something more than I truly was. I knew she had experience with this type of thing. But I didn't want her to see me that way, stumbling through books and scribbling on paper like a toddler. I wanted her to remember me as she saw me now.

I didn't want her pity.

I opened my mouth to tell her thank you, but that I would decline.

She seemed to anticipate my answer and brought my fingers to her lips. She brushed kiss after soft kiss to each of my knuckles and whispered, "Please, Achille. Please let me do this for you. You have given me so much. Please . . . please let me at least try."

I leaned my head back against the pillow and closed my eyes. I thought of my father sitting by the fire, reading to me. I would hang on his every word, wishing I could track my eyes over the page with the same ease as he did. Wishing I could be transported to far-off lands and other worlds, sitting by the fire, a glass of wine by my side.

I wished it didn't have to be so hard.

"Why does it have to be so hard?" I asked, flinching in embarrassment when I realized I had spoken my wish aloud. My voice held a tremor, and my throat was dry.

"What?" Caresa asked softly.

I shrugged, thinking of the last few weeks I had with my father, watching him fade before my eyes, my hero leaving me day by day. Watching him stare each night at the picture of the mother I loved but never knew. And I thought of all those nights he had tried to help me read, but grew helpless and sad when nothing he did ever worked.

Until he tried no more.

Until *I* had tried no more.

"Everything," I said quietly. "Everything just always seems . . . difficult. Nothing comes easily." My gaze drifted to Caresa, bare and with me in my bed, and I immediately wanted to refute my claim. Everything with her was confusing, yet came easily at the same time.

But our situation was not easy. She was marrying the prince. She had only returned to Italy to marry into House Savona, to take her place as the next "queen" in the so-called royal succession.

Our situation was complex, yet I knew that falling in love with her would be the simplest thing in the world.

"Achille," Caresa murmured. She reached up and ran her hand down my cheek. "Let me try and ease some of this for you. Please . . . I'm begging you to let me try. You *can* read and write, we just have to find a way through the fog."

I looked out of the window, seeing the rainclouds beginning to move away. The stormy sky parted, allowing stray beams of moonlight to flood the vines. Stars started to appear in the dark heavens, flecks of silver in a velvet sea of black.

"Even after tonight, you should still come and ride Rosa." I focused back on Caresa. "I see the passion on your face when you practice your dressage. It lights you up. It makes your heart content." A dull ache formed in my chest at the thought of walking away from her, from this night. But it was worse when I thought of her losing the joy she gained from riding my father's treasured Andalusian. Losing the smile on her beautiful face as she danced around the arena, free from worry.

"Okay," she replied. I could tell by the roughness of her voice that I had taken her by surprise. It was a selfish offer too. Because I didn't know how it happened so hard, so fast, but I couldn't imagine a week going by without seeing Caresa, her finding me amongst the vines . . . the sound of her trotting around the arena as I crushed the grapes.

As hard as it would be, I *could* live without touching her again. I couldn't live without occasionally bearing witness to her bright smile.

"And the winemaking?" she added. My eyebrows rose in surprise. A shy expression set on her face. "There is still a lot more of the process for me to observe. I . . . I don't know if you've noticed, but I'm rather passionate about your wine."

I couldn't help it. I laughed, and as she laughed in return my heart jolted toward her just that little bit more. "I know," I said, running my thumb over her bottom lip, trying to memorize exactly how she looked right then. "I know how much you adore my wine."

"I don't just adore your wine," she whispered, and by the blush on her cheeks, I knew she hadn't meant to say that.

She dropped her forehead to my stomach, then after a deep breath, lifted her eyes. "You are allowing me to ride your horse, allowing me to study the process of your award-wining wine. Please, Achille. Just give me a few weeks to try and help you with your reading and writing. Allow me the chance to show you that it is not a lost cause. Just . . . for me. Please, if not for yourself, do this for me."

My pulse raced with nerves and discomfort. She would see all my flaws. She would see me completely exposed. But . . .

I resolved I would do it for her.

Caresa waited, breath held, for my response. With a defeated sigh, I nodded, giving her the answer she so badly wanted.

"Thank you," she whispered. She crawled above me and pressed her lips against mine. The surprise act of affection caught me off guard, but not enough for me not to respond. My hand cupped the back of her head as the innocent kiss deepened with our escalating need.

Wanting to have her again, craving another moment of being joined so closely, I rolled her onto her back, crowding the space where she lay. Caresa broke from my mouth and looked into my eyes. "We can only have tonight."

"I know." I turned to look out of the window at the high moon, then back to her. "But the night is not yet over. The sun is still asleep."

Caresa's fingers brushed through my hair. "Then kiss me again."

I did as she asked, exploring more of her than before. I kissed every patch of her skin, stroked every strand of her hair. This time it was slower. We savored each second, nothing rushed, everything unhurried.

But eventually sleep came calling for Caresa. It didn't for me. I held her tightly to my chest, breathing in the peach and vanilla from her hair, the floral notes from her expensive perfume. I watched the unwanted sun begin to rise behind the distant green hills of Umbria and heard the birds bring their morning song. With every ray of light chasing shadows from my small bedroom, a little piece of me died.

I couldn't stay here.

I couldn't be here when she woke. I couldn't see the flecks of gold in her eyes that I had never known were there before, nor the freckles peppering her cheeks that had grown more and more prominent with each day she spent with me in the fields under the sun.

But worse, I couldn't hear her goodbye.

I would see her again of course, when this night had passed. When I didn't have her scent on my skin and the fresh memory of what she felt like under me, in my bed, cradled in my arms.

As gently as I could, being careful to not rouse her from sleep, I laid her down on the mattress, pulling the comforter over her naked bronzed skin to stave off the morning chill.

I dressed in jeans and a red flannel shirt then left her to sleep. I needed fresh air. I slipped on my boots and went outside. The minute the door was shut, I inhaled a much-needed deep breath. I tipped my head back, drinking in the dawn sky. Purples and pinks slashed through the fading black, the stars being forced to bed. I heard the distant sound of tractors already in the fields; the winemakers' and farmers' day had already begun. I shook out my hands and began the painstaking task of buttoning up my shirt and jeans—another simple task that never came easily to me.

Ten minutes later, I had tacked up Nico and made my way past the perimeter of my vineyard and out into the mass of the estate's acres beyond. I rarely left the security of my home. I couldn't remember the last time I had been out here. I was always out here as child, playing in the trees with my best friend, or fishing in the fully stocked man-made lake.

I arrived at the edge of another vineyard. I let my eyes drift over the already harvested vines. This was one of the mass-produced reds. I shook my head as I squeezed Nico into a steady trot. I couldn't imagine being such a winemaker. Not being at one with the earth and

154

the vines.

I could never be so distant or unappreciative of anything in my life.

That thought brought the image of the prince to mind. I hadn't spoken to him in years. He hadn't even come to my father's funeral. Somewhere over the years he had changed from fun and kind to cold and stuck up. He looked down on everyone on this estate. He looked down on Umbria. He ignored the raw unkempt beauty of the region in favor of Tuscany's pretty, perfectly landscaped views. The king had spent most of his days here. Zeno spent all of his days in Florence.

I knew nothing of the business side of Savona Wines. But I knew my wine was essential to the royal family's wealth and status in the wine world. I was paid a small, living wage, though I rarely touched anything I earned. I knew it was nothing to the profits that the king, and now the prince, would be making from my blood, sweat and tears. But I cherished my home, my horses and my vines. Most of what I ate came from the land. I didn't need much else.

At least the king would visit us twice a month, asking me to show him the work my father and I had been doing. He would sit with me and eat lunch while my father continued his work in the fields. He wouldn't speak much, but I didn't mind his company—he was cold in demeanor, standoffish, but not unkind. At least he cared about getting to know his employees and took an interest in the work we did on his land.

Prince Zeno couldn't care less.

He didn't deserve this place. Knew nothing of this rare jewel he now owned. My head convinced me I was referring to these sprawling vineyards, but my heart knew I referred to something—*someone*—else.

Because he didn't deserve *her* either. I knew of his reputation. Even as a child he had been cocky and arrogant. He would never know Caresa's worth. She would just be another shiny toy to add to his burgeoning pile.

The thought of her being treated this way almost caused me to scream out in frustration.

She deserved more.

She deserved someone who would love and cherish her . . . who would never be parted from her side . . . not even for a moment.

Needing to feel the rush of cool air on my face, I pushed Nico into a canter. We sped along the dirt track, kicking up the still-wet mud in our wake. We pushed on until we reached the end of the long track. I slowed him to a trot, and I saw we had arrived at the botanical gardens. Greenhouse after greenhouse stretched for the length of the land. Nico walked us past the nearest greenhouse, and I noted the rows and rows of rose bushes inside—full white flowers standing proudly on deep-green stems. These greenhouses provided fresh flowers for both the main house and for the Savona florist in Orvieto.

I scanned the area. There was no one in sight.

Acting on impulse, I dismounted Nico, tied him to a fence post and jumped over the fence. I rushed toward the greenhouse and slid back the glass door. The intense smell of the roses hit my nose like a tidal wave. There was a pair of shears on a wooden table; I took them and cut the fullest, purest white rose from a bush. I ducked back out of the greenhouse and scampered back to Nico like a thief in the dawn.

I tucked the rose in my shirt and cantered all the way back home. As I arrived, the sky was turning from purple and pink to blue. Fluffy white clouds chased away the remaining gray, promising a bright, warm day. I untacked Nico and let him and Rosa out into the paddock.

When I approached my cottage, I peered though my bedroom window. My chest tightened. Caresa was still lying in the spot where I had left her, her dark, now-wavy hair splayed out over the pillow, her chest gently rising up and down in sleep. I had never seen anything more beautiful.

I clutched the rose in my hand as I simply watched her sleep. Ordering my feet to move, I entered the cottage and padded silently into the bedroom. My hands shook as I sat on the edge of my bed, careful to not wake Caresa. She murmured in her sleep, the comforter slipping down to reveal her bare full breasts.

My cheeks blazed on seeing her body this way in the daylight. It reminded me that what had happened last night was *real*. We had kissed and explored and made love. She had smiled at me, cried for me, and let me hold her close.

As I placed the fragrant white rose on the pillow beside her, I wondered if she knew what she had done for me too. I wondered if she could tell that she had been my first. I wondered if she knew that I had never touched anyone the way I'd touched her. That what she had given me was more than I could ever have prayed for.

She had allowed the barriers around my heart to finally fall . . . just as quickly as I was falling for her.

Caresa moved her arm, her delicate fingers with their purple nails landing right beside the white petals of the flower. It was an appropriate symbol—white petals for my innocence, beside the hand that had taken it as its own.

I had to turn away when the stabbing pain in my stomach became too much. The rose was a pitiful token for the gift she had given me. But nothing I could give would ever be enough. She was a duchessa. I was just me—no titles, no money.

Just me.

A Marchesi would never be enough for an Acardi. It was a fool's dream to even entertain such a thought.

I cast my head down, running my calloused hand over my face. My eyes fell on the drawer of my nightstand. Before I knew it, my hand was moving to the drawer. I opened it up, withdrawing its solitary occupant. My father's letter sat heavily in my hands. And like I did once a day, I clumsily took it from the envelope and unfolded it.

The same wave of frustration and anger surged through me as my eyes tried in earnest to read the cursive script. And like every day, I could make out a few simple letters before they all became a jumbled mess of confusion on the page.

The letter shook along with my hands. I had no idea what my father had left me in this letter. Several months of wondering and guessing and praying for the ability to just hear from him again. He knew I couldn't read yet he had left me a letter. I struggled to understand what he had been thinking. Why would he taunt me so?

My father was the kindest man I had ever known; there wasn't a cruel bone in his body. Nothing about this made sense.

I averted my eyes from the letter, searching for some calm. My eyes fell on Caresa, sleeping. The sight was an instant balm to my anger. As I felt the sheets of paper between my finger and thumb, I wondered if I could get her to read it to me. I . . . trusted her. I knew she would do it if I asked.

But I knew I wouldn't.

If my father needed to tell me something in a letter, I wanted it to be me who read it.

Then I thought of her offer. I thought of what she said could be wrong with me. That the wires in my head were simply crossed, my path blocked with fallen branches. That we could find a way to get around them, to help me see words and write them down—together.

"Okay," I whispered, so quietly she didn't even stir. "Okay, Caresa. I want you to show me the way."

It was several minutes before I put the letter back in the envelope and forced myself to leave the sanctuary my bedroom had become. Falling back into my old routine, I went to my vines, with my cassette player and my grapes. And I did what I did best.

Only with Caresa's scent still on my skin . . .

. . . and the memory of her lips against my own.

Knowing that, for a brief moment in time, we had been two halves of one whole.

*****

Two days came and went without a word from Caresa. Then on the third day, when I arrived in the barn to begin crushing the grapes from the final two rows of vines, I found her near the fire, a long table pulled close to its warmth, two seats tucked underneath.

A mobile whiteboard was standing in front of the table; pens, pencils and piles of paper were stacked upon the tabletop.

My blood cooled when I saw all the reading and writing supplies. Then it warmed when Caresa lifted her head, as beautiful as ever, if not more. Flashes of our night together instantly filled my mind. I idly wondered if she had liked the rose. When I had returned that night Caresa had gone. She had not come to say goodbye to me among the vines.

But the rose was no longer on the pillow.

I didn't know why, but it made me feel ten feet tall.

"Achille," Caresa called in greeting, her voice slightly breathless, her tanned skin rosy. She was casually dressed in jeans, brown heeled boots and a simple white blouse. Her hair was pulled up into a high ponytail, wisps of baby hair framing the edges of her face. It made her appear younger than twenty-three.

She must have seen me staring at her hair, because she lifted her hand and explained, "I thought today called for a power ponytail." She laughed at her own joke.

I had no idea what a power ponytail was. Yet I smiled at the amusement she found in herself. I placed the bucket down near the crushing barrel, needing to tear my eyes from her face. I thought this moment would have been easier than it currently felt. I found myself wanting nothing more than to march over to where she stood and take her in my arms. I wanted her heartbeat pounding in tandem with my own, and her warm lips back on my mouth.

"Sorry I have not been here for the past couple of days," she said. "I had to go to Rome. There is an American school there. It was the only place I could find what I needed. My old professor's colleague is the principal, and he arranged for me to meet him."

My back tensed as she spoke. I straightened and faced her. "You didn't have to go to Rome to get these things. It's not that important."

Her expression fell. "It *is* that important, Achille. And no matter how many times you try to divert me from doing this with you, it won't work."

My shoulders sagged in defeat.

Caresa came closer until she was right before me. I had to clench my hands into fists at my sides to stop them from reaching for her. I could see the torment flickering on her face too, the understanding in her eyes when they fell to my tensed arms.

Neither of us said anything out loud. Both of us were trying to change poles on the magnetic draw that always pulsed whenever we were near one another. If possible, it was even stronger today. Now it had a taste for what we felt like joined, it refused to have things any other way.

It could never happen.

"You are nearly finished?" Caresa broke the silence first, stepping back to point at the bucket of grapes.

"It's almost time for putting the fermented wines into the aging barrels."

"I'm excited for that," Caresa said and smiled. And it was a genuine smile. I could tell by the way two tiny lines creased at the corner of her eyes. "How is Rosa?"

"Missing you," I blurted, the air between us thickening again. We both understood the subtext. *I* was missing her. I was missing her more than I'd imagined was possible, as if a hole caved in my heart a little bit more with each day she was gone.

Caresa lowered her head, and with such sadness in her voice, confessed, "I missed her too."

She lifted her head. Her beautiful dark eyes caught my gaze and held it for a long moment.

"Moka?" I offered, walking to my coffee pot, desperate to put some space between us.

"Thank you." Caresa moved to the table she had set up. When I came back, coffee in hand, she said, "I hope you can take a break now and we can start this." Her pretty face was so hopeful.

It was the last thing I wanted to do, but I found myself agreeing. I wondered if she had any idea of the effect she had on me.

"Good," she said excitedly. "Then maybe I can help you crush the grapes later tonight?"

My hand froze as my cup of coffee was just about at my lips. Memories of being in the barrel a few days before were suddenly all I could think about. "I'm . . ." I cleared my throat. "I'm not so sure that's a good idea, Caresa."

Her face beamed with redness, and a nervous laugh escaped her lips. "No," she sighed. "I suppose it's not."

She sat down and patted the chair beside her. I sat warily, my eyes raking over the sheets of paper she had brought. I stared at the pens and pencils, and the strange rubber casings placed over them.

"They are tripod grips. They're designed to help your grip when you write," Caresa explained. I tensed, realizing she must have been watching me closely. She picked up a pencil and held it in her hand—just like all the kids at school had done with ease.

It was pathetic really, but I envied her. I envied anyone who took these small, simple things for granted. "I got these from Rome. They help your fingers find greater purchase on a pencil or pen. We can assess whether you are showing signs of dyspraxia. If you are, these will help." She offered the pencil to me. As she did, I saw her eyes focus on the way I was holding my cup. My fingers were not on the handle as they should be; instead I was grabbing the small ceramic cup with my whole hand.

Clumsily.

As if to highlight how hard holding this tiny cup was for me, my fingers slipped from its sides and it crashed to the ground. It shattered into pieces on the concrete floor, splashing the last few drops of my coffee under the table.

I jumped from my seat, the chair legs scraping loudly on the floor. My heart slammed against my ribs in embarrassment. I turned on my heel, trying to get away, only to stumble over the chair that I had pushed behind me.

"Achille!" Caresa called out as I righted myself and rushed out of the barn. My chest was so tight I felt as if I couldn't breathe. The hit of fresh air helped. I hated being inside. I didn't like to be cooped up.

I didn't like trying to fool myself that the things Caresa had brought would do a jot of good.

"Achille." Caresa's breathless voice sounded softly from behind me. My hands were balled at my sides as I tried to calm myself down. Without looking back at her, I said, "I . . . I don't think I can do this." My voice cut out when my throat became too clogged to speak through. I swallowed, trying to push the suffocating lump away. "It's hopeless, Caresa," I whispered. "Just . . . let it be. I've got by this far. I'm . . . fine."

A strong gust of wind whipped around me. The days were cooling rapidly now, the autumn weather closing in. I took the shirt from around my waist and put it on, fighting to snap the fasteners down the front. It was always a challenge, but my hands were shaking more than usual, making the task damn near impossible. When the shaking became too much for me to contend with, I just let the shirt remain open, the cool breeze biting at my torso.

Light footsteps sounded from behind me, and Caresa moved into my peripheral vision. I still didn't look at her. I couldn't . . . I was . . . I was humiliated.

But she didn't let me withdraw. She moved into my line of sight, strong and brazen. When she laid her hand on my chest, I couldn't help but look down. Her eyes were focused on the fasteners as her slim, unhurried fingers fastened them. When she had closed the last one, her long lashes fluttered, and she finally met my eyes. Her hand was still pressed against my flannel shirt, right over my heart.

"Achille Marchesi, I think this is the first time since we met that I've seen you wear something on your torso." My stomach was tight, mortification still ran thickly in my blood, yet, at her light teasing, I found myself smiling. It wasn't much of a smile but, for a moment, she had chased away my pain.

A teasing expression played on her face, before it fell as she said, "You don't wear a shirt much because of the buttons, do you?"

All the fight left my body. "I have many shirts that have no buttons, that are easy to put on. But over the years I found myself unable to give in. I gave up trying to write, gave up trying to read. My father always wore these shirts. And I don't know why, but I was damned well going to wear them too. I always get there in the end. I buy the snap fasteners to make things easier for me."

"Normal buttons are too challenging?"

I nodded curtly.

"Your jeans have that fastener too," she stated. "Unusual on jeans. I thought so the other night."

I sighed. "Eliza . . . she modifies them for me. Has done since I was young. She and her husband, Sebastian, know that I have . . . limitations."

Caresa stepped closer. I wanted to kiss her forehead. I wanted to be the person who was allowed to freely kiss her lips and confide in her my greatest fears. But I wasn't, so I remained stock still.

A heavy silence stretched between us. I broke it by saying, "I am a hopeless case, Caresa. Ride Rosa, help me with the wine, but let this go. I have. I have come to terms with the fact that some things in life I simply cannot, and will not, do."

"No," she argued, a hint of fire in her hardening voice. "Don't give up, Achille. I know it is scary, facing something that has burdened you for so long. I don't know who encouraged you to stop trying, but you can do this. You just have to trust me." Caresa took one more step closer until she was pressed against me. I closed my eyes at the feel of her warmth, at her peach scent filling my nose. "Do you trust me, Achille?"

I heard the nervous tremor in her voice.

I realized she *wanted* me to trust her.

She was worried that I did not.

"Yes." I spoke honestly. "I trust you."

I opened my eyes and saw relief and then happiness flood Caresa's beautiful face. Her hands ran down my chest until they fell from my body. But before I could miss her touch, her hand wrapped around mine.

"Come back to the barn. Trust that I can help."

I stared at her delicate fingers, so slim and soft, caged by my large rough ones. "I'm so embarrassed," I confided, feeling my pride take the heavy hit of this confession. "You're going to think I'm stupid."

Caresa's hand squeezed mine tighter. "Achille, seeing you face a demon that has held you in its grip since childhood will not make me think you are stupid. In fact, quite the opposite. Taking this on, accepting a challenge as great as this will be—it is the single most impressive thing you could do. You are a magician when it comes to your wine, a master; anyone can see that. But do me a favor. Just . . . just close your eyes."

I was puzzled, but did as she asked. "Picture yourself in your barn when the labels for next year's vintage arrive. Picture yourself reading the beautiful script, proudly reading *Bella Collina Reserve*. Imagine the moment you see the words that will announce to the world that this is *your* wine." I could see it. I could see it so vividly in my mind's eye that I almost believed it was real. And I felt the rush of happiness it brought, to actually be able to read the words for myself.

"Now imagine being in your cottage, beside the fire." She stopped. I wondered why. Then she spoke again, and I knew. "Imagine having your wife by your side, lying in front of the fire, her head nestled in your lap. Imagine you are reading to her in the firelight, the wood crackling in the hearth and the smell of the burning oak filling the room. You are stroking her hair as you read her your favorite story. And she has her eyes closed, cherishing the moment, knowing she is the happiest woman on earth."

"Plato," I said, my voice graveled and torn. "I am reading from Plato's *Symposium*, about split-aparts and completed souls."

Caresa was silent, completely silent, yet my mind was alive with thought. Because in my vision, the one she was painting so perfectly, there could only be one woman listening to me speak. She had dark hair and dark eyes and the kindest, purest soul. It was her. Caresa, as my wife, lying with me by the crackling fire, listening to Plato, my hand running through her hair.

My missing half.

Caresa's breathing hitched. Just as I went to open my eyes, she instructed, "Then imagine your child, a little boy, just like you. You are reading him Tolkien, as your father had done with you. Imagine how full with life and pride and joy you feel. Because you have overcome your reading challenges for him, and for her—whomever she may be."

Caresa's voice cut out. I opened my eyes, and her eyes were glassy. "I see it so clearly," I said. "I see them both so clearly." I left out that it was her I could see, and the boy made by us.

"Good," she said in a faltering voice. "Then hold on to that image. When you feel like giving up, let the image of this future give you the strength to keep going. Because it is possible, Achille. Everyone deserves the chance to read and write. Especially you."

My head fell forward. I couldn't take looking at her any longer. I was afraid that I might kiss her lips if I did.

"Come back inside," Caresa said. "Let me assess where we are, then let me begin to help." I blew out a long breath of air, but nodded, allowing Caresa to lead me back into the barn.

She did not let go of my hand until we were seated at the table. She picked up the pen again and held it out for me to take. With my heart beating wildly and sweat coating my palm, I took it in my hand. I concentrated on holding it correctly. Caresa shifted my fingers until they were in the correct position. A jolt of surprise ran through me when the pen didn't slip. When, helped by the rubber casing Caresa had put on, the pen stayed in my hand. It didn't exactly feel right. But it didn't exactly feel wrong either.

"Does that help?" she asked cautiously.

I blinked; my vision had suddenly become blurry. "Yes," I said, moving my wrist, feeling the added grip of the pen between my fingers.

"Good!" Caresa exclaimed. She took the pen from my hand and placed it on the table. Next she placed a piece of paper in front of me. I could see the words written on it.

Caresa inched closer. "Try and read the first word for me."

I glanced away, hating that the written word made me feel this way. A warm comforting hand covered mine, chasing away some of my nerves. I pulled myself together and turned back to the page. I ran my eyes over the first word. I could see the first letter was a *V*, but I struggled with the second. Within moments my eyes were straining. I sat back from the table and ran my hand down my face. "I can see the letters, but I don't understand how the word sounds. I can't hear it in my head. Without hearing it, I don't understand it." I looked at Caresa, who was listening attentively. "Does that make any sense?"

"Completely," she said. "But we can help with that. We can use the multi-sensory approach." She edged closer. "People with dyslexia often obtain a greater grasp of the words by using three things." Caresa lifted her hand, and I swallowed when she touched her index finger to my eyelid. "Seeing the word." She moved her hand to my mouth, and my blood rushed faster through my veins. "Saying the word aloud." Finally, she brushed her hand past my ear, and shivers broke out across my skin. "And hearing the word repeated back."

She drew back her hand and took different colored pens to the page. She ran a red pen over two letters. "We can also color-code the vowels and the letters that give the word its sound. We can help you phonetically. We can help you identify the syllables. You will eventually understand the words by sounding them out in your head."

"Really?" I asked doubtfully.

Caresa pushed the paper back before me. I ran my eyes over the letters: *V I N O.* I didn't quite know what it said, but the different colors helped me make out the different letters.

"Can you decipher the letters?" Caresa asked. I told her what they were, using my finger as a guide on the paper.

Caresa's responding smile was wide and bright and free. "Achille," she whispered. "You are not illiterate. You understand letters. You can *read* letters."

"I attended school until I was thirteen, before the king suggested I be pulled out."

Caresa's face became a mass of confusion. "The king encouraged you to leave school?"

"Yes. The teachers said I needed more help than they could give me—the school wasn't equipped. It was a small village school. My father asked the king for help as we didn't have the money to afford specialized treatment on our own. The king sided with some of the teachers who agreed I was just slow. He thought it better that I followed in my father's footsteps and poured myself into learning the craft of winemaking, especially the merlot. He promised my father that he would get me tutors to help me along as I worked. But it never happened. By the time my father had had enough and demanded the king make good on his promise, too much time had passed.

"If I had gone back into the mainstream school, I would have been two or more years behind, and I just couldn't bear the thought of that. I fought with my father over it. It was the only time we had ever fought. In the end, he agreed to school me at home. He tried, but in the end, my issues were beyond his grasp. He had a vineyard to run, and time just slipped away. I never knew why the king did what he did. It was as though he wanted me kept out of sight. Eventually, my father and I got used to my lack of academic abilities. I threw myself completely into winemaking, and a few years later I became the head winemaker. At age sixteen I made my very own vintage. I did it all myself; my father simply looked on."

"2008," Caresa murmured, that same hint of awe in her voice that she'd had the first day we met.

"Yes. How did you know?"

"That year is historic for the Savona Bella Collina merlot. It is the year the wine became better than ever before. Achille, the 2008 vintage is the most expensive bottle of merlot in the world."

"It is?" I said in surprise, not daring to believe it was the truth.

"How can you *not* know this?" she asked in amazement.

"Because that part of the process doesn't interest me. For me it is about the making and aging of the wine, not the price."

A loving expression blossomed on Caresa's face. "I know," she said quietly. "Then you don't know that the winner of the International Wine Awards will be announced at three p.m. on the day of Bella Collina's grape-crushing festival. You may well win again. You have not lost in years."

"The king has always accepted the acclaim." I laughed to myself. "I have never even seen the awards. King Santo always kept them to display over in the main estate."

"Achille, that is awful." Caresa was appalled, and I didn't think she even noticed that she had once again put her hand in mine.

"I don't mind. I don't like being the center of attention. King Santo was good at it. Prince Zeno will be no different. If we win, he will take the praise and the award. And I'll be content with knowing that I have produced the best wine possible. I am happy with my quiet life, Caresa. I am not born for balls and parties, crowds and big affairs. In fact, I couldn't think of anything worse."

I didn't mean to upset her. But I knew I had when Caresa turned her head and pointed back to the word on the page.

"Caresa?" I asked, wanting to know what I had done wrong.

She batted her hand in front of her face and threw on a smile. It was fake. I could see it was fake. I wondered if this was the polished face of the Duchessa di Parma I was witnessing.

I decided right then that if it was, I preferred my Caresa.

Caresa's gaze drifted out of the barn doors, then back to the sheets of paper on the table. "Let's get on with this. I don't want you to have to sacrifice too much time with your beloved wine."

Minutes later, and after a long process of sounding out which letters made which sounds, I smiled. "*Vino*. The word is *vino*."

"The most authentic learning comes when there is a connection between the student and the subject. This way, the words are familiar to you and will therefore help you better understand the rules of spelling and sounds. You are every inch a winemaker, down to your very soul. It made sense to me that we should use these familiar words."

My chest constricted at just how much thought and energy Caresa had put into this task. A task she got nothing from.

"Thank you," I said, knowing these two words were inadequate to describe the depth of my gratitude.

Caresa passed me another sheet and the pen from before. Two hours later, I had completed a worksheet where I had to trace out the shape of letters. We had gone through eleven words on the reading sheet, and I was now the proud owner of an iPod.

"It is filled with audio books so at night you can read along with the actual books." Caresa had brought me a stack of books that she wanted me to try and read a sentence or two from each night. The audio book would read along with me so I could see and hear the words. Afterwards, I would sound them out—*eyes, lips and ears*. "It has voice control so you can ask for the book rather than have to find it by the written title. I have put them in the same order as the books so you won't accidentally read the wrong one."

The iPod, she told me, also had on it every opera and concerto piece that I could imagine. She told me it would be easier to listen to in the fields than the old cassette player.

Over a week later, after days and days of intense schooling, she brought her laptop and uploaded some more music. As Beethoven's Fifth Symphony played through the portable speaker she had brought, she turned to me. "Have you ever heard this symphony by Beethoven before?"

"Yes," I said, listening to the vaguely familiar music.

"Do you know that this symphony is regarded as Beethoven's best?" I shook my head. Caresa sat beside me as we listened to the dancing strings. "I wanted to share this with you." She nudged me affectionately. "I know how much you love opera, but I have never heard you play music outside of the Italian greats." She winked at me. "*Some* people might think you show a strong bias to our fellow countrymen."

I huffed a laugh. "*Some* people may be right."

Caresa giggled, the sweet sound filling both the room and my veins. "When I was researching more techniques for us to try, I suddenly remembered Beethoven." She nodded toward the speaker. "Beethoven wrote nine symphonies. This one is the most complex, the most celebrated and the most famous. It was the standout work of his life."

"It's beautiful," I agreed.

Caresa turned to face me. "Beethoven lost his hearing, Achille. One of the world's greatest composers lost his hearing. A composer, a man who wrote music, listened to music, *lived* for music, lost the very sense essential to his work."

"That's awful," I said, shaking my head in sympathy.

"No," Caresa said forcefully. "In the end, it was arguably his greatest blessing. Achille, he wrote this symphony when he was deaf. His greatest masterpiece was produced without the ability to hear sound. Don't you see?" I waited with bated breath for her to continue. "What challenges us, what should break us, can in the end be our greatest blessing. Because our failures can *make* us great. Our most basic of human adversities can inspire within us an almost superhuman strength. Our weaknesses are simply our untested wings waiting to be flown."

In the week that followed, with every new sentence learned and new word written down, I listened to the symphony, allowing Caresa's words to circle my mind.

One night, as I tried to read by the fire, with Beethoven playing in the background, I realized that what and how Caresa was teaching me was working. I let myself imagine the future Caresa had helped me to visualize that day outside the barn.

And I knew that she was right. My wings were simply untested, but each and every day, they were readying themselves for flight just that little bit more.

To fly toward Caresa, the woman who was rapidly becoming my sun . . .

. . . to Caresa, the woman who was lighting my way from the dark.

Chapter Ten

Caresa

"It will be long-sleeved, as all royal dresses should be, yes? Lace sleeves and a v-neckline and a silk skirt?" I stood on a raised plinth as Julietta, my wedding dress designer, took my measurements. She whipped around me like a cyclone as she measured my legs, my waist, my chest and finally my arms. When she was done, she linked my arm and brought me to the table and chairs in my living room.

She turned to another page of the sketchbook lying on the tabletop. Her flawless design for the dress of my dreams had been on page one. Her ideas for my hair and makeup were on page two. And when she turned to the third page, I felt the tears immediately fill my eyes.

"Your dream veil, no?" Juiletta asked, in English. Since she had arrived, she had insisted that she speak English. She said she needed the practice. I had only spoken Italian in weeks. Only over the phone to Marietta did I use English. It was nice to feel my tongue wrap around such familiar-sounding words.

My finger ran along the design, sketched out in charcoal pencil, except for the silken vines that were drawn in shimmering silver. It was floor length with a long train, exactly like I had always dreamed. It had Spanish lace around the front, perfectly suited to a Catholic duomo ceremony.

It was everything I had ever wanted.

"Well?" Julietta said. "Is it good?"

I nodded, my throat struggling to push out any words. But it was not because I was left speechless by the design—even though it was as if she had taken the picture straight from my mind—but because of the heavy ache I felt in my heart as I stared down at the veil I had envisioned wearing since I was a little girl. The veil I would wear when I married my prince.

It was all coming true. I was getting the veil. I had the prince . . . but I knew the reason for the ache in my heart.

I wasn't marrying the *right* prince.

The truth was, I didn't even want a prince at all.

"Bene!" Julietta said, slipping back into Italian. "I will get these back to my studio in Florence, and we shall begin to put it all together. We will have a fitting in a couple of weeks, then again a couple of weeks before the big day."

I hadn't realized I was staring off at nothing until Julietta waved her hand in front of my face. I blinked and forced on a smile. "I'm so sorry, I was in a complete daze for a moment there."

Julietta laughed. "No doubt imagining marrying Prince Zeno in just a couple of months. You're quite the envy of Florence."

"Yes. So I've heard," was all I said in response.

Julietta bade me a good day with a casual wave of her hand and left me alone in my rooms. I needed fresh air. I made my way to the balcony doors and stepped outside. The cool breeze flicked up my hair and sent shivers down my back. It was early November, and the delayed summer air seemed to have finally cooled. I walked to the edge of the balcony, and, like I did each time I came out this way, I let my gaze drift out to Achille's small vineyard, tucked away in the valley in the distance. And like every day, I felt an urge to run down the steps and along the fields until I got there. I could even smell the burning oak from his fire and hear the opera serenading him in his barn. It amazed me that even though I had only known him for four weeks, it felt strange not seeing him every day. Those first couple of weeks spent by his side—harvesting, riding and crushing the grapes—were some of the best and most cherished of my life.

And that night . . . the night we had made love . . .

A symphony of hustle and bustle sounded from around the estate, pulling me from that heated memory. It made me wonder what Achille was up to right then. It made me wonder if he had managed to read last night.

I was so proud of him. I didn't think I had ever been more proud of anyone in my life. Every time we worked on his reading, he struggled. Sometimes the words were so frustrating for him that my heart wept. I knew he came close to giving up at times, but, time and time again, he would prove to me just how strong he was when he refocused, took a deep breath and tried again.

And I hated that I couldn't be there more. I . . . I *missed* him. Felt as though I could barely breathe without him being close by.

I should have decided to stay away long ago. I should have cut all ties from that second day when he had showed me how he hand-harvested the vines. But like the fool that I was, I kept going back, over and over. I had tried to fool myself that I returned simply to help him read and write.

But both God and I knew that was a lie.

I was sure Achille knew it too.

I jumped at the sound of a plate crashing to the ground. The mansion was in chaos. It had been in chaos for the past eight days, as the staff outside readied for the grape-crushing festival, and the staff inside prepared the great hall for Zeno's coronation banquet.

The banquet was tonight.

The festival was today.

Zeno had yet to return.

Today was also the day that the judges of each category of the International Wine Awards would, at three p.m., call the winner to award them the prestigious prize.

As Achille had predicted, the call would come to Zeno, and Zeno would publicly reap the reward. But I knew if Bella Collina's famed merlot won today, that honor went to one person and one person only.

And I knew he wouldn't come. Achille never really left his home apart from when he had to get a few groceries from Orvieto. He barely even left the vineyard but for the occasional ride outside the perimeters of his land. I knew from his expression and tone when we had discussed the awards that he would not be here today.

I wrapped my white cashmere cardigan tighter around my body to stave off the cold. A knock sounded on my door. I guessed it would be Maria, here to order me to get dressed for the festival or prep me on all the important names and faces that would be attending Zeno's coronation dinner.

I opened the door and my mouth fell open in surprise. Zeno stood before me, as handsome as ever, styled and groomed to perfection. He wore a navy-blue designer suit, white shirt and red tie. And in his hands were a dozen blood-red roses.

My immediate thought was that they were not white. That these twelve expensive roses didn't hold a candle to the single white one Achille had left on my pillow the morning after we made love. The one that was now pressed between the pages of Plato's *Symposium*. I had found the book in King Santo's library on the second floor.

Strangely, it had still been out on his desk, the pages worn and well read. It was curious. I had never even heard of that book before I came here to Italy; suddenly it was all anyone seemed to be interested in.

I had taken the book back to my room, where I had read it cover to cover. Every time I read about split-aparts and lost, missing souls, I would yearn for Achille until it became almost unbearable.

"Zeno," I finally said in surprise when his black eyebrows had begun to draw down at my muteness.

He thrust the roses into my hand. "Duchessa." He leaned in to kiss both my cheeks. As his lips met my skin, I wanted to push him off. I didn't want him this close. It felt as if my body was repelling his affection. Achille and I were magnetic; Zeno and I were opposing poles.

"You're finally back," I said, heading back into my room and putting the flowers into a large vase that sat in the center of the table; I would arrange them later.

"Just returned," he said tightly. There was an edge to his voice that made me turn and face his direction. Zeno had walked a couple of feet into my living room. Gone was the relaxed, confident man I had met that first night here. In his place was a man who was stiff and cold.

He even seemed . . . sad.

I made myself smile. "I'm glad you're back. I thought I was going to have to host the grape festival and your coronation alone. The festival I could have managed. But the coronation? Well, I think they may have detected an imposter king in me."

Zeno walked to my open balcony doors and stepped outside. I followed, unsure what was wrong with him. His hands were resting on the ornate stone balustrade, his back tight and arms tense as he looked out over his land.

I stopped beside him, once again finding my peace in the view of Achille's vineyard. Zeno pointed to the track I used most days. "I used to play on that track as a child. These fields were my home each summer when I was younger. Then my mother left my father and moved back to her parents' home in Austria, and I was sent to Florence permanently."

I knew Zeno's mother and father had been married on paper alone. It was yet another truth that the aristocracy pretended wasn't real— that Zeno's mother had left her husband and son and never once returned. Of course, divorce wasn't an option in our circles, certainly not in our devoutly Catholic society. My heart cried for Zeno in that moment. His mother had left him. I was sure from what my own mother and father had said that they were still not that close.

"Is your mother attending tonight?" I asked.

Zeno looked at me and laughed. Harsh, painful laughter. "No, Duchessa. She is not. My mother hasn't graced Italy with her presence in over a decade."

"But you're her son," I found myself arguing.

Zeno's laughter stopped. "I'm my *father's* son." He cocked an eyebrow. "Haven't you heard of my reputation, Caresa? I'm the 'Playboy Prince of Toscana', following in the footsteps of my equally promiscuous father."

"I have never heard your father referred to in such a way," I said, conveniently leaving out that, of course, I *had* heard that said of Zeno.

"He was," Zeno said plainly. "In his early life, and even when he was first married to my mother, his vice was women. It was only after she left us for Austria that he settled down, threw himself into the vineyards and the production of wine. But we were alike in more ways than I can count."

I was surprised. I knew King Santo as many things, but a philanderer wasn't one of them. "I didn't know."

Zeno nodded his head, but didn't say another word on the matter.

"Are you excited for the coronation banquet tonight?" I asked, just to try and change the subject. The topic of his parents' marriage was clearly a sore point.

"Ecstatic," he droned sarcastically. Zeno loosened his tie from his neck and turned to lean his back against the railing. He looked at me, arms folded. "What have you been doing since I've been gone? The staff seem to think you are a little wild in your ways, preferring to traipse through the vineyards for hours at a time rather than hold lunches and dinners."

Panic surged through me. I didn't want him to know where I had been and what I had been doing. But then I thought of Rosa and the fact that many of the staff had seen me ride her daily. "I do prefer being outdoors," I said with a nonchalant shrug. "And one of the winemakers has a horse that I ride. An Andalusian. They have allowed me to school her in dressage. I met them in my first few days, and we agreed I could ride their horse as it needed the training."

Zeno smirked and shook his head, presumably at some internal joke. "Another dressage enthusiast? My father was the same. Always away with the Savona dressage and show jumping team when he wasn't here."

I was glad he didn't push me for more information about the winemaker. I didn't want him to suspect Achille of anything. Then again, I was unsure if Zeno even knew the name of the man who made this estate's prize-winning wine.

"Horses over luncheons, hmm?" Zeno mused. "Maybe bringing you here to Bella Collina was a good idea after all."

"Oh, I went to a couple of lunches with local ladies. And I hosted one luncheon. It was interesting, to say the least." I pretended to think hard, then said, "Baronessa Russo spoke of you a great deal."

Every part of Zeno froze, and then he sighed. "I'm sure she did."
He leaned in, so far that my nostrils became full of his expensive
cologne. "I'm sure she did," he said again, then, eyes lit with curiosity,
asked, "Were you jealous?"

Zeno had told me we should always speak the truth, so I replied,
"Not even a little bit."

His eyes widened at my brazen honesty, then he laughed. Head
thrown back, he laughed hard. He shook his head and turned again to
stare out across the fields. "What a pair we make, Caresa." *Caresa*. I
found it interesting how he had dropped "Duchessa" and now called
me by my name. Silence fell. I felt as if he wanted to say something,
to talk of whatever was on his mind. But in the end, he straightened
without confiding a word. "I had better go and get ready. The festival
guests will be arriving soon."

"Yes, me too," I agreed. Yet I wanted to question Zeno further.
Wanted to ask him if he thought this whole engagement was a farce
too. But I bit my tongue. He already looked defeated, for some
reason. I didn't want to add to his troubles. And I thought of my
father, thought of how disappointed he would be if I questioned my
duty.

I had been born for this.

Zeno nodded his head in goodbye and left. I dressed in the knee-
length Versace dress that had been selected for me, slipping my arms
into the long sleeves and smoothing the burgundy fabric over my
hips. I paired it with my favorite black heels—ones I knew wouldn't

cause me any pain. Maria came through a short time later with a hair and makeup stylist. In less than an hour, I sported a fall-inspired makeup look and had my hair drawn back in an elegant low bun.

"The prince is waiting for you downstairs." Maria directed me out of my rooms. As we walked the long hallways to the main set of stairs, she said, "This will consist of mostly local people, but some guests—wine enthusiasts, sommeliers—come from all over the world just to say they have crushed wine on Bella Collina's famous land. And of course, we will have many of the aristocracy in attendance. Some have come early for the coronation and want to see the festival. They have been awarded rooms in the east wing of the house or in the guest lodgings in the courtyard."

I nodded, trying to breathe through the sudden onslaught of nerves that flooded my stomach.

"You and the prince will start the grape-picking contest, and afterward award the winners on the stage in the courtyard. We have planned it all around the phone call at three p.m. from the Wine Awards. Of course, we are hoping and praying that we will win. I have organized for the guests of the festival to have a glass each of the merlot if we take the coveted prize." She laughed. "I'm sure that's why they are all here anyway, so they can have a glass without paying through the nose for a full bottle."

We reached the top of the stairs; Zeno was waiting below. He had changed into a fresh but similar blue suit. He looked every inch a Mediterranean prince. Maria smiled as he moved to the bottom of the staircase.

Before we descended, Maria placed her hand on my arm. "Make sure you smile a lot today. Listen attentively to anyone who speaks. This is the prince's and your first public outing. We want the attending media and your guests to see you as a strong couple." She leaned in even closer. "It will also help ease the buyers' worries to see an Acardi on Zeno's arm. Believe me, we need all the help we can get right now."

I frowned, about to ask her what she meant, but Maria had pulled back and greeted Zeno before I could.

Was that why Zeno was so forlorn? So down? Were things even worse than before?

As I reached the bottom step, Zeno offered me his arm. "Are you ready?"

"Yes," I replied. We walked through the large house until we reached the exit to the courtyard. I could hear the sea of voices coming from outside. Music from a live band was playing, and I could smell the heady scents of succulent roasting meats, garlic and herbs floating in the air.

Zeno gave me one last look. He inhaled deeply, plastered a smile on his face and pushed through the doors. The minute we entered the courtyard, I felt as though we had been transported back a hundred years to before the royal family's abolishment. Everyone turned to watch us enter. My hand tightened on Zeno's arm as my legs suddenly felt a little unsteady.

I was used to fancy events, but I wasn't used to being so under the microscope. Avoiding the stares, I looked around at the courtyard.

Green shrubbery and vibrant fall flowers climbed the stone walls. The rich smell of autumn trees filled the air, and the sun shone down on the cobbled floor like a golden spotlight.

As Maria led the way to a small stage at the north side of the courtyard, I scanned the crowd. I saw lots of smiling guests who had turned out—some in fancy dress and some in team t-shirts—for the contest. The aristocrats were even easier to pick out. They stood away from the locals and tourists, watching on with amused expressions. A few faces I recognized from the luncheon. I wasn't surprised to see Baronessa Russo here, but a genuine smile formed on my lips when Pia waved at me from her place to the left. Her sister, Alice, was with her, as was Gianmarco, her nephew.

I waved at the young boy, and he gave me a small wave back. I had worked with him several times over the past couple of weeks. Pia had brought him to the estate rather than have me go to Florence. As predicted, he suffered from dyslexia, but he was already making progress. He was a sweet, shy boy, who had simply needed a little help.

As my eyes stayed locked on his timid face, my heart clenched. I wondered if this was what Achille was like as a child. A small boy hiding behind his father's legs because the world outside the comfort of his vineyard was just too overwhelming and daunting.

Gianmarco was struggling being in such a big crowd; I could see it. But he would be okay. I wondered whether, had Achille been given the help he needed at this age, he too would have been brave enough to come to festivals such as this, rather than hiding away from the world, starving people of both his beautiful personality and looks.

A gentle squeeze on my hand forced me away from thinking of Achille again. I realized that I did that too often. He was never far from my mind. Or my heart.

I met Zeno's eyes, and he raised an eyebrow in question. I smiled to let him know I was okay. I heard some of the women at the front commenting on how I looked at him so lovingly. So adoringly.

If only they knew.

Zeno walked to the microphone at the front of the stage. The guests quieted.

"My friends, my fiancée and I would like to thank you all for attending the annual Bella Collina Grape-Crushing Festival." The guests cheered. Clearly used to years of this kind of attention, Zeno smiled a regal smile and nodded his head at the cheers and shouts. When the noise died down, he said, "Today is not only about the prize money of one thousand euro, but about celebrating this region's exceptional wine and all of the work that goes into making it the best there is!" Zeno waited for the crowd to calm from their newest cheer. His smile fell a little, and his voice became strained and somber. "My father . . . my father loved this estate. He chose to spend his time here over our palazzo in Florence. And he loved this festival. Loved seeing his treasured land filled with such an outpouring of love from his guests." Zeno paused, then said in a rough voice, "And I am no different." He gestured to me, waiting behind him. "My fiancée adores this land and has spent every day since her arrival exploring its beauty. We both welcome you here today. So let's get this contest started!"

Zeno stood back from the microphone as the infectious excitement began sweeping through the courtyard. Zeno held out his arm again, and I threaded my arm through his. He led me to the opening of a field of vines. The organizers of the event rushed to place the contestants at their rows. They had eight buckets to fill full of grapes, and the quickest team of two would win the money and a crate each of Savona wines. After the competition, the crowd was invited to stomp the grapes to celebrate the harvest. The wine produced from this would then be gifted to the church in Orvieto.

Maria led us to a central spot and handed Zeno a flag adorned with the Savona crest. But Zeno passed the flag to me and said, "Why don't you do the honors, Caresa?"

I felt every pair of eyes on me as I nodded and walked to the spot Maria had marked out on the grass. I lifted the flag, holding it high in the air, and then dropped it. The contestants rushed to their buckets and scrambled down the rows of vines.

I laughed at the hectic melee before backing away to a corner to watch the contestants competitively harvesting the grapes. Zeno came to stand beside me. "You did well," he said, clapping his hands as a nearby group were the first to drop two full buckets at their starting marks.

"This is good." I gestured to the many people cheering and watching the contestants. "You should encourage this type of event more. Bella Collina is loved. Of course you should protect the more private sections of the vineyards, but this, involving both the local and world's wine communities in what we do here, would only make them more dedicated to you."

"You think?" Zeno said. At first I thought he was being dry and rejecting my idea, but when I looked at his face I could see his expression was contemplative.

"You know, the monarchs of old were disliked for a good reason," I continued. "They were not one with the people. They kept themselves at bay. Maybe that is why the abolishment happened, because their great estates were national treasures, yet kept away from the public eye."

Zeno flickered his gaze to me, then away again without saying a word. I wasn't sure if I had crossed some arbitrary line by suggesting that, but it was true. Plus, what Maria had said to me earlier played heavily on my mind. I knew the situation with Zeno and the buyers was tense—this rushed wedding was the result of that—but I wondered how dire things had truly become.

Zeno wandered off to talk to some of the dukes and barons that had just arrived for the banquet this evening. Somebody moved beside me, and I was relieved when I saw it was Pia and Gianmarco. I kissed Pia's cheeks and smoothed back Gianmarco's hair. I bent down, melting when the timid dark-haired boy gripped tightly to Pia's legs. "Hello, Gianmarco," I said softly.

"Hello, Duchessa," he replied, his little voice strong and brave. He looked up at Pia.

"Go on, give it to her," she said.

Gianmarco reached into his pocket and pulled out a piece of paper.

I looked down at the messy two-word message written in blue crayon: *Thank you.*

Tears rushed to my eyes when they ran over the messy scrawl. Gianmarco was watching me with huge eyes. "You did this?" I said softly. He nodded his head. "Then I'll treasure it always," I whispered through a thick throat.

Gianmarco's mother came over to take him back to the courtyard for gelato. As he left, Pia said, "When we told him we were coming here today, he asked if he could write you this note." Her hand fell on my upper arm. "We are extremely grateful for the help you have given him. And for Sara." Sara was an American educational psychologist I knew in Florence. I had arranged for her to give Gianmarco more intense tutoring than I ever could. With the approaching wedding, my time was becoming more and more limited.

"You're welcome," I said, my voice finally clearing of emotion.

Pia released my arm and cast her gaze to Zeno, who was talking with a tall blond gentleman. "So, he's returned?"

I sighed. "He arrived back this morning for the festival and banquet, but I'm sure that he will leave again shortly after. This place makes him uneasy for some reason."

"At this rate, Caresa, you might have only spent a few days in your husband's company by the time you marry."

"I know," I replied. I felt numb.

"How is the horse you've been riding?" Pia asked out of the blue. My head snapped up at her words, and my heart began to race. I had told Pia in confidence about Achille's vineyard and Rosa. I had not told her about Achille . . . anything about us . . . about what had happened.

"She's good," I replied evasively.

Pia's eyes narrowed. "And the winemaker?"

I knew my face must have blanched. I could feel the warm blood draining from my cheeks. "I don't . . . I'm not sure . . ." I stumbled over my words. My strange response seemed to be all the confirmation Pia needed. Her eyes softened and she nodded knowingly.

"Will he be coming here today?"

I should have kept it from her. I should have denied everything, all her suspicions, but something within my heart wouldn't let me. I couldn't deny Achille. It pained me to do so. He had been pushed aside his entire life; I didn't have it within me to add to that rejection.

I shook my head. "I don't know how it happened," I whispered. "But he somehow became embedded in my heart and connected to my soul. It . . . I don't know how it happened . . ."

"Oh, Caresa," Pia said softly. "You love him?" I froze, completely froze, opening my mouth to most certainly deny that claim.

But my mouth and my heart appeared to be in agreement that I would not deny this either.

Because . . . I . . . I loved him.

Mio Dio, I loved Achille . . .

"I don't think you realized it, but every time I came here with Gianmarco, you always talked about the horse you were schooling in dressage, but more, the winemaker. You said nothing obvious. I'm sure no one else suspects a thing. But I heard something different in your voice when you spoke of how he taught you about his wine. About how you would ride and talk for hours. The tone in your voice and the happiness in your eyes gave your affection for him away."

"You can't say anything," I said sternly. "I ended it. It happened one time, and we knew that was all we could be. We both agreed we had to leave that one night as a single moment in time."

"I wouldn't ever say a thing," Pia said, just as vehemently. She sighed and, taking me by the elbow, pulled me out of sight behind a wall. I was flustered, my body consumed by an overwhelming need to protect Achille. He had no one looking out for him. I was all he had. I couldn't let society gossip hurt him.

"First," Pia said firmly, "I consider you a friend. I may have only known you a little while, but I like you. We share the same views about certain things and, in our world, that is something I cherish— people like you are few and far between." I relaxed a little, my hands shaking just a little less than before. "And secondly, I feel for you. You have found someone your heart calls for, yet you are stuck in this farce of an engagement. That is heartbreaking by anyone's standards."

"I have no choice." I dropped my head in defeat. "I think . . . I think that Savona Wines is in worse condition than I knew. It is our family's livelihood. This marriage needs to happen."

"If the business is worse than you thought, then I am not so sure your marriage will be the remedy. Zeno is at the head of Savona

193

Wines now. It is up to him to keep that position or give it to someone who actually wants to do it. Who knows this industry and knows about the wine it produces. It would not surprise me if Zeno didn't know his Shiraz from his Chianti, even if it were poured over whichever new gold digger was vying for his attention that week. Your marriage is not the fix; *he* needs to be."

I blinked at hearing her fight so hard for me and Achille. She looked me in the eye. "I fell for a teacher two years ago, Caresa. I was on the Amalfi coast for the summer, and so was he." She dropped her gaze, but not before I saw the pain in her eyes. "I fell for him hard, so much so that my heart breaks now even thinking of him. Like there is something missing in my soul."

"Split-aparts," I whispered.

Pia furrowed her brow at my cryptic remark, but carried on. "When I told my father I wanted to be with Mario, to move to his home in Modena to be with him, I was forbidden. I was told that if I married so far below my station, I would be cast from our family." She met my eyes. "I adore my family, Caresa. My sister, little Gianmarco. So in the end I chose them. I lost him and chose them."

"Pia," I murmured, reaching down to hold her hand.

"As much as I love my family, if I had to do it again, I would have left. I would have been with him. I would have chosen not to live with this pain in my chest as I do now. Breathing, existing, but not living. Attending these ridiculous ceremonies and luncheons as if any of it even matters."

"Then find him," I said. "Go and find him. Be with him."

"He has someone else now," she said, her voice cracking. "He moved on." A tear fell down her cheek. "I broke his heart so badly. I killed the possibility of us when I let this pathetic title of mine stand in the way of our happiness. Now someone else is making him happy, repairing the hole in his heart that I caused."

I squeezed her hand as she looked away into the distance and dried her face of tears. "People think they understand our world, Caresa. They see the titles, the money and the family histories and think we have it easy. I am not a spoiled little rich girl crying because she didn't get her way. I know people have it harder in life than we do—it would be silly to try and say otherwise. But these titles are a leash, a tight leash to our happiness. Look at the late king. He was miserable most of his life, his wife taking refuge in Austria, living like a hermit so she wouldn't be judged for wanting another life. Zeno looks as though he wants to bolt from this festival, and has done from the minute you entered the courtyard. And you, you stand so rigidly next to Zeno, a false smile on your face because he is not who your heart wants."

Her words were a dagger to my heart.

"Tell me," Pia said and moved right before me. "Are your parents happy? I assume they were arranged. Does your mother look at your father with nothing but adoration? Does your father dote on your mother?"

I pictured my parents and immediately knew the answer. "No." I stilled. "They love each other, respect each other, and love me. But they are not in love. They don't even sleep in the same room. They haven't done since I was a child."

Pia leaned back against the wall of the courtyard. "What a tangled web."

I was silent for a moment

"Are you staying for the dinner tonight?" I asked eventually. Pia looked at me, and I saw the disappointment in her face. I could see I had let her down by not entertaining this topic any further.

She released my hand. "Of course. Can't miss the new king being officially crowned, can we?"

I stepped forward to say something to her, to tell her that my mind was a jumbled mess, torn between love and duty and panic and worry. But just as I did, a horn sounded, announcing there was a contest winner.

"Caresa?" Maria came scurrying around the corner, in the constant fluster she always seemed to be in. "We must get to the main stage to award the prize." She checked her watch. "The phone call will be coming in soon, in about ten minutes."

Without looking back, I followed Maria to the stage, congratulating the rest of the contestants for their efforts on my way. Their faces were bright from the exertion of the competition, glasses of wine in their hands—not yet the coveted merlot.

When I got to the stage, Zeno was already there, chatting smoothly with the winning pair. He moved to the microphone and introduced the winners. I handed over the check, and we all posed for the picture that would be printed in tomorrow's newspaper.

When the winners left the stage, a hush fell over the crowd. All eyes fell on the phone that sat on the small table at the front of the stage.

I let my eyes drift across the assembled crowd as we waited for the clock to strike three. Then, at the far back of the courtyard, hidden in the tunnel that led to the fields beyond, I saw a familiar figure. A figure so well-known to me that my heart pumped faster the minute my eyes fell on his messy black hair and bright blue eyes. He was dressed as he always was these days, in jeans and a green flannel shirt.

I wanted to run to him. To stand by his side as the call came in. I wanted every person here to know that the wine they were all here celebrating belonged to the genius of one man.

Yet I didn't move.

But I saw the moment he knew I had seen him. Achille pushed off the wall and stepped further into the light. My lungs struggled to find air as his warm eyes met mine. Then my stomach fell when I saw the pain in their depths—deep pain and sadness. I didn't understand it, until I felt Zeno at my side, his hand on my back. I went to move, to pull from under his hand, when the phone began to ring.

In my peripheral vision I saw Zeno answer the phone, but my gaze stayed locked on Achille.

And his on me.

I heard Zeno's deep voice in the background, but to my ears, it sounded as if he were underwater, words muted and blurred. Then the crowd broke into loud shouts of celebration, and I knew.

Achille's wine had won again.

Achille blinked and cast his stunned eyes around the celebrating crowd. And I saw it, I saw the moment he realized he had won, and I saw the pride and passion flare on his handsome face.

But my heart broke anew as he looked around him, as he stood alone, no one to share in his joy. No one to tell him that he deserved this, that they were proud of him for all that he had achieved.

That he was worthy of all this adoration.

Looking lost and so very alone, he stumbled back into the shadows. He turned and made his way down the tunnel. The crowd descended upon the servers that had appeared with small samples of the award-winning merlot. Acting on instinct, I left the stage and rushed toward the tunnel.

Pia was beside the mouth of the tunnel. I met her eyes as I passed. They narrowed at my hasty retreat toward the fields. But I didn't stop. I kept running through the tunnel until I arrived at a field and saw Achille disappearing through a far row of vines.

Not giving up on my chase, I stumbled over the uneven ground until I hit the row. He was almost at the other end. "Achille!" I shouted. He froze in his tracks.

He didn't turn around as I hurried to meet him, but he didn't run away either. When I caught up to him, out of breath, his shoulders were tense.

"Achille," I said again. I reached out my hand and pressed it against his back. Achille heaved out a long sigh and turned. My hand slid to his stomach. But his eyes never met mine. They stayed focused toward the sounds of laughter and music coming from the courtyard.

Distant.

"Achille," I repeated one last time, stepping closer to him. I wanted to close my eyes and savor his addictive scent. But I kept my composure. "You won, Achille. Your merlot won again." He didn't seem to react. His face was blank, only the slight crinkles around his eyes showing that he'd heard my words.

His skin under my palm was scalding, the muscles hard. This was as close as I had been to him in weeks. When we'd studied lately, I had forced myself to keep my distance, as difficult as that was. But right then, I wanted nothing more than to be close. I wanted him to look at me and smile. I wanted to share this special moment with him.

But that was all crushed when his jaw clenched and he said, "You looked good together on that stage, Caresa."

His eyes finally found mine. Pain, raw and uncensored pain, shone back at me. "Achille," I whispered, hearing my voice crack. He made himself smile, but if anything that was even more devastating. Because I had seen Achille when he was happy.

This was nothing like that.

"You had better get back to your guests," Achille said. "The prince will be looking for you."

He moved to turn away, but I found myself wrapping my arms around his waist and holding him as close as I had wanted to from the minute I saw him in the tunnel. I pressed my cheek against his chest and refused to let him go. Achille was a statue in my arms, until, with a pained sigh, he wrapped his arms tightly around my back.

"I'm so proud of you," I whispered into the warm fabric of his flannel shirt.

I squeezed my eyes shut and fought back the rising lump in my throat as his lips brushed a soft kiss to the top of my head. I held him tighter. I wasn't sure how I would ever let him go now that I had allowed myself to fall once again into the safety of his arms. "You deserve this. I'm so very proud."

"Thank you," he murmured, a rasp in his voice. And then he pulled back. My arms dropped to my sides as he gave me one last long, agonized look and left the row of vines for the protection of his small, isolated vineyard.

I felt cold without his warmth.

I let the tears that had built fall. I allowed myself to face the truth— I was completely, soulfully, in love with Achille Marchesi.

And that had just complicated things exponentially.

"Caresa?" I turned to look back toward the courtyard, only to see Zeno at the bottom of the row wearing a confused expression. As I walked toward him, I schooled my features, once again the duchessa approaching her betrothed. "What are you doing down here?" he asked, searching the now-empty vines for clues.

"I just needed to get away for a moment. The atmosphere in there became very overwhelming."

I could see Zeno carefully assessing my answer. But then he shrugged. "You are expected to be present to mingle with the guests. Some of the ladies from the furthest points of Italy were looking to meet you. Maria said we have about an hour before we must get ready for the dinner tonight."

"Of course, the coronation," I said dully as we walked back through the tunnel that, moments ago, had led me straight to Achille. Now it was guiding me back into the life of a duchessa, the future queen.

A future queen whose heart was currently trailing behind its counterpart as he trudged alone, back to his simple life, with tears in his eyes and, it seemed, a fracture in his heart.

*****

"Your father was a great king, a true leader for those of us who still regard true Italian history and heritage as a priority."

I feared my face would twitch with the effort of sustaining my smile. As I glanced at Zeno beside me, I could see he was living the same lie.

The lie that we were happy.

Barone De Luca sat in the seat next to Zeno, holding up his glass of champagne. There were at least fifty people at our table. The decorations were grand and the courses many. The great dining room was swathed in red and gold, hung with oil paintings dating as far back as the Renaissance and before. This room had seen many monarchs.

I wondered what those days had been like. Coronations back then would have been public, of course, but then the king or queen would have been brought back to celebrate quietly in estates such as these. I wondered what these oil paintings would tell us of those coronations, if they could talk. Would they speak of money and politics and crowns and elegant jewels? Would they talk of palaces being constructed, red velvet cloaks and gilded thrones?

Of course, in this relatively modest gathering, there was nothing of the sort. No crown was being placed upon Zeno's head. No orb made of gold sat on Zeno's lap. No golden staff was in his hand, no ampulla and spoon anointed his head, declaring to God and country that he was the newly chosen, holy king.

Instead there was a dinner, speeches that reminisced about monarchs of old. There was wine and laughter, and talk of the "good old days" before the people overthrew the royal family. But it was nothing like I imagined tonight would be. I actually felt sad for Zeno, sitting at the top of the table, listening to how great his family once was, knowing he was failing in his family's business now.

"Your father was a great man, Zeno. And I am sure you will be just the same. The country may have forgotten the true ways of Italy, but we in this room have not. We bow to you as our true king." The barone raised his glass. "*Il re è morto, lunga vita al re!*"

The king is dead, long live the king!

Every glass was raised, the toast was echoed and we all took a cementing sip. Barone De Luca sat back down. Zeno signaled for the table to rise, and we slowly adjourned to the great room next door. Pia fell in step beside me. I knew whatever tension had arisen between us today had passed.

Pia linked her arm through mine. She was dressed in an elegant white and black Chanel dress with her hair pulled back in a French roll. My long-sleeved, floor-length gown was silver and encrusted with Swarovski crystals. I wore my hair pulled up at the sides by two delicate 1920s diamond clips. The gown was perfectly fitted and shimmered like glass in the light of the low-hanging chandeliers, the low back of the dress leaving my skin completely bare to the bottom of my spine.

"You look beautiful," Pia said. She looked over at Baronessa Russo, who was pawing her hands all over Zeno, desperate for his attention. "It's why she's acting that way, I'm sure," Pia said, tilting her head in the baronessa's direction.

But as I looked at her, all I felt was pity. No doubt she had been raised to believe she could have one day married the much-coveted prince. Every day I was here her chances of that fell greatly.

"I feel sorry for her," I said aloud. Pia just laughed and shook her head.

Pia and I sat down across from the fireplace with Contessa Bianchi. The guests milled about the room, making idle conversation. After a while, Zeno moved toward the roaring fire, and the sound of a spoon hitting a crystal champagne glass chimed around the room. The chatter stopped, and when I looked up, I saw that Zeno had his head cast down, waiting for the room to hush.

He lifted his head and looked around at his guests. "Tonight is not only a memorable night for me, but one for my fiancée too." My muscles became blocks of ice, and a trickle of unease ran down my spine. In my peripheral vision, I saw Pia's head turn to face me in alarm, but my eyes were locked in Zeno's direction.

Zeno smiled and met my eyes. "The wedding date is set, and our two houses will soon merge." He paused—for effect, I was sure. "Could you please come up here, Duchessa?"

Quiet murmurs ran around the room like a slow rolling wave. But I stood and made my way to his place beside the fire. He turned to face me. I was sure my eyes were wide as I waited for what would happen next.

Zeno took my hand. "Duchessa, we have been betrothed since we were children, and now have a wedding set for only weeks away." I swallowed as he reached for my hand—my *left* hand.

My *bare* left hand.

Zeno's thumb ran over my ring finger. He smiled. "We are engaged, yet you have still to receive a ring to let everyone know that you are mine. I think this is long overdue." I shuddered as he said the word "mine". It was as though my heart physically rejected his claim. And of course it would. It already belonged to another.

The room was tense, the air thickening with expectation. Zeno reached into his pocket and, in front of the blazing fire, dropped to his knee and stared up into my eyes. "Caresa Acardi, Duchessa di Parma, would you do me the honor of becoming my bride, the woman who will live her life by my side?"

Zeno opened the red velvet box in his hand, and the ladies in the room gasped. Inside was a princess-cut diamond ring. The gold of the band shone like the brightest of suns, and the huge diamond threw its reflection around the room like a spray of perfect little rainbows.

It was at least five carats.

But all I could see when I stared down at this most impressive ring was Achille. All I saw when I looked into Zeno's face was Achille's blue eyes as he praised me for choosing a bunch of grapes correctly. I saw his timid smile as he allowed himself to laugh at one of my jokes, at the moments my upper-class breeding caused me to say something superficial and Achille, with his quick wit and sarcasm, reminded me of how silly it sounded. But more than that, as Zeno kneeled before me, all I saw was the dream of it being Achille who was asking me to be his bride. To be the woman who would help him harvest the grapes then lie with him at night in front of the fire. And he would read to me . . .

. . . of Plato and split-aparts.

My throat was thick as the vision in my head became so very real it tricked my heart. Tears ran down my cheeks, but not for the reason the guests believed.

Because this moment was my ruin.

This moment, where the reality of what my life would become hit home.

This ring, this symbol of eternal, never-ending love, as beautiful as it may be, felt like a prison collar as Zeno slipped it onto my finger. An expensive collar, but a collar nonetheless.

The room broke into rapturous applause, taking my tears as a sign of being overcome with happiness. The duchessa finally getting a token of love from the prince.

They couldn't have been more wrong.

Zeno's eyes narrowed as he got to his feet. He knew I did not care for him in a romantic way, and I knew he grew suspicious of my tears.

"*Bacio!*" a member of the crowd called out, prompting murmurs of agreement from the rest of our guests.

Kiss!

I didn't want it. I never wanted his lips to remove the taste of Achille from my mouth. I didn't want to betray the night I had spent with Achille with this farce. But then Zeno cupped my face and pressed his mouth to mine, abruptly eradicating Achille from my flesh . . . eradicating all I had left of the man I loved.

And I hated it. I hated how his mouth moved against mine. I hated how his tongue swept around my lips and dipped slightly into my mouth. I hated Zeno's grip on my face. But worst, as our chests touched, I hated how his heart beat. Out of step with my own—no symphony, no in-sync rhythm . . . just unmatching and distant.

Zeno pulled back and dropped his hands from my face. He was pale, as if the reality of our situation had just hit him too.

He moved away from me as the ladies rushed around me, holding up my ring for their inspection. Zeno was being slapped on the back, but he looked a little lost underneath his usual confident mask.

"Duchessa!" the women cooed. "It is the most beautiful ring I have ever seen! You are so lucky!"

I smiled, nodding my head and giving rote answers when I could find the strength. And I played the part for another two hours, until at last I could make my excuses to leave. I said my last goodbye and darted for the stairs.

With every step, my heart seemed to drain, until it was a desert in a drought, starved of life and thirsting for any kind of relief. The ring felt like a ten-ton weight on my finger, pulling me down. And with every step, Zeno's kiss blazed hotter and hotter on my lips, ripping away the memory of Achille's kiss that I had clung onto, with a heady desperation, for weeks.

And now it was gone. I had pushed Achille away, giving us just that one, special night, but now all I could think of was being back in his arms. I wanted him in every possible way. I wanted his arms and lips and skin on my skin. I wanted him inside me, loving me just as much as I loved him, hearts beating in unison, blood rushing for the vital touch of the other.

As I reached my room, I let the tears fall. But I also gave in to my heart. I fled through the balcony doors, allowing my pumping blood to guide my feet. The cool breeze snapped at my wet cheeks as I ran as fast as my heels would allow to Achille's home.

The night was dark, the stars creating a blanket of diamonds and glittering golds. It was late, *too* late, but I had to get to Achille. Like Cinderella, I too was running from a prince at midnight. But where she had run reluctantly back to her rags and simple life, I was running *into* the arms of a man who boasted just the same. Cinderella could keep the jewels, the carriage and the prince. I wanted the vineyard, the faded jeans and the golden touch of a beautiful winemaker.

I slammed through the gate of Achille's cottage, the solar lamps leading me to his wooden front door. I rattled the handle, fighting for purchase with my shaking hands until it opened and invited me inside. I ran straight through, into the living room. The fire was burning, a single chair sitting before it. The books I had given Achille to read were stacked beside it, along with a pen fitted with the tripod grip and a pad of paper.

My chest ached at the sight.

Did he sit here every night, learning and trying?

Alone, always alone.

Pavarotti played quietly from an old record player in the corner. Flickering lamps and the fire's orange embers coated the whitewashed walls in a warm glow.

This was Achille's life. Music and wine and loneliness. He deserved more. He deserved more than anyone could give him.

"Caresa?" Achille's rough voice came from the doorway. He stole my breath; he was damp from the shower, his black hair wet, water dripping down his back. A towel was around his neck, and he wore black pajama bottoms.

I felt a sudden wash of peace travel through me at just being near to him. Such peace that it was a healing balm to my pained soul. A peace that I knew, with everything that I was, only Achille could give me.

Something had happened in the universe the day we had met. There was a cosmic shift, some destined alteration to the very fabric of who we were. The sun and the moon had aligned and cast us into one another's hearts, never to be torn apart.

"He said that once you find that person, your 'split-apart', you are blanketed by such belonging, such desire, that you will never want to be without it . . . as Plato said, '. . . and they don't want to be separated from one another, not even for a moment'." The memory of Achille's words circled my mind.

Belonging.

Desire.

They don't want to be separated . . . not even for a moment.

Were we those wandering lost souls reunited at last?

"Caresa? What is wrong? What happened?" Achille stepped forward, worry etched onto his perfect, beautiful face.

I threw myself against him. My arms wrapped around his waist, and I held on tightly. I felt his hot skin on mine, our bodies perfectly aligned, just like the stars that had guided us to this very moment.

To this vineyard.

To each other.

"Caresa? You're scaring me," he whispered as he held me tightly against him. I wanted to punish myself. How could I have walked away from this? How could I have ever left this feeling? How could I have ever left this man?

I'd seen the pain in his eyes today as Zeno was touching me. I had seen him searching for someone to smile at him as his merlot was deemed the best in the world.

That should have been me. It all should have been me.

But I had no idea how any of this could or would play out. We were destined for different paths. We were from such different worlds, yet shared the same soul. It all seemed so very impossible.

"Just hold me," I whispered as I turned my cheek to press against his warmth. I closed my eyes, and just allowed this man to embrace me. I allowed his hands to run through my hair as he pressed tender kisses to my head.

Eventually, Achille guided me back to face him and cupped my cheeks with his palms. He searched my eyes as a tear rolled down my cheek. He caught the tear with his thumb. "What has caused these tears? Why are you so sad?"

I didn't think my actions through. I didn't think anything through at all. Instead I rose onto my tiptoes and pressed my mouth to Achille's. Achille groaned as I brought our mouths together in prayer, my hands pressing in worship to his cheeks. I had barely tasted his lips or absorbed his warmth before he pulled away and staggered back from me.

His blue eyes were wild and afraid. His arms were rigid at his sides. His nostrils flared as he drew in ragged breaths. I took a step toward him, but he held out a hand. "Caresa," he said, his small whisper of my name both a reverent benediction and a curse. "No." He shook his head, his warring emotions flashing across his face—hurt, desperation, passion and confusion. Every single one was a stab to my heart.

"Achille," I pleaded, physically feeling my heart breaking.

"You said we had to stop this." He shook his head, his eyes lost and fearful. "You said we could have only one night . . . I can't do this . . . my heart can't . . . I can't take it . . ."

He turned his back, moving out of my sight, and I found myself confessing what lay in my soul. "I love you."

Achille stopped dead, as if my words were tight leashes to his legs.

My heart sprinted as the realization of what I had just admitted seeped into my bones. But I could not regret the words. They were the truth.

Achille needed to hear them just as much as I needed to express them. Every day they were kept inside was a day filled with pain.

I watched each muscle in his back cord with tension. I waited in silence for him turn around and face me. To look into my eyes and see the truth of my words reflected back. And now those words had been released, set forth into the night air, I felt a sense of freedom.

As if my soul had arrived home.

Achille turned around. He blinked, and twin tears rolled in parallel down his stubbled cheeks. "You . . . do?"

I let out a sob at the sight of his bewildered expression. As if he couldn't believe that someone could love him. But I did. My love for him was embedded in my every cell; it inspired my every breath and heartbeat.

He was me, and I was him.

A true whole.

"Yes," I whispered, taking a step forward.

Then he opened his eyes, and, just as he was about to say something in return, his gaze fell to my hand.

My left hand . . .

. . . and whatever he was about to confess was lost to the silence.

Any morsel of hope I had been holding on to evaporated into the air when his pupils dilated at the sight of that ring. His pale cheeks flushed red. His feet found life and stumbled away from me. I tried to give chase, but he fled the living room, and I heard the back door open. The cool air surged inside and circled around me. The flames from the fire roared and flared with life as the fresh air invaded its space.

The slam of the wooden door pushed me into action. I rushed after Achille, heart thundering in fear—fear that I had lost him. I burst into his garden to see him disappearing toward his vines.

I followed him, past Rosa and Nico in their stables. I burst through the trees he had just run through and found him on the third row of now-empty vines, head tipped back as he stared up at the moon.

His breath was white as it collided with the cool of the night. His damp olive skin bumped and shivered, and his toes curled into the soil beneath his bare feet.

I went to speak, searching for the right words to say, to explain, but he spoke before I could.

"My . . . my heart can't take this anymore."

His words slayed me, cut me where I stood. He still hadn't turned to face me. I wasn't sure if he could. His hurt was evident in his voice.

"I knew . . ." he whispered, so softly, so roughly, "I knew I saw something within you not long after we had met. Then I foolishly allowed my heart to fall, too hard and too fast. I let it happen. I let it happen because it was you and it was me. That's how I saw it in my head. These vines, the horses and you and me."

His breathing hitched and his voice became broken and coarse. "When you were beside me I felt strong and whole. When you were gone, I was empty and sad. There was a hollowness in my chest, and I found it hard to breathe." He dropped his head, evading the moon's soothing light. "Then we made love." He raised his hand, and

212

even though I couldn't see it, I knew his finger lay over his lips. "We kissed, our mouths touched, and it changed something inside me. I felt it happen. I felt it like I feel the hot sun on my face each day, like I feel the vines in my hands and know they are ripe . . . You asked me once how I knew when the grapes were ready for harvesting, and I told you I *just knew.*" He turned to face me. He lifted his fingers to his head, his heart and finally held out his hands toward me. "I know because I know it in my head, I feel it in my heart, and I touch it with my hands."

I felt my lips tremble at the innocence of his explanation, the sadness in his voice.

"With you it was exactly the same. I didn't see it at first, fooled myself into thinking my soul hadn't discovered you as its own, but when we made love, when I held you in my arms, in my bed, skin against skin, I knew. I was changed. I knew it in my head, I felt it in my heart, and I knew it by our touch . . . it was . . . it was . . . destined."

"Achille," I cried. I wanted to move to him, to touch him like he had just described. But he shook his head slightly, begging me not to approach.

"That night, I knew that would be all we ever had. Even before you spoke those words and they met my ears, I knew." He dropped his eyes, and the defeat in his beautiful body broke my heart. "We are made of the same soul but not of the same life. I knew that we were one of the lost causes my father told me about. Not the all-consuming, not those who find their forever peace in the other, but those whose circumstances don't align. The unfortunates that in an alternate universe would be the happiest of hearts but are forever broken and lost in this." He finally met my eyes. "So I can't hear this from your mouth, Caresa . . . I can't do this anymore . . . it hurts . . ." He laid his hand over his heart. "It hurts so much that I can't bear it."

He pointed at my engagement ring. "You are not meant for me after all. You are marrying the prince. I have let myself pretend that it isn't happening, but soon, you will marry the prince. You will become his under God's eyes. Never mine."

"No." I ripped the ring from my hand. Achille watched me with wide eyes as I held it up in front of him. "He gave me this tonight." I gestured to my dress. "He gave me this to impress his guests. It is an empty promise, not given through love. I don't care for this ring, or this damn marriage." I threw the ring to the ground.

Achille was rooted to the spot. But in the light of the moon I could see his face reddening, his hands fisting at his sides. He raised one fist and pressed it against his forehead in frustration.

"Achille—"

"I can't give you what he can," he said, his voice deep and hard. His hand dropped back to his side. "I can't give you jewels and banquets and festivals in a mansion." He slapped his hand on his naked chest. "I could give you me, and my vines, but that is all. I have little money. I know nothing of the world you have traveled. I know Umbria and Italy, and I know my small house and horses." His face screwed up in pain, and he gasped, "I can't even read or write. I am not what you should have."

"You're enough," I whispered, my softly spoken words seemingly daggers to his heart. Because they didn't fall on accepting ears; they were fuel to an already sparking flame.

Achille reached for a vine beside him and ripped it from its branch. He marched toward me and took my left hand. He wrapped the brown vine around my ring finger three times and knotted it.

He knotted it.

The hands that he so struggled to use for smaller movements had tied a ring to my finger. "There," he said harshly. "That is what I could offer. A ring of vines and earth, not diamonds and gold. Is that enough for you, Duchessa? Is this simple life enough?"

I wanted to shout back. I wanted to hit his chest and release my frustration at his cutting tone. But I looked into his eyes and saw nothing but embarrassment and agony, and I knew this was just like when I discovered the secret of his reading. This anger was his shield, his way of coping with a truth that hurt him deeply, irreparably . . . it was how he planned to push me away.

Achille watched me, nose flaring, waiting for me to go, to leave him alone. But instead I reached out and ripped off another tendril of vine. I lifted his rough left hand in my own, and wrapped the brown thread around his finger.

His finger that was shaking.

Shaking so hard.

Achille held his breath as I tied the knot, securing the vine in place. Even when I was done, I didn't let go of his hand. I stroked my fingers over his knuckles, then guided his hand up to my lips and grazed the delicate vine ring with my kiss.

An exhale escaped his lips at my touch, its warmth ghosting over my face. Without lifting my eyes from his work-roughened hands, I said, "If my ring is made of a simple vine born from this earth, then so is yours." A strained sound caught in Achille's throat. I lifted my eyes, making sure I held his attention. "I love you, Achille Marchesi, winemaker of the Bella Collina merlot. I found you, my missing part, here amongst the vines, and nothing you say will ever change that fact."

"Caresa." Achille's eyelids drifted shut as the fight left his tired body. I edged closer, so close that my lips hovered over his chest. Needing to taste him, to have Achille eradicate the feel of Zeno's lips, I brushed a kiss over his chest . . . exactly where his heart lay.

It beat in perfect sync with my own.

Achille hissed at my touch, and as if a dam broke inside him, his hands threaded into my hair and tilted back my head. His mouth came crashing down on my own, a loud groan sailing from his throat. The instant his taste hit my tongue, my blood spiked with fever, my hands gliding to Achille's back to rake at his bare skin.

He groaned as I strived to get him as close as I possibly could. We were frantic and untamed as we drank each other down, starving for the other's touch. I broke from Achille's mouth, searching for breath, and his mouth continued south, laying kisses over my jaw and my neck.

"I need you," I whispered. "I need you now. I need you close."

Achille pulled back and searched my eyes. His were almost black, his blown pupil eradicating the sweet blue. The next minute I was in his arms as he dropped to his knees, placing me gently on the flat, cold ground. But I didn't care. I would have let him take me anywhere, just to feel him inside of me again. Just to feel his chest against my breasts and his body on mine.

Achille crawled over me, his warm skin seeping through the material of my dress. The crystals on my expensive gown sparkled in the moonlight—jewels on a bed of earth.

Achille stilled as he stared down at me. I shifted, feeling nervous at the way he studied me. As if I was everything in his world.

I was in his head, his heart and his hands.

Achille lifted his hand and stroked it down my cheek. He pressed his forehead to mine. "Did you know that you were my first? That night, when we made love, did you know it was you I had been waiting for?"

I didn't think it was possible for me to want or need Achille more than I had. I didn't think it was possible for my heart to expand any further. For my soul to mold any closer to his.

But I was wrong. I was so wrong. Because as his cheeks flushed pink when he drew back his head, everything magnified on an impossible scale. Like a dream, my love for him was endless and boundless. And like the simple vine ring wrapped around my finger, I knew it was eternal.

"I knew," I said as I ran my thumb over his kiss-swollen lips. "I knew, and I was honored. I . . . I still can't believe it was me you chose. It is me who was given a gift. Your heart."

Achille turned his face into my hand, his cheek nuzzling the palm. He bent down and brushed his lips past mine. *"Mi amore. Mi amore per sempre."*

My love. My love forever.

I crushed my lips to Achille's. I shivered as he pushed up the skirt of my dress. He shifted until he was completely above me. And then he was filling me. He was taking me, our souls and hearts bared, and no secrets left inside. My back arched as he filled me completely. His arms shook at the side of my head as his eyes closed.

And then he moved. He rocked into me, slowly, purely, on the soil he tended, under the naked moon and twinkling stars. The rich smell of the surrounding vines merged with the fresh smell of his skin and the peach scent from my hair.

My hands explored his bare back, my fingers running through his hair as his rhythm increased and his breathing grew labored. His eyes opened, and they stared down at me with such intense admiration that tears built in my eyes.

"I love you," I said, needing him to hear those words again.

Achille groaned and took me deeper, making me his own.

"Mi amore," he murmured over and over as he increased his speed, my hands clutching onto his hair as a familiar pressure built at the bottom of my spine. Shivers exploded through my body, and Achille stilled.

Heads and hearts and hands.

When I opened my eyes, Achille was gazing down at me, his skin glistening in the moonlight. "How do you say it?" he asked. I blinked, unsure what he meant. "In English," he asked. "How do you say '*Ti amo?*'"

I smiled. "I love you," I said in English, slowly, so he could hear each word.

"I . . . love . . . you . . ." he echoed, his heavy Italian accent bringing such life to such beautiful words.

"Why did you want to know it in English?" I asked as he lifted my left hand and ran the tip of his finger over the vine ring.

"Because I wanted to be able to say it in both of your languages." His familiar teasing smirk came to his mouth. "Though I believe it sounds better in Italian." His smile fell. "I love you forever," he said tenderly.

Ti amo per sempre.

I agreed; it sounded better in Italian.

"I love you too." I wanted him left in no doubt of how I felt. But I could see the disbelief in every part of his face. I could see the slither of doubt in his eyes. I vowed to make it so I never saw it again.

He brushed back my hair. "I want to take you in front of my fire, in my home."

I nodded. Achille got to his feet, then lifted me into his arms. "Can't have the duchessa's feet getting dirty," he teased.

I laughed, deciding this playful side of Achille was my favorite. For it was as rare as a shooting star, but no less memorable. "I think they already are."

Achille shrugged as he carried me with ease toward his house.

"Then I will just hold you in my arms. You look right there. You feel right there too."

I let my head fall against his shoulder and my arms wrap around his neck as we entered his pretty garden. He didn't put me back down until we were in front of the fire. My feet landed on the soft sheepskin rug that sat before the hearth. Achille disappeared into his bedroom and returned with his comforter and two pillows. He placed them down before the fire. I went to sit down, but he took hold of my hand and drew me to where he stood. Silently, he pushed the sleeves of my dress off my shoulders, the delicate fabric falling to the floor. I hadn't worn underwear, the dress's fit not designed for anything to be worn underneath.

Achille's eyes flared as his gaze roved over my naked body. He brought his thumbs into the waistband of his pants and stripped himself of them.

We were both bared, in both body and soul, before each other and the climbing fire.

It was perfect.

I kicked my dress to the side. Achille sat on the floor in front of the fire and held out his hand. I went to him in an instant, letting him draw me down until my back lay against his chest. He brought the comforter over us both and piled the pillows behind his back.

Blanketed by the fire, Achille and his warmth, I stared into the flames and watched as they danced, swirls of oranges, yellows and reds. I wasn't sure how long we sat there in silence, but it could have been eternity. I had never been more content than to simply sit in contemplative silence.

Achille's hand drifted to my stomach. I stilled; it resembled how an expectant father would hold the stomach of his pregnant wife. "Caresa?"

"Don't worry, I am on birth control."

Achille exhaled a long breath. "I would not feel worry if you carried my child," he said quietly.

My heart swelled.

Achille shifted his hand, and the next thing I knew, a book was placed on my lap. The title read *Greatest Wines of the World*. I glanced up from where my head was tucked into the crook between Achille's shoulder and neck. His long black lashes kissed the tops of his cheeks. He chewed on his lip as though he was nervous. But I waited, with a racing heart, to find out why he had brought out this book.

Achille had improved so dramatically in the weeks that I had been helping him with his dyslexia. But having seen his pile of books earlier, I knew that was mostly down to him. He must have been reading every night, searching for the words that had been out of reach his whole life.

He was a fighter.

He wasn't giving up this time.

Achille cleared his throat, and with careful concentration, opened the book to a bookmarked page. Achille lifted the book, placing his finger on the chosen sentence so he could track the words. I felt him swallow deeply, then take a deep breath. With my breath held and my eyes wide, I listened as he read. "It is ar . . . argued . . ." He paused and collected his thoughts. "That . . . the best . . . merl . . . merlot . . . in the world . . . do . . . does not co . . . come from France . . . but fr . . . from . . . Um . . . Umbria, Italy." I didn't move as he gathered his composure again and continued. "The most sou . . . sought-after wine . . . hai . . . hails from . . . Sav . . . Savona Wines' . . . Bella Collina estate." Achille read the final part of the sentence silently to himself, then said, "2008 is re . . . regarded as the best . . . vin . . . vintage . . . to date."

Achille released a heavy sigh and lowered the open book. His chin rested on my shoulder as he reached down and ran his finger under the words "Bella Collina".

"Bella Collina," he said proudly, earning every ounce of that pride in his voice. "Bella Collina. My home. I can read the name of my home."

This time there was no hiding the tears in my eyes, nor the thick emotion in my voice. I turned in Achille's arms and got to my knees, hearing the book thud to the floor. I pressed my hands to his cheeks and watched as he searched my eyes. "I love you," I whispered, then brought my lips to his. "I am so proud of you, Achille. So proud I can barely even breathe."

Achille kissed me back, and we made long, sweet love before the fire, the flames warming our bodies as they joined on the sheepskin rug. We slept in each other's arms, a newfound peace settling in our hearts.

I woke to Achille's sweet lips pressing kisses to my neck. "Mm . . ." I murmured, arching my neck so he could caress me more.

"*Mi amore*," he whispered, his minty breath filling my nose. "Come with me."

I struggled to open my eyes, wanting nothing more than to make this morning last just a few hours more. I didn't want to leave this fire, nor this rug, nor his arms.

"Please," he begged softly, moving his lips to the edges of my mouth.

"Where are we going?" I asked, wiping the sleep from my eyes.

"I want to show you something." I sat up. Achille was already dressed in his jeans and a shirt. He held out some old black jodhpurs and one of his familiar red flannel shirts. A pair of leather ankle riding boots lay beside me.

"They were my mother's. The shirt is mine. I didn't think you would be able to ride in your gown."

I playfully stuck out my tongue at Achille and was rewarded with a laugh and wide smile. I was fully awake now.

Achille handed me the clothes. He had even included socks and a pair of his boxer shorts for me to wear. He chuckled to himself as I put them on. The jodhpurs fit well enough, as did the ankle boots, but Achille's shirt hung low, and the sleeves drowned my hands. I rolled them up to my wrists. I stood before Achille and held out my arms. "Do I still look like a duchessa to you?"

I was teasing. He knew I was teasing. But when he moved forward and kissed my lips, he still said, "You will always be a duchessa. But now you are *my* duchessa. And that I can live with." He held out his hand. "Come, I've already tacked up the horses."

Achille led me outside. Nico and Rosa were waiting for us beside the paddock. I glanced up at the sky. "Achille, it's still dark," I said. "What time is it?"

"Early." He helped me mount Rosa and then swung himself on to Nico's back. "But I want you to see something. I . . . I wanted to share a moment with you."

"Okay," I replied at the hopeful expression on his face.

Together we walked the horses out of his vineyard and onto the track outside. The birds were beginning to wake from the trees around us, but the rest of the world was still asleep. There was me, Achille, the horses and his vines. All he claimed he could offer, yet in that moment, I needed nothing more.

We walked side by side until we turned right and began climbing a hill. We climbed and we climbed at a leisurely pace until the horses were breathless and we made it to the very top.

Before I had the chance to see the view, Achille had jumped off Nico and tied him to a nearby tree, slipping his bit from his mouth so he could graze on the grass. He came over to me and Rosa and flicked his head. "Come on." I smiled at the excitement on his face, and waited for him as he tied Rosa up beside Nico.

He placed his hands over my eyes. "Let me show you why this estate got its name."

I laughed, pulse racing, as Achille led me forward. "Keep your eyes closed until I say so," he said as he guided me down to sit. He sat down behind me and wrapped me in his arms.

"Can I open my eyes yet?" I asked as I melted against his warmth.

The flannel shirt smelled so much of him that he was all I could feel in all of my senses.

I had never been so happy in my life.

"Not yet . . . just . . . wait . . ." he said as though he were waiting impatiently for something. So I waited, eyes closed, as he tucked me closer, keeping me safe.

"Okay, *mi amore*," he whispered. "Open your eyes."

I opened my eyes and blinked in utter amazement. We were up on the highest of hills, Achille leaning against a thick tree. We had a perfect panoramic view of the Umbrian countryside around us. Vast, seemingly unending, rolling hills stretched for miles into the distance, the valleys painted with Mother Nature's autumn browns and deep forest greens.

"Bella Collina," I whispered.

"It was why it was named Bella Collina, because of this view. Because of this spot, right here. *Beautiful hill.*"

"It is perfect," I said, quietly, so I didn't disturb the tranquil peace of the dawn.

Achille pointed over a far hill, and I gasped when I saw the golden brow of the sun rising to bring in the break of day. The horizon shimmered as the sun cast out its red and orange rays—not yet yellow—as it too roused from sleep.

As I watched the waking sun grow higher in the sky, Achille's hand landed on mine and gently stroked over the vine ring.

He was so worried that he couldn't give me what Zeno could, that he didn't have money and status and a mansion. But not even the greatest riches in the world could give me this.

Only Achille could give me this moment. Brought here on the back of my dream horse. Being held tightly in his arms. Being roused from sleep after a long night of making love to the other half of my soul in front of his fire.

Money, titles and mansions had absolutely no place in my happiness at all. Even if I could have only this, I would still be the richest woman to grace the earth.

We stayed that way until the sun was in perfect view, a golden orb hovering in the blue sky. "I need to have this," I said aloud. Achille tensed behind me. I turned my head to face him. His jaw was clenched as he watched the sun . . . as he avoided my gaze.

"Why are you marrying the prince?" he asked, still without meeting my eyes.

My gaze narrowed at his question. This time it was my hand that sought out his vine ring. I let my fingertip ghost over it. I let it give me comfort when sudden nerves and doubt accosted my heart. "It was an agreement from our childhood, but now it is mainly because of the king." I inhaled, feeling the intrusion of the rest of the world raise its head. "Savona Wines has not been doing well since Santo's death. My father can only do so much from America to help. My marriage to Zeno will help strengthen and stabilize the business here in Italy. But it's also just what we do in our circle, Achille. Status marries status."

"So it is mostly to help your family?"

"I guess," I said quietly.

Achille leaned his head back against the tree. I scrambled to sit up and face him. This time he had no choice but to meet my eyes. "Achille, *amore*," I murmured echoing his endearment back at him. His eyes softened as he heard it. "I want *you*. Yesterday, last night— the ring, the banquet, the festival—they all made me realize that I don't want this. None of this. I want you and only you." I gripped his left hand and brought it to my lips. "Zeno doesn't love me. And I certainly do not love him."

When he still didn't speak, or even react, I pressed, "Tell me. You're scaring me. Why aren't you speaking to me?"

"What about my wine? My home? My horses? My vines?"

He seemed so lost as his blue eyes searched mine for answers. I sat back, casting my eyes to the horses grazing beyond the peak of the hill. "I don't know. I don't know what will happen when I tell my parents, tell Zeno. But I won't deny you."

A loving expression engulfed his face, swiftly followed by an expression so fearful my heart dropped. "The Marchesi family has made wine on that land for decades. It was my father's home. It is my home. That land is in my blood. I . . ." He winced. "I would not know what to do with my life if I did not make the merlot."

I didn't know what to say to that. I tried to imagine Achille without his land and his simple but worthy life here at Bella Collina. It would devastate him to lose it. And Savona Wines would never recover if the merlot were lost.

"Then we buy more time," I said, desperate to try and think straight. Of a plan. Of something . . . "I will talk to Zeno. I will talk

227

to my parents. I will make them understand. As harsh as it sounds, this marriage is about money. Your merlot is essential to my father and Zeno's business. They wouldn't let you go . . . not even for this, I think."

Achille's shaking hand cupped my cheek. "I won't come between you and your family. Family is the most important thing. You will not know this until you have to live without it."

"Achille," I whispered sadly.

"Wait until this year's vintage is complete. I . . . I need to concentrate this month on finishing the process. Then comes the bottling . . . then . . ."

"Then we can tell them," I said, realizing that would give me until mid-December. It was close to the wedding, but I hated how fearful Achille was of losing all he ever knew. So we would wait. What were a few weeks anyway?

"Okay," I said soothingly, pressing my forehead to his. "We will wait. But there's no going back now, Achille." I dropped kisses to his cheeks, to his head and finally to his lips. When I broke away, with his hands running through my hair, I said, "I need to kiss you and touch you and make love to you. I will help with the wine, your reading and writing, and the horses. And I will find a way to love you each night, until I can have you forever."

"You promise?" he said, so quietly that I lost my heart to him all over again.

"With everything I am."

Achille brought his mouth to mine, and I kissed him against the breathless backdrop of an Umbrian dawn. I kissed him until the sun's rays began to caress the back of my neck and the brightening sky told us it was time to go.

As we rode back toward his house, we passed the botanical garden. Achille abruptly dismounted Nico and jumped the fence. I panicked, wondering what he was doing, as he disappeared inside a greenhouse. But that question was answered when he walked out clutching a single white rose. His lip hooked shyly up at the side as he stood beside me and offered the rose to me.

I took it, as I always would. "Thank you," I said, smelling the fragrant delicate petals.

Achille jumped back on Nico and we continued our ride back to his vineyard. He picked up Zeno's engagement ring from the field. "You will need this for now," was all he said as he tucked it into my pocket. Then I left Achille with a long slow kiss, a promise that I would see him soon.

My walk this morning was slow. I allowed myself the luxury of time, drinking in the countryside around me. I held my single rose in my hand, breathed in Achille's scent from his shirt. I kicked up the dust from the track and tried to imagine Zeno playing on it as a child. I wondered if he knew Achille. If he had ever even spoken to him. And I tried to imagine what would be said, weeks from now, when I told my family I wouldn't go through with this marriage. When I told Zeno that I chose my heart over wealth.

And I prayed that, whatever happened, Achille didn't regret me.

That would be a punishment worse than death.

When I entered my rooms, I went straight to the bathroom and showered. I was hungry from the long, sleepless night, so I decided to go downstairs and get an early breakfast.

I made my way along the hallway and down the stairs, taking the route through the study to the back door of the kitchen. As I entered the study it was dark, the long red velvet drapes blocking out the early light.

I wondered why the housekeeper had forgotten to open them. I pulled them back, allowing in the light, when a voice from behind said, "Leave them."

I spun around, hand on heart, only to see Zeno slouching in the large leather chair next to the unlit fireplace. "Zeno, you scared me," I said, trying to calm my heart.

I moved toward him and saw he was clutching a full glass of scotch, an almost depleted crystal decanter on the table beside him. He was still dressed in last night's suit, but his tie was gone and his jacket was crooked. His hair, for once, was a mess, the dark ends sticking up in every direction.

"Zeno." I said, moving to stand before him. "Have you been here all night?" It took him a while to lift his head. When he met my eyes, his were unfocused. "Are you drunk?" I asked, beginning to worry.

"Not enough," he slurred and threw back the remainder of the scotch in his glass. He quickly refilled it with what was left in the decanter.

"Why have you been drinking all night?" I folded my arms over my chest.

Zeno raised an eyebrow at me with a cocky smirk. "Why, Duchessa? Are you suddenly interested in me? In my welfare?"

"Don't be absurd, Zeno. Of course I care for you. And I want to know why you are drinking yourself into a stupor."

Zeno reached out sloppily and patted the chair next to his. "Sit down, *fiancée*."

I cautiously did as he said, smelling the strong scent of liquor on him the minute I was beside him. He tried to smile at me, but it was another forced grin.

I was tired of all the pretense.

"Stop it, Zeno. There is no one here for us to lie to right now. Just tell me what is on your mind."

"What is on my mind . . ." Zeno trailed off and bowed forward. I saw him freeze, then look at me. "Where is your ring? Cost me a pretty penny, that did. But I had to make sure my duchessa was impressed." He leaned closer still. "I even made you cry." He pulled back. "Or was that just a good act? I know you weren't crying from happiness. Did I make you cry in sadness, Duchessa? Because you were tying your life to me?"

I'd had just about enough of this, so I shifted my chair to face him directly and took the scotch from his hand. Zeno's face clouded with anger, but I held up my hand and said, "Tell me why you've been here in this room all night. And don't try and joke or charm your way out of it. I want the truth."

Zeno tried to stare me down, but then sagged back in his chair and ran his hand over his face. "I know you think I have been in Florence all of this time, screwing anything that moved, but you are wrong." I stayed quiet, waiting for him to carry on. He leaned to the side of the chair, defeated, his head resting against the headrest. "I haven't. I was there a couple of days when I had to be. But I have been all over Italy to our buyers, trying to convince them to stay with Savona Wines over our competitors." He laughed a humorless laugh. "Turns out they don't trust me. They grilled me, asked me questions about our production that I couldn't answer. Asked me about a plan for the future—one I didn't have. They questioned me on everything, and I didn't know a thing. I, the prince, was put to the test by wine buyers and merchants and made to look a fool."

Zeno sighed, reining in his anger. "And if I have to hear from one more person that I am not the man my father was, that I am not as dedicated to these vineyards as my father was, I will scream."

"Does my father know?" I asked, feeling my face pale with worry. "Does he know that we are losing business?"

"We?" Zeno said patronizingly. He flicked his hand. "He knows some. I haven't told him of the rest."

"Zeno." I rubbed my forehead. "How many buyers have you lost?"

"Mm . . . close to seventy percent," he said, and I instantly felt sick.

"But how? That's crazy!" I exclaimed. "And the merlot? That is not selling? I thought there was a waiting list?"

"The merlot is fine," Zeno said, staring into the unlit fire. "It is expensive, but with the small quantities produced, it doesn't bring in enough revenue to even sustain this place." He sighed. "Caresa, we have eleven properties all over Italy and own hundreds of thousands of acres of land. *All* our wines must sell, not just the merlot. We have lost winemakers to our competitors. They took other offers when my father died because they did not know me or trust me."

"Why didn't you work with your father to learn the business?" I asked, feeling my anger taking hold. Zeno was a twenty-six-year-old man. How could he have lived so carelessly?

"I had no interest in it. He wanted me involved, but it didn't appeal to me. In the end he told me to take a break and he would handle things. So I did."

"You spent your time drinking and partying instead of learning the family business? Is it any wonder the buyers are jumping ship?"

Zeno's fingers tightened on the arms of his chair. "And what the hell would you know?"

"I know that since I have been here, you have made an appearance at this property twice," I snapped. "I know that on those days you have never once walked through your land, getting to know the people that put their blood, sweat and tears into your wines. I have been here but a short while, and I know more of the farmers and winemakers than you, who has had this estate in your life since you were born!"

I got to my feet, staring Zeno down. "You have a gift in this land, Zeno, in all of the land you own. Your winemakers are exceptional, as is the product. If the buyers are leaving, it is down to you and you alone. These wines are better than any of the competitors can provide." I was shaking with rage. "Maybe instead of traveling to the South of France with whichever baronessa had taken your fancy that week, you should have been here with your father, sharing in the business that allows you to live in such a way. My father moved, Zeno. He left his beloved Italy to expand the business he built with your father. As his daughter, I am ashamed that all he sacrificed is going up in smoke. And this sham of a marriage isn't going to fix it!"

"Are you finished?" he hissed, his face reddening with fury.

"No, there is one more thing." I stepped toward him until I could see perfectly into his eyes. "It is time you started to care about this business before you are its ruin. Many people will suffer, thousands will lose their very reason for being if you let this ship sink." Drawing one last fortifying breath, I pointed at him and spat, "It is time you began living *for* this vineyard, instead of living *by* it. You happily reap the rewards yet do nothing to earn them." I dropped my hand. "So start trying!"

I stormed back toward my rooms, my anger chasing my hunger away. Because I was seething. I was so angry at how Zeno had been allowed to live his playboy lifestyle when Achille had worked his whole life, his lifeblood growing in this earth. And he could lose it because of Zeno's lack of responsibility.

I thought back to Achille this morning, to the devastation on his face at the thought of losing his small vineyard, his home and land.

So I had admonished Zeno for him. Because Achille's happiness was now my own, and his vineyard was the key. I couldn't imagine him taken from his land, no longer listening to his opera music in the fields as he hand-harvested the grapes.

Before Achille, I never knew there could be such beauty in the simple act of picking grape from vine. It was art in living color, grace so pure and true. Through him, I saw such flawless divinity in the most understated acts—the way his hand lay so softly on mine, causing my heart to stop in my chest. His lips brushing a kiss against my lips, stealing every last drop of air from my lungs. And the way his warm breath ghosted across my skin in reverence, lighting my body like embers in a fire. Achille thought himself inferior to the likes of Zeno, but I knew differently.

He was a better man. Period.

I closed the door to my rooms and slumped on my bed. I had no idea what to do. Achille wanted me to wait to call off this engagement. And now the business was failing, Zeno crumbling, falling apart.

What a mess.

It was all such a mess.

I didn't know what I could do to help, but I had to try and do something. I had to learn more, study Achille's work in greater depth. Because he couldn't lose this, whether through Zeno or me.

As my finger ran over the simple vine ring lying on my nightstand, Zeno's expensive diamond still in my pocket, I knew I had to find a way.

There had to be a way we could all rise from these dark shadows. Because I wanted that forever with Achille by my side.

And that's how I fell asleep.

Hearing Achille's soft voice echoing through my mind . . .

. . . *Mi amore per sempre* . . .

Chapter Eleven

Achille

I ripped the unneeded vines from their stems and discarded them in the buckets at my feet. All the wine was now aging in its barrels. I would leave it there until December, when it had to be bottled.

The clouds above were gray, the rain threatening as I finished pruning, readying the land for the planting of the next crops.

Caresa had come to my cottage again last night. She had an appointment in town today with her friend so couldn't be here to help. And I missed her. She had only been out of my sight now for about six hours, but I felt her absence seep into my heart.

As the bucket filled, my thoughts drifted to next year's harvest. I froze, my eyes staring blankly at the soil beneath my boots, as I wondered what next year looked like. What next month would look like. What would happen when Caresa told her family about us?

I lifted my eyes and ran them over the now-bare vines. I couldn't imagine not having this, not waking each day to the rich smell of the bustling leaves, or the sun rising over the distant hills.

But I also couldn't imagine my life without Caresa.

I didn't understand why this all had to be so hard. I loved her and she loved me. That should be enough.

It had been five days since the night Caresa had come back to me. And every night she had come to me and I had read to her by the fire. We had drunk wine and cooked food and made love all night long.

My stomach fell. Because I hadn't realized until this week just how much of life I had been missing. I hadn't realized how lonely I had been. Hadn't realized why my father had sat staring at my mother's picture each night when I was growing up—he was only half a heart without her. And although he had me, I now understood how much pain he must have been in. Caresa and I had only been truly together for a little less than a week, yet it brought agony to my heart to think of losing her.

But I let in the light again when I thought of how she had left me this morning, with a soft kiss and a promise to return.

Beethoven played through my headphones while I worked. I lifted the bucket to take it to the heap of dead vines I would later burn, and when I turned, I stopped dead.

A man stood at the end of the row. He was dressed in a suit and looking my way. He waved and indicated to me to take out my headphones. I dropped the bucket of vines and did as he asked.

The prince—I supposed technically he was the king now, but I couldn't get my head to accept that fact—was in my vineyard.

The minute Beethoven was silenced and the familiar sounds of my vineyard enveloped us, Zeno put his hands in his pockets and strolled toward me. I didn't know what to think.

"Seems the apple didn't fall far from the tree." Zeno stopped a few feet from me. As I narrowed my eyes, wondering why he was here, I couldn't help but think of Caresa. He didn't deserve her.

He couldn't have her.

I waited for him to continue. Zeno smiled and raised his eyebrows. He pointed around the vineyard. "You and your father. Seems whatever ran in his blood runs in yours too." Zeno tilted his head to the side. "Though you look nothing like him. Your father was short with fair hair. You're tall and dark. But the winemaker gene was clearly more dominant than his coloring."

I stayed silent. Zeno laughed and shook his head. "What, Achille? No greeting for your old best friend?" He gestured in the direction of the track beyond the trees. "We used to play on those roads as children, yet you have nothing to say to me now?"

"Prince," I said coolly.

Zeno narrowed his eyes. "It's Zeno and you know it. You were the only one who never cared about my title when we were children. Don't start now."

"Why are you here?" I asked, not interested in reminiscing about our childhood, or how he was my very best friend and just one day stopped coming by.

"Straight to the point, I see." He laughed. "Well I guess you haven't changed all that much."

"You have," I snapped back, then shrugged. "Or at least you seem to have. I wouldn't know. I haven't seen or heard anything from you in years." I picked up the bucket and walked past him. I dumped the vines in the pile I had made over the past few days.

I heard him following behind me. When I turned, he was rubbing the back of his neck as though he was nervous or uncomfortable. When he caught me looking at him, he sighed. "Look, Achille. I know I haven't shown much interest, or any interest, in the wines or the people here in this vineyard, but I want to start now."

Shock rippled through me. Zeno dropped his hand from his neck and said, "How is this year's vintage coming along? Do you think it will be as strong as the last?"

"Stronger," I replied and headed toward the barn. Zeno followed, his expensive polished leather shoes no doubt being scuffed by the rough dirt.

As we entered the barn, I pointed at the barrels stretching the length of the building. "They are aging now, then they can be bottled. This year was a good year."

"Good," Zeno replied.

I motioned to my moka pot. "*Caffè?*"

Zeno nodded and walked over to the two chairs that sat beside the fire. He sat down in the one that was now Caresa's. I wondered if he had any idea she came here every day. I wondered if he would even care.

From what Caresa said, I was sure he would not.

I brought the small cup toward him and sat down. It was awkward and uncomfortable. I could talk to Zeno as a child, when he was my friend. But now, as adults living two very different lives, I scrambled for something, anything, to say.

"I'm sorry about your father," I said eventually.

240

Zeno's hand stilled as he brought his cup to his mouth. He cleared his throat. "Thank you." He shifted uncomfortably on his seat. "Sorry about yours too."

I nodded my head in thanks and took a sip of my own coffee. Zeno was studying the barn. "You really did it," he said. He must have seen my confusion, because he added, "The Bella Collina merlot. You used to talk of being its head winemaker one day. And you did it."

"I made my first vintage at sixteen, Zeno."

"You did?" I saw the realization appear on his face. "2008," he murmured. He shook his head in disbelief. "*You* were the difference? You're the reason why it changed? For the better?"

"That was the year I took charge," I said. "Though my father guided me for many years to come . . . until the day he died."

Zeno finished his coffee and placed the cup on the floor beside his chair. "My father would have loved you to have been his son. He loved wine, all wine, but especially *this* wine, *your* wine."

"I know."

"You know?"

I nodded. "The king would come to see us frequently. This was his favorite part of the vineyard."

Zeno sat back, deflated. "He should have left this business to someone like you. Not me."

I couldn't believe what I was hearing. "I can make wine. I know nothing about the sale or promotion of it."

"But you see," Zeno said, "that is all I have been asked about since I have been meeting with the buyers. They wanted to know that I

241

understood how everything worked. I didn't. I don't." He sat forward, elbows on his knees. "It's why I'm here now. I want to know the winemakers that produce the wines. I want to understand the business." He sat up straighter. "You produce our most famous wine, Achille. And . . . and I knew you once. We were best friends. So I wanted to start with you." He gave a short laugh. "I have recently been told that I should start living *for* the business instead of *by* it. Let's just say that the message got through."

"The workers will appreciate you taking an interest."

Zeno nodded, then got to his feet. "I'll leave you to it." He walked out of the barn, and I followed behind. As Zeno walked past the paddock, Nico and Rosa trotted over. He went to them. Nico gave Zeno his attention for about a minute before walking off, but Rosa stayed close.

Zeno patted her neck, then moved toward the gate. Just as he reached my garden, he stopped in his tracks. He glanced at me over his shoulder with a strange expression on his face. "That gray horse? Is she an Andalusian?"

"Yes," I replied, wondering why he seemed so curious about her breed. I had never known Zeno to care about horses in his youth.

An unreadable look flashed across his face. "Is something wrong?" I asked.

Zeno's eyes tightened, his shoulders tense, but he placed a smile on his lips and shook his head. "No, I just remembered something that's all. Something particularly interesting."

With that Zeno walked away, but I didn't move. I didn't like that strange look in his eye as he left.

Feeling the rain beginning to fall, I finished as much of my work as I could before the heavens opened. By the time I had arrived back home, a storm raged outside. I knew if it held up, Caresa wouldn't be able to come here. She was out today until late, and I didn't want her to have to walk to me in the rain.

I lit my fire, made myself something to eat and then walked into my bedroom. I sat down on the edge of the bed and stared at the nightstand. My reading was better now. The things Caresa had taught me had helped me more than anything had in my life. I still struggled; I knew that. Writing was still hard. The pen in my hand never felt right, but I practiced every day. It was . . . improving, but not great. I would never dare write anything to her yet. But maybe one day.

I opened the drawer and saw my father's letter inside. I took it out and laid it on my lap. My hands were damp, and my heart fired a canon in my chest when I looked down at the envelope, and after focusing on it for a while, saw my father's writing.

I *saw* and *read* my father's writing.

I choked on a sob when, for the first time, I understood what these once-jumbled letters said. They spelled my name. On my lap, before me, was my father's writing, spelling my name.

"Papa," I whispered, running the tip of my finger over the cursive lettering. "I read my name," I added, as though he could hear me. "I've . . . I've met someone, Papa." I smiled through the tears that filled my eyes as I brought up Caresa's face in my mind. "She taught me that I wasn't slow after all. My brain just works differently to most. And she's helping me, Papa. I can read some now. It's slow going, and at times I get frustrated, but I can see the words better. Caresa has helped me learn to read."

I brushed the falling tears from my cheeks, and the letter in my hand shook. I wanted to read it, I wanted to finally know what was inside, but . . . I took a deep breath. I wasn't ready yet. I knew that. The letter was long, and my reading wasn't perfect yet. When I read my father's last words to me, I wanted to be able to read them without having to concentrate on each and every word.

And if I was being honest, I wasn't ready to say goodbye. This letter was the final thing my father would ever say to me. Even though he'd been gone for all of these months, I treasured this letter. Because after this . . . there would be no more him. He would be truly gone.

Visions of his last few hours filled my head, and I couldn't breathe . . .

I walked to his bed and sat on the edge. The cancer had ravaged his body. He had always been small, but now his slight frame was withered and weak. His dark eyes that had always been so bright were dull and tired. He could barely lift his hand to hold onto mine.

His breathing was slow and labored, and the doctor had told me it would be soon. My father hadn't wanted to die in hospital. He had wanted to come home and pass on to the next life on his land. This land was everything to him.

He was *everything to me.*

His hand trembled in mine as I held it tightly.

He coughed. "How did . . . the work go today? Is . . . everything almost . . . ready for the planting in the . . . spring?"

"Yes, Papa," I replied, reaching out to prop his pillows higher under his back when he began to cough and struggle to breathe. "Everything will be good. I have planned everything just as you taught me. We will bring in a good harvest this year."

My father's eyes seemed to glaze with sorrow. "You will bring in a good harvest, Achille. This year it is all down to you."

A pit carved in my stomach and a hole burrowed in my heart. I nodded my head when my words failed me. I didn't want to lose him, I didn't want to say goodbye, but he was too sick. I didn't want him suffering anymore.

I looked at the picture my father held in his other hand, tucked safely against his side. My mother. My mother smiling to the camera as she stood next to her horse. She had just won a dressage championship, and anyone could see in her face that she was happy.

"She will be the one to greet me," my father said, clearly seeing me staring at the picture of the woman I never knew. "There is no one else who I would have welcoming me home but her." My father smiled, tears filling his eyes. "I imagine heaven to be much like our small vineyard at Bella Collina. A place where I can still tend the vines as your mother rides in the paddock behind me, dancing her horse to the sound of Verdi."

I squeezed his hand; my sorrow was too much of a barrier for my words. My father tuned his face to me. "And I will tell her of her son. I will tell her of the man he became and how proud she should be of him. How proud I am of him. A good man who has a big heart. A man who is kind and caring, and the best winemaker I ever knew."

"Papa," I whispered sadly.

"It is true, Achille. You have surpassed anything I could have taught you. You

are more talented and natural at this life than any man I've ever known." My
father shifted and gripped my hand as tightly as he could—his touch was nothing,
proving how weak he truly was.

"Achille, when I am gone, you must go out more. You are tied to this land just
as surely as I am, but I also had your mother and you. This life is hard at times,
and you have the ability to love so deeply. There is a woman out there for you, son.
Your split-apart, the woman your soul will remember, the one you will love your
whole life." He tugged me closer. "Promise me, Achille. Promise me you will
live."

"I promise."

"And learn to read and write. Challenge yourself to learn. You love literature.
You love books. And I think . . . I think I have sheltered you too much. I should
have insisted you got the help you needed. I should have insisted the king came
through on his word."

My father coughed again, but this time, true fear ran through me. It was worse
than before, and I could see him fighting to stay conscious. But he never let go of
my hand. Even as his eyes rolled, fighting sleep, he said, "You live a lonely life,
Achille. And that is no way to be. When . . . when you find her, be sure you fight
for her. Promise me . . . promise me . . ."

"I promise," I choked out, and that answer brought a smile to my father's face.
As his eyes closed, for what would be the final time, he whispered, "Your mother
will smile when I tell her that, son . . . your mother will smile . . ."

As I came back to the present, tears were streaming down my face.
A few hours later, with me sitting by his side, my father had taken his
last breath and joined my mother, his missing half.

I had sat with him awhile after that, unable to move from his side. I knew when I moved that it would mean he was truly gone. And I wasn't sure I could face the world without him in it. I wasn't sure what our small cottage would feel like without his music, his coffee, his voice reading aloud from his precious books.

Then, weeks later, my father's attorney brought me a small inheritance check from a pension I didn't even know he had, and a single handwritten letter.

The letter I was still too scared to read.

Taking a deep breath, I stared out at the torrential rain beyond the window. I placed the letter back in its drawer to read another day. I stood from the bed, my father's passing still so clear in my mind, and hated the silence that filled my empty cottage. Every day, for the last five days, I would work, then Caresa would come to me at night.

I was no longer alone.

Yet today, I felt it. The storms and rain came harder in this region during this time of year, and there was a good chance of snow toward Christmas. Caresa and I had decided that on days like today, she should not come to me so late at night. As I checked the window again, seeing the rain had not yet let up, I knew she wouldn't.

But I needed to see her. The memory of my father's last hours, and Zeno's strange arrival at my vineyard today, had set my mind racing.

And I didn't want to be alone.

I threw on my boots and headed to the door. A white rose lay on the side table in the living room. I had retrieved it today for when Caresa came to me tonight.

She wouldn't be coming, so I would take it to her.

Tucking the rose into my shirt, I stepped out into the rain. Within minutes I was drenched, so I walked, not bothering to run, along the dark track toward Caresa's rooms. She had told me which rooms were hers, and that a private balcony led straight to her door.

I arrived at the stairs of her balcony unseen and climbed my way to her door. Through the slightly open drapes, in the dull lamplight, I saw Caresa, sleeping in a large four-poster bed. She was so beautiful that I didn't even care if the rain had soaked me through. It had been worth it just to see her like this.

Lifting my hand, I tapped on the glass of the door. I was quiet, so as not to draw attention, but loud enough that it would hopefully rouse Caresa from sleep. Caresa's dark eyes fluttered open and fell in the direction of the tapping—they fell directly on me.

She blinked in confusion before a wide smile graced her lips, and she leaped from the bed. She padded over to the door and pulled back the drape. I gazed at her through the glass. She was wearing a short silk nightdress, and, even with her usually perfect hair in slight disarray, she was flawless. I couldn't believe she was mine.

The lock turned on the door, and Caresa opened it quietly, a look of disbelief on her face. Before she could speak, I reached into my now-sopping shirt and brought out the rose. It was wet too, the petals limp. I shrugged as I handed it over. "It looked better before the rain." I couldn't help the small smile that pulled on my lips when Caresa covered her mouth to mute her sudden laugh.

She took the flower and held it to her chest. "I love it," she whispered. "Limp or not."

Reaching down with her free hand, she took hold of mine and guided me inside. I ducked into her room, and my eyes widened as I took in the size. This was just her bedroom, yet it was at least twice the size of my entire cottage. Paintings in gold frames adorned the walls, and the rich hardwood floors were covered in expensive rugs.

Caresa ducked her head. "Achille?"

I glanced down at my wet clothing. Caresa tried to coax me forward, but I stayed in my place. "I'm soaking," I said, backing toward the door. "This room . . . I should go. I just wanted to see you and give you the rose." I dropped my head. "I . . . I missed you tonight."

"Hey," Caresa said and placed her hands on my face. "You're not leaving. You just got here." She glanced behind us to a set of doors that I assumed must lead to yet another room. "The doors are locked from inside. No one can come in. No one ever comes in anyway. We won't be caught."

I felt out of place in this room, in this mansion. In all the years I had lived on the land, I had never once been inside. Other winemakers had been here, at dinners and such, but my father and I had never been invited.

"My clothes are too wet. I don't want to mess up the room," I said. Rainwater was already pooling at my feet.

Caresa glanced down at the expanding puddle and stepped closer. "Then let's get you out of them."

I followed her to the bathroom. Like her bedroom, it was opulent and extravagant, all white marble and gold finishes. I stopped beside

249

the bathtub, and Caresa placed a towel on the floor. I stepped onto the plush white towel and shook my head. Water dripped down my face. "What is it?" Caresa asked as her hands began unsnapping the buttons on my shirt.

"Nothing," I said hoarsely as she peeled my shirt from my back and discarded it in the tub. Her rooms, although vast, were warm. Her gentle hands fell to the waistband on my jeans. She snapped open the modified button, pulled down the zipper, then pushed the jeans down my legs until I was naked. Her hands ran up the damp skin of my legs, my waist and my stomach. I hissed as she leaned in and pressed a single kiss to the middle of my chest.

She took another towel and dried every inch of my bare skin. And as she did, I couldn't stop staring at her face. If I hadn't already known she loved me, I would have known in that moment. The way she silently cared for me. The way she cherished my body. The way she rose onto her tiptoes and ruffled the towel through my wet hair. She took the towel off my head and smoothed back my hair that had fallen in front of my face. "There," she said reverently. "Now I can see those beautiful blue eyes I adore so much."

God, I loved her too.

She tied another dry towel around my waist, took my hand and led me to her bed. It was huge, twice the size of my bed. When I had arrived at her door tonight and seen her sleeping, all I could think was that she looked so small. The woman who owned my heart drowning in a sea of white.

Caresa climbed in and held up the comforter for me to climb in too. I dropped the towel and shuffled forward until I was in her arms. I closed my eyes as my head lay over her chest.

Her heart beat quickly.

"Is everything okay?" she asked as she stroked her hand over my forehead.

I held her a little closer. "I needed to see you. I . . ." I swallowed, trying to chase away the remaining sadness. "I kept thinking of my father tonight . . . of when he died." Caresa held her breath. It was the first time I had ever mentioned his passing to her. "I kept thinking of things he had said. I kept thinking of how weak and frail he was." I sucked in a quick breath. "I . . . I needed you. I . . . I didn't want to be alone . . . not tonight."

"Achille," Caresa whispered, shifting on the bed until she lay on her pillow opposite me. She held my hand in the space between us. Her grip on my fingers was iron tight. "Then I'm happy you came," she said and bowed her head to lay a kiss over my knuckles. In an instant, I felt better. Just being beside her, being in her presence, was all the balm my soul needed to heal.

"I'm glad I came too." I looked around the room. "It's good to see where you stay when you're not with me."

"You have never been in the mansion?"

"No." I shook my head and couldn't help the smile that appeared on my lips. "I feel very out of place here. I'm afraid I'll break something priceless."

Caresa shifted closer still, her warm body pressing against mine. "The only thing in this room that is priceless to me is you. So you don't have to worry."

"I love you." I brought my lips against hers.

"I love you," Caresa said when she pulled away.

We lay there in silence for a while, content to just stare at each other.

"The prince came to see me today," I said.

The shock was evident on Caresa's face. "Zeno came to your vineyard?"

I nodded. "He said he wanted to get to know the winemakers on his land more. Wanted to understand the products better." I thought back to us sharing a coffee, of how awkward he was. "He seemed different to when we were children. The same in some ways, but . . . different."

Caresa's brow furrowed. "When you were children? You knew Zeno as a child?"

Exhaling a long breath, I said, "He was my best friend. Zeno was the only friend I ever really had. He would come to Bella Collina in the summer, and we would play on the tracks and in the nearby woods. We would fish and ride bikes." I shrugged. "Then, one day, he just stopped coming around. I asked my father if I could come to the mansion and ask where he was, why he didn't want to be my friend anymore, but my father told me to leave it be." I blinked away the memory. "I never spoke to Zeno again until today. He took me by surprise. I never thought I'd ever speak to him again in my life."

"You were best friends?" I could hear the disbelief in her soft voice.

"Yes. My only friend . . . until you."

Caresa's eyes glossed over. Then she looked away and said, "I never knew you knew Zeno, Achille. You never said."

"Because I don't know him anymore. We were children. He left the estate for Florence, and I never had any contact with him again . . . until today." I pressed my forehead to hers. "But I am thankful to him."

"Why?"

"Because he brought you to me. He left you here on my estate, and God made it so we would cross paths. So although I don't know him anymore, I am thankful to him."

Caresa's lips found mine. When we broke from the kiss, she said, "I can't believe he came to see you. I'm glad. I'm glad he is trying."

"I guess so." I laid my head back over her chest. My arm wrapped around her waist and, just as my eyes began to close, pulled by sleep, I saw an old book on her nightstand. A book I knew very well. "Plato's *Symposium*," I said and felt Caresa still.

"I have been reading it," she confessed. I caught the embarrassment in her tone. But all it did was make my heart explode.

"Mi amore?" I asked.

"Mm?"

"Read to me," I requested. She didn't move for several seconds, but then she leaned over to the table and retrieved the book.

I closed my eyes as Caresa's soothing voice lulled me to sleep. As I drifted off, I thought of the room she stayed in, of the expensive nightgown she wore, and wondered if I was enough.

But then, as she spoke of jealous gods and drifting souls, I let all my worries float away. She was here with me now. That was all that mattered.

The issues we had to face would still be there tomorrow. So for now I let her words wash over me, until I fell asleep, completely content.

Chapter Twelve

A few weeks later...

Achille

I heard the music coming from the mansion as I put Nico and Rosa back in their stables. Even through the thick trees that blocked my view of the house, I could see the Christmas lights sparkling against the evening sky. I could see every window in the house was lit, and I could hear the music blaring from within.

It was the first day of December, and the day of the annual Bella Collina Christmas masked ball. Every aristocrat from Italy had come to the prince's home for the event. A tradition that had been upheld by the Savonas for over three hundred years. A night where the lords and ladies of Italy gathered in Renaissance dress and Venetian masks to dance and drink and remember that they are someone.

Caresa had not been able to get away for the past four days. So I had waited for her in her bed every night, a single white rose on her pillow.

The past month had carried on much the same as normal for me. My wine was almost ready to bottle, and then ... then I didn't know.

But for Caresa, things had only grown busier. Every day she had to discuss wedding plans, go to lunches and attend dinners with Zeno . . . and every day she grew sadder and sadder. She clung to me every night, made love to me as though she would lose me. And it killed me.

But I had to get this year's wine made. And if I was being honest, the thought of her declaring to her family and friends that she was choosing me over the prince scared me to death. I didn't want to lose this life, but I didn't want to lose her.

The thought made me feel sick.

As did the thought of Caresa now in the mansion, dressed in a beautiful period gown, on the arm of the prince. I wanted nothing more but for her to be on mine—she *should* have been on mine—but I had no place in a party such as that.

An hour later, as I sat at home trying to read, the music and my curiosity got the better of me. Throwing on my boots and a shirt, I took a single white rose from the always-stocked vase I kept at the cottage and stepped out onto the path. Gently falling snow landed on my face as I trudged up the hill toward the mansion.

When I reached the highest point, I stopped and looked down at the bustling estate. Christmas lights hung everywhere. The gardens were scattered with lights, illuminating their perfect landscaping. Then my eyes fell on what I knew was the great room. Inside, I saw people dancing, swirling reds and golds and greens.

I made myself move again, wanting a closer look. I ducked past large shrubs to avoid the attention of the increased security that had been brought in to protect the exclusive guests. I came to a large window and peeked inside, making sure to stay in the shadows.

And my eyes widened. The ballroom was a mass of color. Venetian masks of all colors and shapes and sizes were spinning around as the guests waltzed to a live orchestra. Laughter rang out over the music. I had never seen anything like it. It was as though I had been transported back in time. In this moment, the royal family was very much alive and well . . . and I was a winemaker looking in at a life that wasn't his.

And then I saw her.

And I saw him.

The crowd moved to the sides of the ballroom and clapped as a couple walked down the stairs. Zeno was dressed in royal blue with an elaborate silver mask. And Caresa . . . *my* Caresa, wore a deep-red sleeveless ball gown, a corset squeezing in her small waist. Her dark hair was curled and pinned up off her face. She wore long golden earrings and a pretty golden Venetian mask with golden feathers bordering the sides. Her full lips were bright red . . . she was a vision.

Then my stomach fell. Because *this* was Caresa, the Duchessa di Parma. This was the woman she had been raised to be. Music began, and like the most perfect couple, she and Zeno began to waltz, their movements as perfect as they looked. The watching crowd clapped and stood in awe of the royals as they danced, as they whirled across the floor.

A part of my soul died.

It had been a fantasy. All of it. Seeing Caresa like this, I . . . I couldn't disgrace her. Because I would. If she chose me over Zeno, she stood not only to lose her family, but her title and her honor. Caresa laughed and smiled as she danced, and even though my heart was breaking, I found myself smiling slightly too.

No one would ever own my heart like Caresa. But that did not mean that *we,* us as a couple, were right for her. My feet backed away from the window, and I forced myself to turn from the sight of the woman I loved in another man's arms. I wandered listlessly to the stairs that led to the balcony. I climbed each step, knowing the door to her bedroom would be open. She always left it open for me now, so I could climb into her bed at night, if she didn't make it into mine.

I slipped inside, and like I did the first night I was here, I drank in the room. The incredible room that suited Caresa's birthright perfectly. It was almost, *almost,* as beautiful as her.

Sitting on the side of the bed—the side where she slept—I ran my hand over the copy of Plato's *Symposium* on her nightstand, then the pillow on which she slept. I laid the rose on her pillow and stared at the delicate flower on the pristine pillowcase.

I wasn't sure how long I sat there for, but I eventually made myself move and leave her rooms. This time I wasn't steady in my walk back to my home; I ran. I ran, needing to feel the biting cold pinching at my face and the ice-cold wind filling my gasping lungs. The surrounding vineyards were white from the newly fallen snow, and the dark sky above was cloudless, the stars like diamonds up above.

In that moment, they appeared just glittering as the masked ball. As unreachable too. Too far out of grasp, unattainable in their beauty . . . just as far out of my world as Caresa's was from mine.

I ran all the way home, the heavy soles of my boots crunching on the icy mix of soil and grass. I darted into my cottage, needing its familiar comforts to calm me down. But it offered none. For months, my father's ghost had haunted these rooms—his seat by the fire, his calming voice in the night. But now, as I looked at the fire, as I thought of my bed, he had been replaced by Caresa. Day by day she had consumed every part of my life just as sure as she had consumed my soul.

And it hurt. It hurt because no matter the plans we had made, no matter the love we shared and the needs of our hearts, it couldn't work. None of this could ever work.

We had been fools to think so. Struck from our senses by love.

And it hurt. It hurt so much I couldn't breathe.

I staggered into my bedroom and slumped onto the edge of my bed. My elbows landed on my knees, and I ran my hands through my hair. As I looked up, my eyes fell to the nightstand . . . and the letter inside called my name.

I needed my father right now. I needed to hear his voice. I needed his help . . . I had nowhere else to turn. My reading had improved so much over the last month. And I . . . I knew I could do this.

I *had* to do this.

My fingers trembled as I opened the drawer and took out the envelope. I took in a long, deep breath, but it took me four more inhales and exhales before I could open the back and pull the four pages from their home.

A wave of emotion overwhelmed me, and I had to glance away. I closed my eyes and imagined my father's face. Smiling at me as he tried to teach me to read and write. Telling me that I could do it. Telling me that I could do anything if I only tried.

With that image in my head, I steadied my hand and let my eyes meet the page. And so I read, trying to make his memory proud . . .

My dearest son,

If you are reading this, then know one thing: I loved you. Most fathers love their children, but you have always been special to me. You were a gift I never expected to be given. But better than that, you exceeded anything I could ever dream.

You may have wondered why I would write you a letter. You may have wondered, why, with the challenges you face, I would be so cruel. But if you are reading this letter, I know it is because you have sought out the help you always should have been given. The help I should have moved heaven and earth to get you.

And know that as your eyes read these words, I am bursting with pride. You are the best winemaker I have ever known, one of the greatest people—with your kind heart and soul—but your reading always held you back. I failed in not taking you into the world more, instead staying close to our vineyard. I know, that even when you read this, what your every day will entail. You are a man who will live a simple life. You will always get by because you always have done. You order your life in a way that you don't have to read or write. You will live off the land or rely on Eliza and Sebastian like we always did, so that your trips into town are limited and you don't have to worry about appearing slow or strange to strangers.

And I confess that I had a hand in that. Not because I didn't want you to better yourself, I did, but because I was so out of my depth with your challenges. But I was also protecting you. Making sure we stayed at the vineyard, just me and my son.

And that was for a good reason too.

You may be wondering what that reason was. And I will get to that, Achille, I promise. But first, there are some things you do not know about your mother, about your mother and me. Things that I kept from you to protect you. To protect your mother's memory.

Your mother was everything to me. Abrielle was the very reason I breathed. She was the dawn and the dusk and all the hours in between. We were soul mates, split-aparts, but we were not without our problems.

You see, Achille, when I met your mother, we were young. The moment I laid my eyes on her, time stopped. When I met her in Orvieto, singing Christmas hymns around the tree on Christmas Eve, with the snow falling around her beautiful face, I knew I had found home. Abrielle glanced up from her hymnbook and looked across the tree, and I knew she had found her home in me too. People like to say that love at first sight is a myth, that instant love is for the pages of a fantasy book.

But it isn't. I lived it. Your mother and I were proof of that fact.

We were married two months later, and she moved into my home at the vineyard. Your mother was a dressage champion, and she quickly became the standout rider in King Santo's dressage and show jumping team.

She loved her life, playing out her passion, and I loved mine. It wasn't long before we wanted a child of our own. We wanted a child to complete our family . . .

But that wasn't meant to be. We tried, Achille. For years we tried, and despite the love we had for one another, the fact that we were not producing a child became a plague between us. The depression your mother sank into took her to a lonely

261

and desperate place. A place to which I could not follow.

We sought out help, answers to what the problem was. And the findings were straightforward. The problem was me. I couldn't have children, Achille. I, the man who loved your mother with everything that I was, could not give my soul mate the one thing she desired most.

I couldn't give her you.

I know you, son. I know as you read this you will question if you have understood my words correctly. And you have. I couldn't have children, and my heart broke as I helplessly watched your mother drift further and further away from me, drowning in waves of sadness.

We lost our way. We lived together, slept beside each other every night, but we weren't okay, we weren't us. We were lost in the heavy rain . . . and that's when your mother was taken on a championship tour with the king.

I couldn't leave the vineyard because of the harvest. And she didn't want to stay. So she went. She went and won every competition she entered, becoming renowned in the equine community and acclaimed in her sport. But her victories, her beauty and her spirit also managed to win the king's affection. In that year, King Santo barely came home, instead choosing to travel with the team. The queen stayed behind with the young prince.

King Santo never came home because of your mother, Achille. King Santo became infatuated with my Abrielle, and, it still pains me to say, she became affectionate toward him too.

I do not blame your mother, Achille. She was young and sad and far from home. And although he never held her heart as I did, I knew that she loved him too. When your mother came home she told me everything at once. Her tears were thick and full as she confessed her infidelity.

It took me a while, but I forgave her. I loved her. She was my split-apart. And I was hers. And despite the crack in my heart her affair caused, it brought your mother back to me. Gone was the pain, and gone was the sadness. I had my Abrielle back. I chose to forgive her. Many wouldn't, but it was my heart and my pain, and I chose the heavy route of forgiveness.

She won her final championship, then came home for good. She told the king they were over, and I finally had her back.

Then a month later we discovered she was pregnant. It wasn't a medical miracle. We both knew how she was with child, and it wasn't my doing. We knew whose baby she carried. I struggled at first, son. It was a dagger to my heart. But when you were born, all of that pain became filled with the greatest of light. When I held you in my arms and you looked into my eyes, I knew I was your papa. You were my son.

And then my Abrielle died. Right in front of me, she died with tears of sadness in her eyes. But not before she told you she loved you and that I was your father. She knew I would love you. She knew you would be safe. She believed her death, the reason we were being torn apart, was because she was being punished. She thought death and not getting to know her son was the punishment for straying.

I never believed that. And I still don't. Because nothing, not even death, could take her from me. She stayed with me through you. You looked so much like her, son. Your mannerisms, your shyness, your kindness were all your mother. Though you carried your father's eyes. His height and his broadness. The older you got, the more I saw him within you.

And then you befriended Zeno. You became best friends with your brother, as if the fates had pushed you together, a winemaker's son and the prince— as if destiny had always known you should have been close. And you loved Zeno like a brother. My shy little boy had found someone he could be himself with. You cherished his visits as you played out on the track.

Then one day the king turned up to my vineyard and saw you both playing in the field beyond. It was the first time I had seen him since your mother died. One look into my eyes and he knew I knew about their affair. He knew we had had a son. And when you came running toward the vineyard, with Zeno in tow, I saw the moment he knew you were his. You and Zeno, laughing side by side. Similar in both hair color and eyes. Same height, same build, same smile.

Both Santo's.

He pulled me aside and demanded the truth. So I told him. It was the scariest day of my life. I feared he would take you from me. I saw in his eyes that he still loved your mother, still grieved for her. We shared in that pain. And then here you were, their perfect mix. A piece of Abrielle living on his land, with his blood running through your veins.

King Santo returned to the mansion with Zeno. Days later, Zeno was sent back to Florence, and a week after that, the queen returned to Austria. She never came back.

Because King Santo had told her of you and how you were a rightful prince. He told his wife that he wanted to publicly declare you as his. He wanted Zeno to have his brother in his life. He . . . he was happy you were his, son. He wanted to know you. He wanted to love you.

But his brother Roberto and his advisers warned him against it. His reputation would be ruined. His wife would be humiliated. I was so angry at him when he chose to listen to them and deny you. But then he never left the estate. He began to visit you frequently. And every time he came, he fell more and more in love with you. And I could see you liked him too.

When your schooling became difficult for you, I asked him for his help. Rumors of how you looked like him had already begun to spread throughout the school you attended when he tried to intervene. He pulled you out, and I trusted him when he said it was because he wanted what was best for you. It quickly became clear that he was hiding you. My beautiful boy was being kept away, a secret, so his affair wouldn't be exposed. And I am ashamed that I allowed it. I know now that I gave in to your request to not return to school because I also wanted to protect your mother. But I was wrong to do so. The king loved you, yet he could not rise against the blue-blood world he ruled to accept you.

Then you became indispensable to him because you were my heir. You would follow me in making the Bella Collina merlot. And you were better than me. I believed the king loved you like a son, but he knew keeping you from reading and writing would encourage you to stay at the vineyard. I could see you wanted that too. But I failed you. I liked you working by my side; I cherished each day. So I let it happen. I will regret that forever. Sometimes I wonder if I was as selfish as the king, keeping you sheltered so I could keep you as my son.

I will always be your father, Achille. You were mine and I raised you the best I could, but you have a right to know the truth. I never told you when I was alive as I knew you weren't ready. You lived in the small world the king and I had created for you, and I knew you wouldn't be ready to hear this truth until you took it upon yourself to seek out more. I knew someday the boy I raised would conquer his demons. I didn't know how or when, but I knew he would. And when that day came, I knew you would finally be ready to hear the truth.

To accept your birthright.

Achille, my son, you are a Savona. For all intents and purposes, you are an ancestral prince of Italy. You were always better than me—sweeter, kinder, and

265

more talented. You are not merely a son of a common winemaker, but a bearer of blue blood from centuries' breeding of kings and queens.

To me, you will always be my son. But you need to know the truth.

I love you.

Your mother loved you

As did the king.

Be great, my son. Be the prince you were born to be.

Your proud father.

As I read the last word, with my heart torn into shreds, I realized I couldn't move. So I sat there on the bed, with shaking hands and tears streaming down my cheeks. Because everything I had ever known was a lie.

For the first time in weeks, I wished I had never met Caresa. Because Caresa had brought me the gift of words and books. But she had also brought me this truth, this truth I didn't want.

So I'd just sit here some more . . . and at some point, when I could muster the courage, I would move . . .

. . . and do what?

I had absolutely no clue.

Chapter Thirteen

Caresa

"I think you're convincing them. *Brava*," Zeno whispered as he spun me around the ballroom, all of the guests looking on with smiles on their faces. My cheeks ached from the smile I wore as we waltzed around the room.

I wanted to step back and tell them all that this whole thing was a joke. I wanted Achille to walk through the main doors. Wearing a suit and tie with a mask adorning his face. I wanted to dance with him as if he were my prince. The prince I loved and adored and wanted to be betrothed to.

When the song came to an end, I bowed at Zeno as the crowd clapped and flooded the floor to dance again. As the people rushed between us, all twirling in one direction, I turned and walked in the other. Zeno didn't even try and stop me as I fled for the main doors.

Pia took hold of my hand as I passed her, bringing me to a stop. "Are you okay?" she asked.

"I just need to go to my rooms for a moment. If anyone asks, tell them I have gone for fresh air."

"Caresa," she went to say, about to tell me again that I didn't have to do this. But I shook my head, silently begging her to not start. She

267

released my arm.

I ducked out of the large doors and went straight up to my rooms. As soon as I was safely inside, I pressed my hand over my corset and tried to breathe. I walked into the living room, feeling a breeze coming from my bedroom. I moved into my bedroom to see my balcony doors open. My heart raced. "Achille?" I whispered, searching my bathroom and closet. They were empty. But he had been here, I was sure.

Then I caught a familiar sight on my pillow. A single white rose lay where I slept. But as I looked around the room again, something didn't feel right within me. Why didn't he stay? Why didn't he wait for me?

I rushed across the bedroom and saw the light in his cottage was on. I struggled with what to do. The ball was nowhere near over. I was dressed in a gown and mask. But I ripped off the mask, and despite the snow and the fact that my arms were bare, I ran off the balcony and toward Achille.

My breath was bursts of white as I ran as fast as I could, slipping on the icy ground in my vintage Renaissance-inspired heels. It felt like it took forever to get there, and with each step I took, I felt an ominous feeling settling in my stomach. Something wasn't right with Achille. I could sense it. He was easy to predict. Ordinarily, he would have waited for me in my bedroom. But he hadn't stayed, which made me think something was most definitely wrong.

I pushed past his gate and through his front door, my chest raw from breathing in the winter air. His fire was unlit, making the small room feel cold and dark. "Achille?" I called out as I dashed through to his bedroom.

I froze in the doorway. He sat on the edge of his bed, holding a letter in his hand. My stomach dropped when I saw that he was deathly still but for the torrent of tears that was flooding down his cheeks. His face was so pale I was sure he was ill. I lurched forward and dropped to my knees before him. "Achille? *Amore?* What's wrong?"

I reached out and placed my palms on either side of his face. He was stone cold. My hands became drenched from his tears. Tears of sympathy built in my eyes too as I waited with bated breath for him to speak. He slowly lifted his head and worked his mouth . . . but nothing came out.

I watched him struggling to find something to say, when instead, he just handed me the letter. I took it from his trembling hands. "You want me to read it?" Achille nodded his head. His eyes locked on mine, as if he were searching for some kind of relief, some respite from whatever was haunting him.

"Okay, *amore,*" I soothed. I sat back on the floor and began to read. And with every new line my emotions became a kaleidoscope— sorrow, happiness, intense shock and sadness . . . and then . . . then . . .

"No," I whispered as his father's secret was revealed. "Achille . . ." I read of King Santo and Zeno, of Achille being pulled out of school and why, and with every word scanned, my heart shattered apart, fleeing my chest piece by piece and leaving a darkness in its wake.

When I had finished the last line, I dropped the letter to my side. Achille was still a statue on the bed. But his eyes were on mine— desperate and hurt and soul-shatteringly destroyed. "*Amore,*" I said as I wrapped him in my arms and held him close. His response was delayed, shock still clearly setting in. Then with a pained sob, he launched into me, his arms around my waist and his head in the crook between my neck and shoulder. And he fell apart as he purged the pain and hurt from his body. The knowledge that he was King Santo's son.

Achille was a prince.

My Achille . . . was born a *prince*.

"Shh." I brushed my hand over his hair. I was so wrapped up in comforting my Achille, that I didn't hear the footsteps enter the house. I didn't hear someone move into the doorway of Achille's room until a voice spoke.

"Well, it's nice to know that my suspicions were correct."

Achille and I froze to the spot at the sound of Zeno's deep voice.

Achille sniffed and moved his head so he could sit back. I gathered my composure and got to my feet. I turned to face Zeno, who was crowding the doorway, his arms folded over his chest. "Not now," I said tersely, wiping the tears from my eyes.

Zeno raised a single eyebrow. "You leave the masked ball not even halfway through the party to come and screw your bit on the side, and you think that's okay?"

"Stop it," I snapped and watched a smirk form on Zeno's lips.

"Despite you thinking you can do whatever you wish, Caresa, our guests were questioning where the future queen was. It didn't take me long to work it out when your balcony doors were open . . . again." I felt the blood drain from my face. "You think I didn't know you were sleeping with Achille? I have surveillance cameras, Caresa, and not to mention you're not exactly discreet when you run over to his cottage at midnight, or he to your rooms." Zeno flicked his chin. "But this ends now. We are to be married in a matter of weeks, and this has to end. You've had your fun and I've had mine. We have the aristocrats of Italy waiting for you to come back. It is your duty."

The blood that was rushing through my veins like rapids turned red hot. "I am not coming back. You can tell them what you want. Tell them I'm ill, or whatever you like, but I'm not coming back. Achille needs me."

Zeno opened his mouth to argue, and I felt Achille get to his feet behind me and take the letter from my hand. I hadn't even realized I was still holding it. Zeno stood straighter and gave Achille a questioning look. I looked back at Achille. His eyes were red raw and swollen from crying.

"Read it," Achille said, offering the letter to Zeno. Zeno's eyebrows drew together. He looked at me, then Achille. And for the first time, I saw it. I saw it as clear as day.

Their resemblance, it was there. Their hair color was the same. Their eye color was exactly the same. Even the way the way Zeno's forehead creased with confusion was the same as Achille's.

"Read what?" Zeno asked suspiciously. I thought of what he was about to discover. About his father, about why he was taken away, and the fact that Achille was his brother. It wasn't just Achille who was going to be torn apart tonight. Zeno's world was about to be blown to pieces too.

"Read it," I found myself saying, after Zeno hadn't moved and the silence became too loud. I took the letter from Achille and gave it to Zeno. "You *need* to read it."

Zeno viewed me skeptically, but then edged toward the light and began to read. I moved to stand next to Achille, who was frozen beside me. But he never took his eyes off Zeno. I slipped my hand through Achille's and squeezed it tightly. I heard his breath catch, but I stayed focused on Zeno. And I saw the moment his face turned ash-white. His hands shook, then he tensed, every muscle in him strained.

Then he read it again. He read the whole letter twice through before lifting his head. "No," he said, his voice low and laced with venom. "What is this?" he snapped and held up the letter. "This isn't true." Zeno shook his head, and I felt Achille begin to shake. But it wasn't in fear or sorrow; it was in anger. I could feel the heat of rage radiating from him.

"This is false!" Zeno spat.

"My father doesn't lie," Achille said through tightly clenched teeth. "He would never lie."

Zeno held the letter in the air as his face reddened further. "Well, according to this, he isn't your father!"

"Zeno!" I shouted, moving to stand in front of Achille, who was breathing far too fast. Zeno was still glaring at Achille, and Achille at him. I looked between them. I was a fool to have never seen the resemblance before now. Because they were most certainly brothers. So similar in certain ways, so alike in looks. "Zeno. *Look* at him. You have the same eyes, the same height, build . . . God, Zeno, he's your brother. You have to see it! His father didn't lie. Why would he lie?"

"To get money? Status for his only, slow son after he'd died? Because he hated my father? Any of those things!"

"He would not," Achille said. I flinched at how low and menacing his voice sounded. He was my quiet, shy and timid man. He never spoke in such a way.

Zeno took a step forward. "You are not my goddamned brother! Your father was a malicious liar, and you're both nothing!" He screwed the letter up in his hands and threw it to the floor.

That was all it took to make Achille snap. As the balled-up paper hit the other side of the room, Achille ran around me and tackled Zeno to the ground. They hit the floor with a thud, and Achille plowed his fist into Zeno's face. But they were evenly matched in strength and height, and before long Zeno returned the blow.

Blood spattered on the floor as they grappled and punched. "Stop! Stop!" I yelled, rushing forward to try and pull them apart. But Achille and Zeno were men possessed, raining blows on one another. "STOP!" I yelled as loudly as I could, catching Achille's arm enough to pull him slightly back, breaking them apart.

Zeno scrambled to his feet and wiped the blood from his cut lip and nose. His hair was disheveled, and his suit was ripped beyond repair. His eyes were wild as he pointed at Achille and snapped, "Get your things and get the hell off my land. You are not my brother and will get no money from me! You're lucky your father is dead, or I would sue him for defamation. Now, get the hell out!"

Zeno fled through the door, and I had to brace myself in front of Achille to stop him from running after him. He wriggled from my hold, rushed to the corner of the room and picked up his father's letter. He placed it on the bed and tried to straighten the pages.

And that's what broke me most of all. A bloodied and bruised confused man trying desperately to hold on to the only father he had ever known, the one who had just told him he wasn't his father after all. Smears of blood began staining the pages. I rushed over and gently guided his hands from the letter. He looked at me, eyes glassy and wild. His lip was cut, and a bruise was already beginning to form on his swelling eye. "My letter," he rasped, so softly it destroyed me. "I need to save the letter."

"I know," I said gently. "But you're staining it with blood." Achille drew back his hands as if the letter was suddenly a burning page. He stood in the middle of the room, looking around, completely lost. He struggled for breath as his tears continued to fall.

Leaving the letter, I stood before him and cupped his cheeks. He couldn't look at me first, but then drew a breath and met my eyes. "We'll leave," I said. He gave me a blank look. "My family have a villa on the outskirts of Parma. We'll take your father's old car and leave tonight. We need to give it some time and work out what to do. We'll get away. Just you and me. We'll get Sebastian and Eliza to watch the horses. Okay?"

Achille was breathing hard, but he nodded, curling his cheek into my palm. I melted, tears streaming down my cheeks as he sought out my comfort. I leaned forward and pressed my forehead to his. "I need to go change and grab some things. You pack a bag. I will return soon, then we'll go. Okay?"

"Okay," he whispered. He drew back his head and searched my face. The sorrow in his blue gaze was heartbreaking. "We'll get through this, *amore*," I said. I kissed him on the non-cut side of his lips and whispered, "I love you."

He kissed me back. "I love you forever."

Ti amo per sempre.

I forced myself to back away and ran back toward the house. I wondered what excuse Zeno had given the guests, if he had even returned at all. But I didn't care; I just kept running. Once in my room, I threw on some jeans and a sweater and packed as much as I could in a bag. I put on my coat and boots and headed back to the cottage. Thoughts of Zeno so angry, and Achille so hurt, swirled in my head with every step. The two of them fighting, hitting each other, spurred on by mutual pain.

It was a mess.

It was all such a mess.

When I entered Achille's house, it was silent. "Achille?" I called out, rushing to check every room. I ran out to the barn, then the stables, searching for where he could be.

And then I noticed his father's old car was missing from the garage behind the barn. I shook my head, backing toward the house. *He wouldn't. He wouldn't have left me. He wouldn't have gone without me.*

I burst back through his house, my heart cracking as the truth began to set in. And then I saw a piece of paper on a pillow on his bed, the pillow I slept on . . . beside a single white rose. My feet were leaden as I walked toward it, my personal green mile.

With trembling hands, I reached down and turned it over, and I dropped to the floor in a confused swirl of devastation and pride. Achille had *written*—he had never written before—but the untidily formed words cut me in two.

> *My love,*
> *I'm sorry.*
> *I love you forever.*
> *Achille.*

A sob ripped from my throat as I was ravaged by a sadness so consuming I wasn't sure I'd survive. He had left, the other half of my soul had left, and he had taken my heart with him too. All I could think of was how much pain he must have been in as he went. And where had he gone? Who else did he have? He was so alone.

I cried and I cried until my throat was raw and my chest ached. Eventually I lifted off the ground and walked back to the mansion. As I arrived at my balcony, Zeno was leaning against the balustrade. He took one look at me, at my crying face, and a strange expression flashed across his face. I almost believed it was one of shared sadness, and maybe regret too, but when he schooled his features back to his usual cold expression, I knew I must have been mistaken.

As I walked past him, I said, "He left."

I was just about through my doors when Zeno said, "Good. Maybe now you'll actually start doing your duty and forget him. We are getting married whether either of us likes it or not. It is what we must do. And it is about time you stopped fooling yourself into thinking you could run away into the sunset with a poor winemaker. It will never happen, Duchessa, not for the likes of us."

With that he left.

Achille had left too.

And as I curled up on my bed, clutching the rose that Achille had brought me, I reread the letter he had written me. I read it until sleep took me, giving me a temporary reprieve from the unbearable pain in my heart.

Chapter Fourteen

One week later . . .

Caresa

"Duchessa, you look beautiful."

I stared at my reflection in the floor-length mirror, yet I felt nothing. I was numb. I had been numb for the past seven days, since he'd left me. Today was the final dress fitting for my wedding day. It was strange really—here I was dressed exactly as I'd always envisioned, in my dream lace dress with long sleeves, a corseted waist and a flowing silk skirt. And wearing the floor-length veil adorned with silken vines that I had wanted since I was a child. Today should have been the happiest of my life.

It felt like the worst. I was in a nightmare I couldn't escape from, and the hero I wanted to come and save me had left me alone. I had cried for seven days straight. Now there was just a deep, dark sense of nothing.

Maria, Julietta and her assistant lost themselves in the excitement, taking pictures for any last-minute alterations that would be made this week. But I stayed silent. I wasn't sure what I could say anyhow.

"Wait until your parents see this, Duchessa! They get in next week, yes?" Julietta asked as she began to unzip me from the dress.

"Yes," I replied. I was making sure I listened to them just enough to answer any questions.

"They will be in love!" Julietta said happily, clearly pleased with her work. As she should be—the dress and veil were exquisite. If I were in any mood to feel excited about such a thing, I would share in her joy of a job well done.

I changed into a robe as they packed everything up. I sat down, sipping a *caffè* as I stared into the flames of the fire that had been lit in my bedroom. It was coming up to Christmas now, and the house staff had decorated my rooms. They smelled of pine and cinnamon from the heavily decorated tree, and the crackling fire was never allowed to die.

Maria came and sat beside me. "Contessa Florentino has called, Duchessa. She would like to arrange a lunch sometime this week." Pia. Pia wanted to see me.

I placed down my cup and shook my head. "No thank you. Please decline. I won't be making any engagements this week."

Maria sighed in frustration. "You cancelled all the ones from last week, Duchessa. And now this week too? It is Christmas soon, and the city expects you to make an appearance. You should have been in Florence days ago. There are festive parties to attend. Our society expects your presence at these functions due to you being their future queen."

"Zeno can go in my stead," I said and curled my legs onto the chair. I turned toward the fire, hugging my waist.

"The king will not leave either. I think he is waiting for you."

I flinched as Maria called Zeno "king". The word made me think of Santo, and the mess he made when he seduced Abrielle Bandini and took her from her husband. When he had a child and refused to acknowledge him as an heir, because our precious society deemed it inappropriate. Then what she said sank in. "Zeno is still here?"

"He has not left in a week either. You both left the ball and have been hiding in your rooms for a week. You are worrying us all. The king will only see his secretary." Maria moved closer. "She said he had been injured. Maybe by fighting. He wouldn't say."

"I wouldn't know," I said vaguely, then turned to stare again at the flames.

"Well, your parents are due to arrive next week. Will you be going to the palazzo to meet them or continue hiding here?"

"I don't want to leave here," I mumbled. *In case he returns.*

"The king has cancelled the Christmas banquet at the palazzo, but the wedding is set for the Duomo on New Year's Eve, and you will have to be there a few days before. There is only so much time I can buy you both." Maria got to her feet and, in a surprising move, laid her hand on my head. The affectionate gesture brought tears to my eyes. I had been so closed off, so devoid of affection since he left, that I didn't realize what someone's caring touch would do to me.

Maria kissed my head. "I know these marriages can be hard, especially on one as young as you. Societal marriages have a way of seeming cold and routine. All any bride wants for her big day is to be loved and have butterflies swirl in her stomach when her eyes land on

280

her groom." She stepped away, leaving the tears tracking down my cheeks. "But the king is a good man. And the fact that he has stayed here when you are feeling so low is testimony to how fond he has grown of you."

Maria turned for the door. "I'll clear your week. But from next week, Duchessa, you must make more of an effort."

The moment she left me alone, I broke apart, wondering how I had got to this moment. And Zeno? Why was he still here? I had not spoken to him once since that night.

Seeing the time was almost eleven o'clock, I got up from the chair and got dressed. I pulled on Abrielle's jodhpurs, a pair of short boots and a sweater. Wrapping myself up in a scarf, coat and gloves, I left my balcony and began the walk over to Achille's home. As with every day since he had left, the closer I got to the cottage, the more mixed my feelings became. I loved this place, found comfort in its small walls, but not seeing Achille in the fields or in the barn was a dagger to the heart.

Yet every day I came. Every day I lived in hope that he would return.

I pushed through the gate and checked the house. It was empty, like every day this week, but it was clean and waiting for his return. I had made sure of it.

Not needing to stay there, I went to the barn and unlocked the doors. I heard the eager sounds of hooves on stall floors, and the briefest of smiles came to my lips. When I arrived at the stables, Nico and Rosa had their heads over the doors. I patted each one on their necks, kissing their noses. "You ready to come out? Sorry I'm late today, I had an appointment I couldn't get out of." I released them into the paddock and put out some hay. The grass was hidden beneath a light layer of snow and difficult for them to eat.

When the horses were happy, I went into the barn and took a deep breath. Today was the date Achille was meant to have started the bottling of the merlot. He wasn't here, so I would have to do. He had talked me through the process weeks ago, and promised that he would let me help him when the time came. This year's vintage, in Achille's estimation, would be his greatest yet. I wouldn't let all this destroy the wine.

This wine was his passion, his life. It needed to be done.

"Right." I took off my gloves. I started the fire and tried to warm up the vast space. And then I began. I sorted the now-corrected labels and gathered the empty bottles and corks that would be used. I got the sanitation fluid and siphon and began the arduous task of cleaning the wine bottles. It took me hours, but I didn't stop. I needed to keep going.

As I finished cleaning the last bottle, someone coughed from the doorway. I lifted my head. Zeno walked into the barn, his hands in the pockets of his dark jeans. He was wearing a sweater, scarf and gloves. Like this, he looked just like everybody else. No suit, no attitude, just . . . normal.

But my anger toward him was still simmering. For how he treated Achille, calling him slow, insulting his late father so brutally. For trying to ruin the letter, and for casting him from his land like he was nothing.

"What do you want?" I asked tersely.

Zeno stopped dead. I waited for him to hiss something back, but he bowed his head in defeat. "I didn't come here to fight with you, Caresa." I didn't say anything in response. Zeno stepped forward, looking at what I had been doing, at the bottles that had been cleaned. "What are you doing?"

"Bottling," I said tightly, then carried on with my task, washing away the sanitizing solution and preparing the siphon to get the aged wine from the barrels.

"You know how to do this?"

Zeno came to stand beside me, watching me with interest. I nodded. "Achille taught me before . . ." *He left*, I wanted to say. But if I did, I knew I would lose control of my anger and take it out on Zeno.

"He taught you the entire process for the merlot?"

I nodded again, then dropped the siphon I was holding. I rested my back against the counter, remembering when Achille had prepared lunch and made coffee for me in those first few days. I had to quickly rid myself of those thoughts. If I let them, they would drown me in sadness.

And I had a job to do.

Zeno rested his back beside me and stared out of the barn doors at the lightly falling snow. "You are here everyday?"

"Yes," I replied. "The horses need caring for, and I knew today was the first day of bottling. I knew . . . I knew Achille would want this done. He cares for this wine like no one would ever understand. It is his entire life." I flicked my eyes up to Zeno. "It is all he has in the entire world. Without this, he would be so lost. The outside world overwhelms him. You . . . you read in the letter that his father kept him sheltered, and why. So your father wouldn't be suspected of being Achille's papa." I swallowed back the burgeoning lump in my throat. "If he doesn't come back . . . if he doesn't ever return . . . he would want this year's wine completed."

I looked right at Zeno. He was looking back at me with an unreadable expression on his face. "He believes this wine will be the greatest yet," I said. "Though I'm sure anything he produces would be great." I shook my head. "You have no idea of the kind of man he is, Zeno. He cares so much, he loves so much and so deeply that I've never seen anything like it." A tear fell down my cheek as I whispered, "He just wants so desperately to be loved back. He *deserves* to be loved back. He doesn't deserve all of these blows life keeps giving him—never knowing his mother, his father dying young, and now all of this." I studied Zeno. "You are not so dissimilar, you know. You have both lost your fathers, never truly got to know your mothers. And you both have had to shoulder these burdens alone." I wiped away the tear and stared at the ground. "But Achille doesn't have the tools you do to cope with things. And he should. Because if anyone deserves happiness and love, it's him. It'll always be him."

Zeno didn't say anything for the longest time, until he ran a hand down his face and whispered, "You love him, Caresa. You truly love Achille."

284

I laughed a humorless laugh and fought not to crumble. "Yes . . . he is my split-apart."

Zeno looked confused, but then said, "I will be gone for a couple of days. I'm going to see my Uncle Roberto in Florence." He paused. "I have to know the truth. I . . . I have thought of nothing else for the past week. How we used to be so close as children." Zeno laughed, but it was pained and short. "I think . . . I think he was the best friend I ever had." He cleared his throat. "Turns out there might have been a reason for that. He may be my brother. My best friend, who I was told by my father and mother I could never see again, could have been the very thing I had always wished for—a brother to laugh with and share my life."

"His father would not have lied about this."

"I know that," he said sadly. "I knew Signor Marchesi. He was a good man. As is Achille."

"And yet you sent him away," I said softly.

Zeno stilled. "I know that too."

He pushed off the counter's edge and walked to the doors. Just as he left, I said. "None of this is real, you know?" Zeno stopped and, with tense shoulders, turned my way. I pushed off the counter too. "All this, the world we live in. It's all a mirage. We live like the aristocrats of old, talking of pride and ancestral honor, but it's all pretend. The country doesn't recognize us as anyone special anymore, just the relatives of people who used to be someone once. Our titles are by name only, the official lineage papers that we add to with each new birth are practically forged.

"We all pretend that we live in castles made of stone, but in reality they are made of sand, one bluster of wind away from crumbling into the sea of the long-forgotten past. We talk of the lowly classes beneath us as though they are no better than dirt on the bottom of our shoes. But like the gods of old to the mortals of Earth, in truth we envy them, because at least they are free. Tell me, Zeno, who lives the better life? Us, sitting on our fake thrones alone, or them, who spend every second with their soul mates beside them, raising families and loving hard? We are fools because we see ourselves as better, when really we are all just miserable pawns in the great chess game that is our heritage."

Zeno inhaled deeply. "Yet you and I are still betrothed. We still do as our parents wish."

The same numbness I had felt all day wrapped over me like a protective blanket, staving off the grief of Achille's absence. "And isn't that just the most curious thing?" I said tiredly. "The most curious thing of all. That we know all this, yet do absolutely nothing about it?"

"It was never my intention to make you unhappy, Caresa," Zeno said softly, and I knew he meant every word.

"I know," I whispered back. "But it was never in your power to make me happy either. That honor belonged to someone else. It was written in the stars, way before we were born."

Zeno bowed his head and turned to leave. As I turned my back too, I said, "He would make a better prince than we would ever make a king or queen. Achille is the kind of man you would want at the helm

286

of your family's legacy. He is the special one here, not you or me."

I assumed Zeno had left when no answer immediately came. But then just as I took the siphon to bottle the first wine, I heard a whisper. "I know that, Duchessa. Believe me, I'm beginning to see that too."

Zeno's whispered words sailed on the wind and struck my heart. And in that moment I wished that the wind were stronger, because then it could drift to wherever Achille was and reach his ears. Because that was the kind of sentiment he should hear.

From his brother.

His onetime best friend.

Someone who should have loved him all his life.

And the brother that maybe now realized he wanted Achille to return . . . nearly as much as I did.

Chapter Fifteen

Sicily, Italy

Achille

"Are those hands still giving you trouble, Achille?"

I froze, holding the wine bottle clumsily in my hands. My *zia* Noelia stopped beside me and put her hands on her hips.

I shrugged but continued bottling, using the techniques I had adopted over the years to cope with how sometimes my hands just would not work they way they were supposed to.

Zia Noelia's hand landed on my shoulder, and then she joined me in bottling her Nero d'Avola wine. When the first bottle was full, I raised it up to the light. This red wine was so much darker than my merlot, the tannins richer and the taste bolder. It was rare, and her vineyard was small. I couldn't help thinking that this could achieve so much more.

Zia Noelia was my father's sister. She too had grown up on the Bella Collina estate. She had met her husband, my zio Alberto, when he came to work on one of the other vineyards on the property, but before long he had found employment in his home town in western Sicily. Zio Alberto was an expert on Nero d'Avola grapes. They made a rare wine, unique to this region. He had followed his heart, and my aunt had followed him.

As I lowered the bottle, my first thought was that Caresa would have loved to have seen this place. My aunt's vineyard overlooked Lake Arancio. It was beautiful, peaceful. The only place I had in the world to come to outside of Bella Collina. Zia Noelia and Zio Alberto were the only family I had left.

At least on the Marchesi side. There was now Zeno on the Savona side, but I was trying not to think of that too much right now. I had been here for eight days. When I had shown up, my aunt had taken one look at my face and knew why I was there. She didn't say anything but "So now you know." But that was mainly because of me. I refused to talk about fleeing my home that night. I hadn't told her about Zeno, our fight, or my . . . . or my Caresa.

Even at the thought of her name, a large rip would slice through my chest. Because I had left her. She was choosing me, but I couldn't go to Parma with her. I couldn't let her run from her life, not for me. When she was with me, she made everything better. She made me feel safe and whole.

But I didn't want to feel comfort or safety right now. I wanted to feel every emotion my father's secret ignited within me. I *wanted* to feel the pain and hurt. I needed time away from everything I loved— my vineyard, my wine, my Caresa—to think clearly. To work out what I was meant to do now.

So I worked beside my aunt and uncle on their vineyard, throwing myself into a new kind of wine production, a new taste, a new process . . . just something different.

I needed change.

As night drew in and the sun began to bow over the distant green hills, every muscle in my body ached. I took my bottle of water and a glass of two-year-old Nero d'Avola to the patio table on my aunt's stone deck and sat down. I breathed in the fresh air as the sun's reflection glistened off the crystal-blue water of the lake. There wasn't a soul in sight, not a sound to be heard. There was only me with my thoughts, my sadness and this wine.

I had sat out here every night for eight days, and nothing was better. And I knew why. Being without Caresa, thinking of how hurt she must have been when she found me gone, ensured I felt no peace. Thinking of Zeno, how he pushed me away, how he denied me as his blood, only served to sink the dagger of sadness in further.

And there was no reprieve from this hollow cave in my stomach. The pain just kept rolling and rolling, wave after wave, as if I were caught up and drowning in a wild, stormy sea.

An arm came over my shoulder. My aunt placed my dinner of pasta ragù on the table. I waited for her to leave me alone, as she had done every night, only tonight she did not. She moved beside me, placing her own plate down on the table.

She gazed over the calming scenic view and, without looking at me, said, "I remember those days like it was yesterday, Achille." My back tensed; she had finally had enough of my silence. She sighed deeply. "I remember the day my brother saw Abrielle singing Christmas hymns in Orvieto. I teased him for his infatuation at first, but after a while we could all see how much he loved her. And it wasn't long before she loved him in return."

My heart was a drum, beating loudly in my ears as she turned to me with glistening brown eyes. "Not being able to conceive a child hurt your mother so deeply. Abrielle was so sweet, so kind and had such a big heart. And it truly broke her when they discovered your father was infertile. It wounded him too, but not as much as when he discovered his wife was pregnant with the king's child."

I shifted uncomfortably on my seat. Zia Noelia covered my hand that lay tensely on the tabletop. "But you see, Achille? Sometimes what we think is the worst thing in the world can really be a blessing in disguise. You became your father's very reason for living. And as much as he cherished Abrielle, I believe he really only came to life when you were born. It no longer mattered how you came to be, only that you fit so perfectly in his arms. And the king loved you too, of that I am sure. We were not raised in that world, Achille. It is hard for us, I think, to put ourselves in their shoes. They have rules and ways that seem bizarre to us. But I saw how the king adored you, and so did his son." She squeezed my hand. "Zeno loved you, Achille. You were both so alike as you played the day away. It made my heart swell with joy to see you both laughing, brother and brother."

"He sent me from the estate," I cut in, and watched my aunt's face fill with sympathy.

"Your black eye and split lip," she said knowingly.

I nodded my head. "He read the letter and said my father told lies. I . . . I hit him when he tried to destroy the letter. If . . . if it hadn't been for Caresa, I don't know if I would have stopped." Guilt flooded my veins. "I . . . I have never been so angry in my life, so hurt, as when he denounced me on the spot." I winced. "He called me slow. He shamed me in front of her. I . . . I have never felt so unworthy of her as I did in that moment."

"Her?" my aunt asked. "This girl, Caresa?"

My chest ached. "Yes."

"Achille?" Zia Noelia said. "Are you talking of Caresa Acardi, the Duchessa di Parma? King Zeno's fiancée?"

I felt my throat thicken. "She found me in my vineyard one day. Then she came back the next. She kept coming back, and before we knew it, we had fallen for one another. It wasn't meant to happen, but . . ." I trailed off, and then, meeting my aunt's eyes, I patted my chest and whispered, "She made me whole. I found her, Zia . . . my split-apart. I was struck with love, and there was no going back."

"Oh, Achille," Zia Noelia said sadly. "And where is she now?"

"At the estate. I . . . she wanted to run away with me, to get away, but I left her, Zia. I left her and came here alone. I left her with just a simple note. A note I would never have been able to write if it wasn't for her."

"She's the one who has been helping you read and write?"

I nodded, and my aunt sat back in her seat, shocked. "Is she still marrying Zeno?"

Her question made my stomach drop to the ground. "I don't know. We . . . we had planned to tell her family about us when I had finished this year's vintage. But now . . . now I don't know." I inhaled deeply. "I don't know anything anymore. But I know that each day I am not with her, it becomes harder and harder for me to breathe."

"You love her," Zia Noelia stated.

"More than life," I replied with an unhappy smile. My aunt reached over and took my glass of wine. She took a long drink and placed the now almost-empty glass back on the table. I couldn't help but smile, a real smile this time, as she shook her head, and said, "I needed that, *carino*."

"What are you going to do?" she asked after a minute.

"I have no idea."

My aunt pulled her chair beside me and placed her hand on my arm. This close, I saw my father in her eyes. And as I studied her face, it was obvious I was not from their bloodline. But I had never seen it before.

"Achille Marchesi," Zia Noelia said sternly. "I am going to say something, and I want you to listen, okay?"

I nodded.

"I loved my brother, I did. He was a great man and cared for me his whole life. It devastated me that I was not there when he passed. That is something I will never forgive myself for. But one thing I always believed was that he did not fight hard enough for Abrielle. He saw her despair and watched her sink into a depression, but, out of love, he let her go away with the king's dressage team. Yes, he had the harvest, but she was gone a while, and he never followed. He wanted to give her time, but I believed he should have tracked her down and made sure she knew she was loved. Promised her that they would find a way to have children. It was the same with you. When your schooling became challenging, he trusted the king would help. When he didn't, my brother, out of love, let it go. Neither situation was helped by his passive nature. And Achille, I am telling you now, if you love the duchessa, if she is your split-apart, you must fight for her. You have fought all of your life, *carino*. And you have been the victor in every battle that came your way. Do not give up now when you face the war. If you want the duchessa, you must go back for her. You must tell her how you feel."

My heart pumped the blood around my veins like a red rapid. "But she is a *duchessa*," I said. "Her father will not allow our marriage. He will not accept us. She is a blue blood. She is different from me in every way."

Zia Noelia's face tightened. "Last time I checked, *you* were a prince of Italy. You are a Savona just as much as Zeno. Your blood runs blue too."

I stared at my aunt, and she stared back, never breaking my gaze. "Zeno won't . . . he didn't want to know or accept—"

"Forget Zeno!" she argued. "If he doesn't want to believe the truth about you, who cares? The king wanted to acknowledge you as his own, Achille. He wanted you as his son, but he let others rob you of your rightful title. Do not rob *yourself* of your birthright. Not if it means you get to keep your duchessa. Forget those who hate, forget those who do not think you belong. If your Caresa is worth fighting for, then fight."

"I do not know the first thing about being a . . . a prince."

"*Carino.*" My aunt put her hand on my face. "The very fact that you believe you will not be a good prince will be the very thing that ensures you are. You sell yourself short, Achille. You are meant for more than what life has awarded you. So take it. Grab it with both hands and never let go."

My body shook with the adrenaline rushing through me and igniting my every cell. "Okay," I finally said and jumped to my feet. I ran my hands through my hair as I tried to calm myself down.

I needed to go home.

I needed my Caresa.

I leaned down and pressed a kiss to my aunt's cheek. "Thank you," I said and rushed toward the house.

"He loved you, you know."

I stopped dead in my tracks and turned around. "The late king," Zia Noelia said softly. "He didn't do the right thing by hiding you away, but he loved you. He adored your mother, and in the end, he had a healthy respect for your father. Benito, Santo and Abrielle's tragic love story was complex and intense. It was filled with love—a messy kind of love—but love nonetheless. I just want you to know that whether you see yourself as a Marchesi or a Savona, you were born from such a deep love. Three hearts from very different backgrounds were broken along the way, some beyond repair. But the light in all of their suffering was *you*. Never forget that, *carino*. Remember that as you take your rightful place as a royal of our country. You were a blessing to them all." She smiled a watery smile. "And you will be just as much a blessing to her." She shrugged. "It's funny how history repeats itself. A Marchesi, a Savona and a girl. Curious, no? Just make sure *you* are the one to win this time, whatever that victory looks like."

"I love you," I whispered, her words dissolving any anger I had left within me. Zia Noelia picked up the wineglass and brought it to her lips. She turned away to stare out across the lake at the last rays of sun.

I ran to my room and grabbed my things. Five minutes later, with the stars appearing in the night sky to guide me home, I was in my papa's car, rushing home to win back my split-apart.

She was the prize.

I would make sure I was the victor.

*****

It took me a day to get home. I had only stopped once to catch some sleep. I slept in the car. It was cold and uncomfortable, but I didn't want to waste time finding a hotel and checking in, only to leave after a few hours. I drove all through the night, and now, as I made my way toward a familiar back road, night was falling again. I passed though the back gate of the Bella Collina estate. As soon as I entered, a sense of peace settled over me.

I was home.

As I passed by the mansion in the distance, this time I truly looked at it. I remembered the golds and the reds and the expensive furnishings. But I refused to let it intimidate me. I was done with feeling inferior. Like my aunt had said, part of me lived in that house, part of who I truly was. The cottage would always be my home—just like my father would always be Benito Marchesi. But I had to accept that there were others who had made me who I was too. Santo Savona's blood ran in my veins. I was a product of two very different worlds.

And I simply had to get used to the fact.

Five minutes later I arrived at my cottage. As I drove the car into the garage and killed the engine, I took a deep breath. *You can do this,* I said to myself. *You must do this for her.*

I got out of the car and grabbed my bag. I walked around to my cottage and opened the front door. For a moment, I expected Caresa to walk out of my bedroom, smiling and throwing herself into my arms. But the house was still and cold.

There was no warmth without her anymore.

I dropped my bag on the hard floor and moved into my bedroom. My heart melted when I saw that it had been cleaned. There was no evidence that a fight had ever broken out.

I sat on the bed and reached into my coat pocket. My fingers immediately found my father's letter. I pulled it out and opened the drawer of the nightstand. I slipped the letter inside, the pages still rumpled from Zeno's savage touch and stained with my blood. And then I shut the drawer, sealing it inside. I would always treasure the final words from my father, but I didn't need to read that letter anymore. I had the information he so wanted to give.

It was done.

I had to move on.

I stayed in that spot, just gathering my composure, for several minutes. Eventually, I got to my feet, left my house and walked toward the barn. The sound of Nico and Rosa in their stables greeted me. I went in to them, both of them immediately coming to see me. I patted them both, seeing that they had been cared for in my absence. I'd hoped Sebastian would have stopped by—it looked as if he had. I had no idea how I would explain my absence to him.

After staying with the horses for a while, I made my way to the barn. I had bottling to do. I was a week overdue. I threw the doors back and flicked on the light . . .

. . . and then I froze. Completely froze.

I cast my eyes along all of the freshly sanitized barrels, stacked and ready for the next harvest. To the right were shelves and shelves of bottled wine, this year's vintage. I moved closer; the labels had been placed perfectly on each bottle. They were corked and they were done.

I stood back, wondering who had done this.

"She has been here every day since you left."

My back tensed as Zeno's rough timbre met my ears. I tried to control my breathing, readying for another fight. And then I spun around to see my . . . my . . . *brother*, resting against the doorframe. He was wrapped up in a long, thick coat, a scarf around his neck and gloves on his hands. The snow fell in small flakes behind him.

He looked tired. His hair was in disarray, and he was pale.

Yet as I studied his expression, he didn't seem angry or upset that I had returned. In fact, if I had judged his features correctly, he appeared . . . relieved.

"Where is she?" I asked, my voice just as rough as his.

Zeno stepped closer and ran a hand down his face. "She is in Parma. Her parents arrived early for the wedding, and her mother took her home to try and make things better. They know everything. When it all came out, Caresa fell apart. She's . . ." He paused, making my heart slam in my chest. "Not doing so well." Zeno stopped in front of me. I allowed myself to truly look at him. Look at his eyes, his nose, his height. And it was there. Our fraternal truth that had been hiding in plain sight.

I could see he was doing the same. When our eyes met again, he broke from my gaze and gestured to the seats in front of the unlit fire. "Do you mind if we sit?"

"You're not throwing me off the land?" I asked, waiting for this too-timid reunion to fall apart.

He shook his head and laughed a humorless laugh. "No. Now, shall we?"

He walked to the seats and sat down. I cautiously made my way over and took my seat beside him. I wondered if I should start the fire, but I was too worked up. I didn't know what he wanted, or . . . "How did you know I was here?"

"I had security on alert for your return. I knew you'd come through the rear private entrance," he said.

"How did you know I *would* return?"

Zeno looked me square in the eye. "Because she is here."

"Yet now I find she's in Parma," I said.

"She is only there for a few days with her mother. Her father is here, at the mansion." His face betrayed the stress he was feeling. "He is here to try and help with Savona Wines too. To see how we can gain back what buyers and business we have lost."

"It is bad?"

Zeno laughed, but it was forced. "I don't know wine. It is my own fault, I know, but I find myself lost. I . . . it is incredibly hard doing this alone."

I glanced up at Zeno and saw him already watching me. His expression made a strange feeling burst in my chest. Something akin to fondness. Something I imagined siblings shared, something reminiscent of the closeness he and I had once had, many moons ago.

"It is not easy doing anything alone," I said, averting my gaze to stare into the unlit fire. "I didn't realize how alone I was until Caresa came bursting into my life." I smiled, remembering the day she appeared in my vineyard, all flustered and fresh from her run. "She made me want more from my life." I sighed. "She made me want *her*. And only her, forever." I risked a glance at Zeno. His eyes were wide. "I don't imagine you know what that feels like. I have heard you don't want for female attention." Something flashed across his face, something I couldn't recognize.

"Just because one is always surrounded, it doesn't mean one is not alone."

"You're rich, and always have people at your beck and call. What would you know of being lonely?"

Zeno turned to me this time and truly looked into my eyes. "Wealth is no protection from loneliness. It is very easy to be surrounded by many people yet feel like you are caught alone in the rain. I—" He stopped himself from whatever he was about to say and sat back in his chair. When he had composed himself, he said, "I think the only time I never felt alone in this world was when we were friends." He smiled, and this time it was genuine. "Do you remember when you fell into the fishing lake? I ended up jumping in after you when I thought you had drowned."

I couldn't help but laugh at the memory.

"Your father was so mad at you for snapping his fishing rod when you ended up having to help *me* out. Do you remember?" Zeno asked.

"I do," I said. "He banned me from that lake for a month."

Zeno wiped his eyes and then shook his head. The levity drifted away, replaced by a heavy silence once again. I had a million questions floating around my head, but I struggled to speak even one. Then Zeno spoke for me, and answered about a dozen.

"I spoke to my Zio Roberto this week. I went to Florence. I kept to myself for a week, and thought of nothing else but your father's letter and our fight. I . . ." He took in a deep breath. "I kept replaying that night in my head. I was so angry. I was hurt, but then" —he leaned forward and rubbed his forehead— "Zio Roberto confirmed everything. He tried to lie to me at first, but I saw through his deception." His eyes met mine. They looked sad. "It was him, Achille. Zio Roberto. He was the one who persuaded my father not to publicly acknowledge you. My father wanted you. Even when my mother left because she found out, he wanted you. But it was Roberto who told him what was at stake. Your mother was not of noble birth. He . . . he thought you a bastard and claimed you would sully the Savona name."

Pain hit me with the force of a thunderbolt. *He thought you a bastard . . . sully the Savona name.*

"I hit him too," Zeno said, and my face whipped to his. He shrugged. "I have never fought in my life, yet I hit two people in the space of a week." He smirked, but it quickly fell. "My father wanted you, Achille. Roberto confessed to me that my father never forgave him for persuading him otherwise, but as you grew older, he thought it was too late.

"He confirmed that the king would come and see you when you were a child, just so he could know you in some way. He asked your father not to tell you the truth so the risk of gossip was squashed." Zeno sagged in his seat. "But you see, it's not even about my father's pain. He was a grown man who should have fought harder for you. It . . . it was that they kept the fact you were my brother from me. They kept it secret, that my best friend shared my blood. And when they sent me away and I protested, they told me that you were not good enough to be in my life any longer. They took you away, my . . . *brother* . . . to protect their reputations."

I listened to every word he said, quietly breaking further and further apart. But the only word my head picked out was "brother". *Brother, brother, brother . . .*

He had called me his brother.

He would have *wanted* me as his brother.

"I . . ." My whisper was barely audible. "I would have . . . liked you as a brother too."

I kept my eyes facing the ground, but I knew Zeno was staring at me. I could feel his eyes burning through me. Eventually, I lifted my head and saw the glint of happiness in his expression. He coughed to clear his throat. When neither of us rushed to speak, he eventually said, "I have never seen anyone in my life pine for someone like I saw Caresa pine for you this week."

At the mention of Caresa, all the pain I had momentarily staved off came back with vengeance. I fought to breathe as my lungs constricted. "I . . . I missed her too. More than I can explain."

Zeno sighed. "You love her too?"

This time there was no hesitation in my reply. "More than you could know." I squared my shoulders. "I won't be without her. I came back for her. Even if you renounce me and take away my land, I won't be leaving without her. Never again."

I braced for an argument, for Zeno to tell me their marriage was set and there was nothing he could do. But instead he nodded his head. "I know. And don't worry, Caresa and I won't be walking down the aisle. Her father only had to watch her fall apart and witness my personal hurt to see that this marriage would never work. So I told him everything."

"You told him about me?" I felt fear, real fear at the thought of Caresa's father disliking me. I knew how much she cherished their relationship.

"And so did Caresa. He never knew. He was one of my father's closest friends, yet he never knew about you. He was angry."

I felt my face blanch. "He doesn't want his daughter with me?"

"No," Zeno said vehemently. "He was angry that *you* were never acknowledged. He was livid with Roberto. And then, when he thought back to those days, he blamed himself for being a bad friend. He said he knew that something was wrong with my" —Zeno cast me a wary glance— "*our* father. He never knew why my mother left. And he never pushed him for answers."

I didn't know what to do with that. Caresa's father thought I should have been acknowledged as Santo's son. Did that mean . . . would he mind if . . . ?

"Society expects a marriage between the Savonas and Acardis on New Year's Eve." I stilled. "That can still happen. Only the Savona groom would be different." My pulse raced and my eyes widened.

Zeno shrugged. "I would have to publicly announce you as a Savona, of course. And I would have to do that soon." Zeno lifted his hand and, after some hesitation, laid it on my shoulder. "I would acknowledge you as a prince of Italy. I would acknowledge you as my brother. Achille, I would announce you as part of House Savona."

My heart was racing out of control as I stared at Zeno. I wasn't prepared for this. I knew nothing of being a prince. All I knew was wine. All I knew was . . . "Then you must also announce me as the maker of the Bella Collina merlot."

Zeno's eyebrows drew together in confusion.

"I know wine, Zeno. I may not know the business side yet, but . . ."

I felt full with pride, confident that what I was about to say was the truth. "But I can learn. I have been working on my reading and writing. And I am . . . I am getting better. You said the buyers and shareholders wanted the Savona-Acardi marriage to happen to secure the business. Well, we can also tell them that I am the winemaker of your most sought-after merlot. Tell them that the houses will still unite, and I am going to help with the business too."

"You would do that?" Zeno asked, his voice thick with emotion. "You would help me with the wines? The business? You would partner with me?"

"Yes." I inhaled deeply. "I have hidden away for too long. But . . ." I pulled a stern expression onto my face. "I want to continue making the wine. I want to stay at this estate. To keep Caresa I will do what is required of me, but I *will* have this. The wine is my life. I need to keep it."

"Done," Zeno said and blinked as though he were in shock.

His hand slipped from my shoulder. He got to his feet. He appeared nervous, an emotion I had not seen from him before. Then he cautiously held out his hand. I stared at his outstretched fingers, knowing that if I got to my feet, my old life would be in the past. But then I thought of Caresa, thought of taking her hand in mine in a church, before God, and it was easy. I held out my hand and allowed Zeno to pull me to my feet.

He hesitated for a second, then awkwardly brought me in to his chest. He embraced me for but a moment, then inched back. He slipped his hands into his pockets. "Who would have thought we would be here one day? Brothers. And you, a winemaker turned prince."

Prince . . . the word circled my head, but it was too big for me to even fathom. "Not me."

"But you're ready to take it on, yes?" Zeno asked.

I stilled, looking around the barn that was once my entire life. I sighed in relief. After tonight I would no longer be alone.

I would no longer be alone . . . I had to hold onto that with both hands.

"Achille?" Zeno pressed. "You *are* ready, aren't you?"

"I will be," I said on a steady, fortifying breath. "For her, I will be."

Zeno smiled widely, every inch an Italian prince. "Good. Because you're coming with me. There's a man in the mansion that you need to meet. And you'll need to ask his permission to marry his daughter." He slapped my back. "No pressure, brother."

Brother, I thought again, and this time allowed its sound to fill my heart. *Brother, brother, brother* . . .

"I feel no pressure," I said confidently. "I love his daughter with all my heart." I nudged him like I would do when we were kids. "And I have you by my side pleading my case . . . don't I?" I asked hesitantly.

"That you do," Zeno said softly, and we walked in companionable silence from the barn.

As we stepped onto the path that led to the mansion, I tipped my head back and stared at the stars above, knowing they were finally, after all these years, aligning in my favor. "Thank you," I whispered aloud to them and whoever was watching from above. Then, heart

slamming, and without turning to Zeno, I added, "Thank you too . . .
brother."

Zeno held his breath, then let out a long, soul-freeing exhale. And
we followed our footsteps to our new life, en route to ask the Duca
di Parma for his daughter's hand in marriage.

And my heart felt full . . .

. . . because I was no longer doing it alone.

Chapter Sixteen

Three days later . . .

Achille

"She is back?" I whispered as I walked into Zeno's study.

Signor Acardi rose from his chair and nodded his head. "Late last night." He slowly walked to the window and gazed out at the still-dark sky. "Take a look for yourself."

I stood beside him and squinted at the distant track. My chest tightened. I couldn't see her properly, but, in the light of the fading moon, I could make out her silhouette walking down the track to my cottage.

"She goes to look for me?"

Signor Acardi nodded again. "When we arrived she was not the girl I knew." He sighed. "On my second day here, I couldn't sleep. I came down to the study to catch on up on some work, and that's when I saw her. I watched my daughter sneak from her room and follow that track. I had no idea what she was doing, so I followed her. I followed her all the way to your cottage, and then again as she tacked up a horse and set off into the dark. She ended up sitting on a high hill, watching the sunrise with tears running down her face."

He looked straight at me. "It . . . it broke my heart."

I closed my eyes as Caresa's silhouette faded behind a set of trees. "I didn't mean to hurt her," I said hoarsely.

A hand landed on my shoulder. Then it gently squeezed. "No one has been saved from hurt in the mess Santo has caused. She just wants you, son. There's no stronger truth than that."

He let out a small huff of laughter. "You know, Achille, when my daughter first tried your merlot, she was sixteen. We allowed her a drink with her evening meal. Our American friends disapproved, but we are Italian. The minute she tasted it, her eyes widened, and she told me that it was the best wine she had ever tasted. She turned to me and said, 'Have you met him, Papa? The winemaker?' I hadn't, of course. When I told her so, she smiled and said, 'One day I should like to meet him. I need to meet the man who can create such perfection.'"

I had no words.

"Go." His hand slipped from my shoulder. "You know you have my blessing."

I rushed through the mansion to the rooms I had been staying in for the last three days. I retrieved my coat, pushed out of the main door of the house and headed for the track. I slipped my hand in my pocket and ran my fingers over the smooth velvet of the box. Swallowing back my nerves, I pushed forward until I arrived at my cottage. I glanced inside the windows; Caresa wasn't there. But she had lit the fire—it was like a beacon calling me home.

I ran through my vineyard and jumped the perimeter fence, landing on the path that led the way to the hill. I walked slowly, seeing the sky beginning to lighten, and thought about what I would say. I didn't know if she would be angry or upset. I didn't know if I had broken her heart beyond repair.

But I had to try.

As I passed the botanical gardens, a small smile pulled on my lips. I climbed the fence, and as I had been doing for weeks, sneaked into one of the greenhouses and cut a single white rose from its bush. A thorn stuck into my finger, drawing blood. It was apt, I thought. A blood penance for the fact that I had broken Caresa's heart.

By the time I arrived at the bottom of the hill, I was wrought with nerves. I turned at the sound of a familiar huff and saw Rosa tied up to a tree. Passing the Andalusian with a gentle pat on her neck, I climbed the steep hill, taking a longer route so I would see Caresa before she saw me.

And then I did, and, like a miracle, the constricting, hollow chasm I had felt in my heart for the past week soothed.

For the first time in days, I could actually *breathe*.

She looked so small as she sat on the cold ground. She looked paler, and she appeared to have lost weight. But it was the sadness that radiated from her huddled form that was truly my undoing. Because I knew she had been devastated by my absence, just as I had been by hers. And I knew that everything my father had done for my mother—his forgiveness of her affair, his acceptance of me—was because he felt this for her. His love was this deep.

Plato had been right. Split-aparts did exist. And they were only whole when each found the other.

A rebel ray of sun burst from behind the hill and kissed Caresa's face, illuminating her beauty. Needing to feel her in my arms, I stepped forward and whispered, "*Mi amore.*"

Caresa stilled. She was barely moving as it was, but now her chest froze as she held her breath. She didn't turn her eyes to me, but I saw her linked hands begin to tremble.

When she didn't speak, when her eyes closed and her face contorted with pain, I moved before her and dropped to the ground. "Caresa . . ."

Caresa's lips shook, her eyes squeezed tighter, and only when a choked sob escaped from her mouth did her eyes open again. I stayed still. I didn't move an inch as those big, beautiful brown eyes searched mine, and tears streamed down her face.

The seconds felt like hours as she remained looking at me as if I were a ghost. My stomach churned with fear, fear that I had left it too late, that by walking away I had lost her forever. But then she launched herself into my arms. Her arms circled my neck, and her grip was iron tight. I held her back, my arms slipping around her waist.

I wanted to speak. I wanted to pour my heart out to her, tell her how much I missed her. But as she cried great, racking sobs, burying her face into my neck, sadness stole my voice. So I just tightened my grip, showing her without words that I had returned for her. That I belonged to her. That she belonged to me.

"Achille," she croaked, her throat raw with emotion. "My Achille. My heart," she whispered over and over again as her tears fell on my neck and her warm breath ghosted over my skin.

"*Mi amore*," I whispered back, and let her exorcise her sadness. I held her for minute after long minute, eyes closed, as the dawn brightened around us. It was only when I felt the sun's heat warming my back, that Caresa pulled back her head. She pressed our foreheads together, keeping her lips just a hairsbreadth from mine and asked in her sweet, soft voice, "Are you really back? I'm not dreaming?"

I moved forward and took her mouth with my own. I tasted her tears on my tongue, but then it was just her. All her as she invaded my every cell, her touch and taste igniting my senses. I slid my tongue against hers, craving her more and more as she moaned into my mouth.

But I slowed the kiss down. This was not the time for wild and desperate. This was me showing her I had come back for her.

This was me declaring my intentions.

I broke from the kiss, breathless, searching for air. I pulled us slightly apart and met her red, swollen eyes. "I'm sorry, *mi amore*. I am so sorry."

She shook her head and cupped my face. "No, baby," she whispered. "*I* am sorry. Everything is a mess. You must have been so hurt. I just . . . I just missed you so much I felt like I was dying." She laid a hand on her chest. "I couldn't breathe, Achille. I couldn't breathe without you by my side."

"Me neither," I said, feeling my every synapse sparking with happiness. "I love you, *mi amore*. I love you forever." I pressed a kiss on her cheek. "And ever." Another kiss on the corner of her mouth.

312

"And ever." And finally to her lips. "For eternity."

"I love you too, Achille. Forever."

I held her close again . . . and I smiled though my tears when I felt it. When I felt our hearts falling into step, beating in their mutual beat.

And when I pulled back and saw a small smile grace her lips, I leaned forward and captured it with mine.

"You are back?" she asked against my mouth. Her hands slid into my hair, clutching the strands tightly.

"Yes."

I ran my nose down her neck until I heard her breath hitch. "Achille," she murmured. I reached down and picked up the white rose I had placed on the ground. Her eyes fell on the flower, and she laughed with pure joy, taking the flower from my hand.

She brought the petals to her nose and inhaled, her eyelids fluttering to a close, and I reached into my pocket. My hands were shaking.

I took out the velvet box. I held it out between us and waited for her to reopen her eyes. When she did, her gaze immediately fixed on the box. She sucked in a quick breath, then her chocolate doe eyes collided with mine.

I swallowed, trying to find the perfect words to do justice to the way I felt.

I took a deep breath and decided to just say what was in my heart. "I know I am not what you thought you would marry. I know I am not quite from your world. But I promise you, Caresa, no one will ever love you like I do. I will live every day to make you happy and, if you let me, will never be without you from this day on." As tears fell down Caresa's face, I whispered, "Marry me, *mi amore*. Make us both whole."

Caresa launched forward and pressed her lips to my mouth. "Yes," she said softly against my lips. "Yes, yes, yes, yes, yes!"

I smiled against her lips and kissed her with everything that I had— deeply, reverently, passionately. When we broke away, I opened the box, revealing an old gold ring with a single small diamond in the center.

I felt my cheeks flame. "I know it is not large and expensive, but" —I took a deep breath— "It was my mother's. My father . . . it was the ring my father gave to my mother."

"Achille," Caresa whispered and ran her hand over the small, worn diamond.

"I know their life, their love story, didn't turn out as it should, as they deserved. But ours will. I want this ring to see soul mates living out a happy life." My voice broke. "I want to give my parents the happily-ever-after they should have had through us. I want it all . . . with you."

"It's perfect." Caresa took the ring from the box. I would struggle with that. And she knew it. I took the ring from her hand, and for once not caring about my clumsy fingers, pushed it onto her ring finger on her left hand.

"It's the perfect fit," she said as she stared lovingly at the simple ring.

A simple ring for a simple man who loved this woman with his simple heart.

She blinked, then blinked again. "I want what you said. I want this ring to see us, happy. I want your mother and fathers, wherever they are, to see their devastating story turn out right." She looked into my eyes and pressed her palm against my cheek. "I want everything with you. Achille, my winemaker. My heart."

"And prince," I said and watched her eyes widen.

"What?"

I rested my back against the tree and brought her against me, her back to my front. I wrapped my arms around her, and cast my gaze over the hill and on the rising sun. As the valley danced with oranges, yellows and pinks, I said, "I have spoken to Zeno. I . . . I have spoken to your father."

Caresa's head whipped around to face me, shock on her every feature. I kissed the end of her nose and smiled. "I . . ." I couldn't believe what I was about to say, but I said it anyway. "I am going to embrace my title. I . . . I am going to be a brother to Zeno." I stroked back a strand of hair from her face. I smiled wider when I saw her cheeks filling again with color. My presence was healing her broken heart. "I am going to be the man you need. I am going to be a prince. And I am marrying my duchessa."

Caresa studied my face, then turned her body to face me. "I will marry you regardless. I will renounce my title, Achille. I will live each day with you in the vineyard, by your side, and I will be the happiest woman there ever was. You need not take on this title for me. I will want you anyway. Rich or poor."

I couldn't resist it, so I kissed her. But when I broke away, I said, "I love you more than you will ever know for saying that. But I am going to do it. I have lived in the shadows for too long. I have hidden myself from the world, and now it's time to break free." I shook my head at how strange it all sounded to my own ears. "Zeno . . . Zeno needs me. Your father, he needs me too. And *I* need this. When I was away, I did nothing but think." I moved Caresa to sit back against my chest and brushed a kiss against her hair. "My aunt told me more of what happened. And I understood them more. I understood that they all . . ." I tried to fight back the lump in my throat, but I was unsuccessful. "They all loved me," I croaked. "And . . . and I just want to make them proud." A single tear fell down my face. "I want to make you proud."

"Baby," Caresa murmured, turning her head up to me. "That isn't possible. I am already as proud of you as I could ever possibly be."

I let her words drift over me. "*Mi amore?*"

"Yes?"

"I want to take you home." I bent down and let my mouth graze over the skin on her neck. "And I want to make love to you."

"I want that too," Caresa replied on a breathy sigh.

I stood and helped her to her feet. I held her hand as we walked down the hill. Caresa rode Rosa home, and I walked beside her, never letting go of her hand.

Then, when we had put Rosa in the paddock, I led my fiancée home and shut us in the cottage, the only place I knew would ever be home to us. The warmth from the fire filled the room. Caresa turned in my arms and shed my coat from my shoulders. She moved to my shirt, and then to my jeans, and with every move she made, I watched the ring shining on her finger, the flames catching the diamond in their light.

I had never felt so complete.

When my clothes had been shed, it was my turn to undress Caresa. And with every item of clothing dropped to the floor, I kissed a freshly bared part of her body—her shoulder, her hip, her lower neck. Caresa's skin shivered with my every touch, and when she was naked, vulnerable before me, I lifted her into my arms, and walked to the rug before the fire.

Happiness shone from the depths of her eyes as I lowered her onto the soft sheepskin and crawled above her. Caresa's hands glided along my back and stroked along my skin. I rolled my hips against her, closing my eyes as I felt her warmth beneath me. I lowered my head and joined my mouth to hers.

"*Ti amo per sempre*," I whispered.

"I will love you forever too," she said with a smile. I skirted my body down over hers and kissed every inch of her olive skin. I ran my tongue over her breasts, Caresa arching into my touch. I continued south until I reached the apex of her thighs.

Caresa's back arched as I brought my mouth between her legs and kissed her most sensitive part. A cry left her mouth. The sound, her taste and her warmth all spurred me on, my tongue lapping and lips sucking as her hands gripped onto my hair. My hands ran over her flat stomach and down over her thighs as I brought her closer and closer to the edge. I didn't want to stop. I wanted to never hear her cries of pleasure stop. With a strangled moan, Caresa tipped her head back and tightened her grip on my head. I kept my tongue on her as she broke apart in pleasure, tasting her until her hands guided my head back north.

Caresa's brown eyes were glazed, her cheeks flushed with red. "I want you," she urged as she guided me onto my back. She climbed on top of me and straddled my thighs. My hands landed on her waist as she placed me at her entrance, then slowly sank down. My eyes rolled closed as I filled her, inch by inch, until I was deep inside. Caresa bent forward and sought out my mouth with her lips. I groaned as her tongue slipped over mine, then she moved, her hips rolling slowly and deeply. Her mouth slipped from mine, and I opened my eyes to see her face right before me. Her lips were parted and her eyes were leaden, but she whispered, "I love you, Achille Marchesi. With my whole heart."

"I love you too." I moaned loudly as her hips increased their speed. My hands on her waist guided her movements as I felt the pressure of my release building within me.

"*Mi amore*," I whispered as her breathing stuttered and her movements jerked.

"Achille," Caresa gasped as my hands gripped her hips like a vise. And then she stilled, crying out with pleasure, taking me over the edge with her. Light exploded behind my eyes as I groaned out my release, striving to catch my breath.

Caresa fell on top of my damp body, her skin hot from the fire's warmth and her hair damp from exertion. She breathed into the crook of my neck as my hands still refused to let her go.

After a few minutes, I shifted her to the side, her head lying on my shoulder. I ran my fingertips down her arm, happy in the fact that I had her back. That I had her beside me again, in my home, beside the fire that she had kept lit for my return.

"*Mi amore?*" I asked, my voice barely above a whisper.

"Mm?" Caresa said sleepily.

"You bottled for me."

"You weren't here," she said softly. "I wouldn't let this year's vintage fail. I . . ." She breathed deeply, stifling a yawn. "I will never let you fail."

Before she fell asleep, I said, "*Amore?*"

"Yes?"

"There is still a wedding date set for New Year's Eve."

Caresa's head snapped up at my words. "What are you saying?" she asked.

I lifted her left ring finger and pressed a kiss to the diamond. I smiled. "This looks better than the vine ring I gave you weeks ago."

"I don't know about that," she said, then ducked her gaze. "I . . . I still have it, Achille. I keep it under my pillow, so that you are always near."

"Caresa," I croaked. Then I laughed. "I still have mine too. In my wallet. I keep it with me always."

"You do?" she asked softly.

"Always." I turned on the rug to face her and ran a finger down her face. "Marry me on New Year's Eve. A Sa . . . Savona." I stuttered, the surname sounding peculiar from my lips. "Marry me in the Duomo, a prince and a duchessa before God and all society. Marry me because I never want to be away from you again. Marry me because you're my split-apart and I will never let you go." My lips curled into a small smile. "Your parents are already here, the invites have been sent. And you already have the dress."

Her eyes gleamed. "And my veil of vines."

"You have vines on your veil?" I asked, my heart stuttering in my chest.

"I always dreamed I would." She smiled. "From a child I envisioned silken vines woven into the Spanish lace veil." She breathed in deeply and laid her head back on my shoulder. "Because God knew I would one day find you. Find you when I returned home, amongst the vines."

Just as I thought she had fallen asleep, she whispered, "And yes, I will marry you on New Year's Eve. I would marry you today if we could. I no longer want to wait to be your wife."

Caresa couldn't see it, but I smiled widely. She couldn't feel it, but my heart exploded in my chest. And she would never know it, but she had brought me back to life. She gave me hope, she gave me grace, and better yet, she gave me her.

I once asked her what I could possibly give her; she had told me she simply wanted me.

And I wanted her.

Walking toward me in a church in a white lace dress.

With her veil of vines.

As she was always destined to be.

Chapter Seventeen

Florence, Italy
New Years Eve

Caresa

"*Et voilà!*" Julietta announced flamboyantly in French as she threw the sheet from the floor-length mirror. I blinked as I took in my reflection. I had seen the dress many times before this day. But today it was different. Because today I was marrying Achille, a newly announced prince of Italy. The love of my life who had recently taken his place in the history books of House Savona's legacy.

I let my eyes sweep down my perfectly fitted long-sleeved white lace dress and to the simple ring I wore on my left hand. My hair was pulled back in an intricate bun. My makeup was flawless—my eyes enhanced with shades of brown, my lips and cheeks rosy. I wore large diamond studs in my ears, but the one item that stole the show was my veil.

My perfectly designed veil of vines.

"You look beautiful, Caresa," my mother said from beside me. She lifted my hand and pressed a kiss on the back.

"Thank you, Mamma," I said, trying my hardest not to cry.

Marietta came to stand beside me and wrapped her arm around mine. "My Caresa!" she said dramatically. "You look stunning." I smiled at my best friend. Her blond hair was tied back in a low bun, and she looked radiant in her lavender silk maid-of-honor dress.

"Are you ready, Caresa?" Pia asked. She too was a bridesmaid, looking beautiful in lavender. "The cars have arrived."

I took a deep breath and, smiling at my reflection, announced, "I'm ready."

The staff stopped in their preparations for the wedding breakfast to watch me as I walked down the hallway. I smiled at them as I passed, nodding in acknowledgment of their support.

The past couple of weeks had been insane. A few days after our engagement, just before Christmas, Zeno had gathered the most important families in Italy at the Bella Collina estate. It was there that he declared Achille his brother. It was there that he informed the shell-shocked crowd that Achille was a Savona. And that he was also the maker of the Bella Collina merlot.

And Achille had stood beside his brother, dressed impeccably in a Tom Ford suit, looking every inch the prince that Zeno was claiming him to be.

Zeno explained that the marriage would still happen, but that I was now betrothed to Achille. I knew the gossips would be in full flight, purporting this to be the scandal of the decade—King Santo's illicit affair with Achille's mother, Achille being acknowledged as a Savona, and our sudden engagement. But I didn't care.

Let them all talk.

As I rounded the hallway to the top of the stairs, my eyes fell on a portrait of the old king, painted when he was twenty-five. And there he was, my Achille staring back at me from the canvas. Zeno had always resembled the king. But as I stared at a young King Santo, looking proud in a traditional regal pose, I only saw Achille. It was clear why he had kept Achille hidden. Anyone who knew the king as a young man would have seen the resemblance in a heartbeat.

Movement from the bottom of the stairs caught my attention. I smiled when I saw my father, my bouquet of Bella Collina's white roses in his hand. The flowers were as beautiful as every rose Achille had ever given me. Yet the best part of the bouquet was the vines threading between the roses—vines from Achille's land.

They matched my veil perfectly.

I descended the stairs, my bridesmaids and mother walking behind me. When I reached the bottom, I had to quickly turn away when I saw tears building in my father's eyes.

"Papa." I whispered. "Don't cry. You'll make me cry too."

I heard him sniff and clear his throat. When I faced him again, his eyes were still glistening, but he had composed himself. He reached out for my hand and brought it through his arm. "You look so beautiful, Caresa," he said and pressed a kiss to the side of my head. "Like a vision."

"Thank you, Papa."

As my father handed me my bouquet, and the familiar, comforting scent of the roses filled my senses, I felt a calmness wash over me.

You are marrying Achille. In just over an hour, you will have soldered your soul to his in every way possible.

Vintage cars were waiting outside. The photographer snapped away as I slid into one. My father slipped in beside me and held my hand tightly.

It was a short trip to the Duomo from the palazzo. We parked behind the Piazza del Duomo and got out of the car. Paparazzi flashes blinded me as my father took my hand and guided me out onto the street. My mother and bridesmaids joined me, and we slowly made our way to the Cattedrale di Santa Maria del Fiore, the vast *duomo* that dominated the center of Florence. The air was crisp from the biting winter chill, delicate white snowflakes falling around us like confetti. The sounds of early New Year's Eve celebrations sailed on the wind to our ears, and the sun shone brightly in the sky above the Duomo, God's blinding spotlight blessing our special day. As we approached the main entrance, tourists and locals out for dinner and drinks stopped to watch us pass by. Many shouted their well-wishes, only attracting more attention to us.

By the time we made it to the entrance, quite a crowd had gathered, taking pictures and videos on their phones. My heart was beating at a million miles an hour as my mother kissed me on my cheek and went into the main body of the church to take her seat.

I could hear the mass of people inside. But my thoughts only went to one person—Achille. All I could picture was Achille in his suit, standing in front of the hundreds of people gathered here today to witness our union.

We waited behind the closed doors. My father kept his head straight forward, but just as the music began to play—Andrea Bocelli's "Sogno"—he squeezed my hand and whispered, "I am so very proud of you, *carina*. So very very proud."

My throat thickened as he moved before me and pulled my veil over my face. The doors slowly opened, and just like we rehearsed, my bridesmaids began their journey down the long aisle.

Then it was my turn to make that leap forward. My legs shook and my heart hammered a symphony as we began our slow walk down the aisle. I kept my eyes forward, trying to focus on breathing, as we passed the first row of guests. Through the thin veil I could see a sea of faces, all blurring into one. I heard their gasps of awe, their whispered well-wishes that echoed off the huge cathedral walls. It was all a swirling whirlwind, until my father squeezed my hand and said, "Look up, *carina*."

I hadn't even realized my eyes had cast down. Inhaling deeply, hearing Bocelli's perfect voice building to a crescendo, I did as my father said. And the minute I did, my body filled with uncensored joy and light and life.

Because before me, waiting for me with a small, adoring smile on his face, was Achille. And everyone else fell away. My feet felt lighter, my heart calmed in its erratic beating and air filled my lungs.

Because this was my Achille.

My heart, my conscience and my soul.

We reached the end of the aisle. My father placed my hand onto Achille's waiting one . . . and I was home.

I closed my eyes and sent a silent prayer to his two fathers and his mother for gifting me this beautiful man. All their pain, all their sufferings, would now be turned into nothing but happiness and love. I promised them I would look after their boy.

He would be safe in my arms.

I felt him move beside me. When I opened my eyes, Achille was lifting my veil . . . my veil of vines, the vines I knew had always represented the other half of my soul. My sweet winemaker of the Bella Collina merlot.

He pushed the veil back from my face, and I sucked in a sharp breath. My eyes grazed down Achille's tall, broad frame. He was dressed in a designer tux, and his usually messy black hair was combed back from his face, showing the beauty of his turquoise, Mediterranean-sea eyes.

And when our gazes locked, I played the story of us in my mind. From the first day in the vineyard, to him brushing his hand past mine, our kiss, making love, and finally being back in his arms after we were split apart. I played it all—the memories a fingerprint on my soul.

Because sometimes, just sometimes, the sun and the moon align, bringing two people to the same place at the same time. Sometimes destiny guides them to exactly where they are meant to be. And their hearts fall in a tandem beat and their souls merge as one.

Split-aparts.

Soul mates.

Two halves, now one whole . . .

. . . Achille and Caresa.

Per sempre.

Epilogue

Bella Collina Estate, Umbria
Three years later . . .

Achille

"Santino, come here, *carino,*" I said, laughing as my two-year-old son let go of his mother's hand and ran down the long row of vines to reach me. As he stumbled his way toward me over the uneven earth, his face was bright, and his infectious laughter carried on the wind. I couldn't help but feel blessed.

Santino fell into my arms, and I brought him to my chest. I stood with him in my arms and kissed his chubby cheek. I took his hand and ran them over a full bunch of grapes, warm from the sun, and asked, "Are these ready yet, *carino?*" Santino's little fingers ran over the skin of the grapes. "Well?"

"Yes!" he shouted. I tickled his waist, and he burst into laughter.

"Very good!" I praised and spun him around as he laughed harder. I looked at Caresa, who was watching us from the end of the row with a look of happiness in her eyes. Her hands were cupping her pregnant stomach as her long hair blew around her in the warm breeze.

We were having a little girl. And I couldn't wait to meet her.

"Shall we run to your mamma?" I asked Santino, and he clapped his hands.

I set off in a steady jog as we made our way to Caresa. "Mamma!" Santino shouted and held his arms out for her.

She lifted him up for a moment, but then placed him back down on the ground. She pointed toward the cottage. "Look who's come to see you!"

Santino turned at the same time as I did. Zeno was standing near the trees, dressed in his usual suit and tie. He waved my way, then crouched to the ground. "Santino! Your favorite uncle has come to see you!"

"Zio Zeno!" Santino screamed and pushed his little legs to their maximum speed as he ran across the field and into Zeno's arms. I laughed as Zeno put him down and began to chase him around the grass.

"He's so good with him," Caresa said affectionately.

I nodded in agreement, then turned to my wife. I cupped her face with my hands and brought her in for a kiss. When I broke away, I pressed my forehead to hers. "I love you forever."

"I love you forever too," she murmured back, then ran her hand down my bare chest. "I love this time of year, because I get to see you dressed like this every day as you bring in the harvest."

"Then I'll always look forward to October," I said and kissed my wife again, because I could.

I threaded my arm around her shoulders, and we walked toward

Zeno and Santino. When Zeno saw us, he picked Santino up in his arms. Zeno kissed Caresa on both cheeks then hugged me. "Are you staying for dinner?" I asked.

"Of course," he replied. We all walked back to the cottage. Since I had taken on the title of prince and become part of Savona Wines, Caresa and I had stayed here on the Bella Collina estate. The main house was ours, but we mostly stayed here in the cottage. Especially during the harvest.

This cottage was our true home.

Zeno spent most of his time at the Palazzo Savona in Florence, but was here often. Together we ran the Italian side of the business, and together we had made the business flourish. Savona Wines was better now than it ever was under our father the late king. And Zeno listened to me as I did him. He trusted my judgment on wines we should produce or vineyards we should acquire. And I was proud of Zeno. Gone were his playboy days. Instead he had thrown himself into the business one hundred percent and had become truly great at what he did.

And he was once again my best friend.

He was my brother.

We sat on the deck as the horses grazed in their paddock. "So," I said to Zeno when Caresa went inside for the food. "How are the sales of the Nero d'Avola?"

"Through the roof," Zeno said with a smirk. "You were right again, brother. The wine is a hit." The first year I had come on board, I suggested Savona Wines acquire my Zia Noelia's wine. They had gone as far as they could alone, and now, with our backing, they were soaring.

"And your love life?" Caresa asked, coming out of the house with bowls of her homemade *cioppino*. It was my favorite.

Zeno laughed. Caresa placed Santino in his high chair and sat down. "I'm married to my job, Duchessa. You know this."

Her hand covered his. "As proud as I am of you, Zeno, you need love too."

Zeno shrugged. "One day. Maybe. But for now, I'm . . ." He sighed contentedly. "I am happy. For the first time in a long time."

We ate our food and laughed long into the night. My brother and I discussed business, and when Santino's energy was depleted, Zeno left with the promise of coming back again tomorrow.

He wanted to help me with the harvest. As he had done last year. Together.

As we entered the house, Caresa went to put Santino to bed. But as the door shut behind us, I took our son from her arms. "I'll put him to bed. You go wait for me by the fire."

Caresa's face melted into the most beautiful, loving expression, and she made her way to the large cushions that lay before the glowing embers.

Santino yawned. I kissed him on the cheek as I led him into his bedroom. I changed him into his pajamas and laid him down on the bed. Before I had even sat down, he scrambled across his bed to his stack of books and brought one back for me to read. As I read the title, I playfully rolled my eyes. "This one again?"

Santino laughed and settled under his comforter. Shuffling beside him, I opened the first page. As I always had to, I focused on the words and allowed them to make sense in my head. And then I read. Santino laid his head on the pillow next to me, his arm around my waist. He laughed when I made the appropriate animal's noises at the right time, but when the laughter stopped and I looked down, my little boy was fast asleep.

Heart melting at his slightly parted plump lips and messy dark hair, I slid from the bed and kissed him on his head, whispering, "I love you forever."

I placed the book back on his shelf, knowing that one day I would read him Tolkien, just like my father had done with me.

I closed the door to his room and made my way back to my wife. Caresa was lying by the fire, her gaze lost to the flames. She smiled. "He fell asleep?"

"Almost straight away. We didn't even make it a quarter-way through the book," I said and sat down beside her. Caresa shifted until her back was against my front. As she settled back, I leaned my back against a large pillow.

A second later a book was in my hand—Plato's *Symposium*. I glanced down to see Caresa looking up at me, her long lashes kissing her cheeks as she blinked. "Read to me."

My heart exploded in my chest at the amount of love in her eyes. Love that only seemed to increase day by day, as impossible as that seemed.

"Always," I said and opened the book to our favorite part, the part

I read to her every night. Caresa snuggled into my chest, and I laid my free hand over her stomach. Then I read. Against the firelight, in our home, with our son in his bed and our daughter listening in, I spoke of wandering lost souls meeting their missing parts and being struck from their senses by love. And as I glanced down at my beautiful wife, my other half, with her hand pressed over mine, I spoke of belonging to one another, knowing Plato spoke of couples like us.

Because from the moment I saw her, and allowed myself to fall in love, my soul recognized her as my own. And . . . *we would never want to be separated from one another . . .*

. . . not even for a moment.

The End

Playlist

Shadow — Birdy

Sirens — Cher Lloyd

Love Like this (Acoustic) — Kodaline

Ships In The Rain — Lanterns on the Lake

Set Fire To The Third Bar — Snow Patrol

Atlas: Touch — Sleeping At Last

Talk Me Down — Troye Sivan

Happiness (Acoustic) — NEEDTOBREATHE

All Again — Ella Henderson

Lost Boy — Troye Sivan

Dark Island Sky — Enya

Dusty Trails —Lucius

Say You Won't Let Me Go — James Arthur

Wishes — RHODES

Autumn — Paolo Nutini

Follow the Sun (Acoustic) — Caroline Pennell

When We're Fire (Cello Version) — Lo-Fang

I Could Never Say Goodbye — Enya

Sogno (Extended Version) — Andrea Bocelli

BITE — Troye Sivan

To listen to the soundtrack, please go to my page, 'Author Tillie Cole', on Spotify.

Acknowledgments

Mam and Dad, thank you for all the support. Mam, I've finally written a book with absolutely no darkness or guttering tears!

To my husband, thank you for encouraging me to write whatever genre of book I feel like writing. *Ti amo per sempre.*

Sam, Marc, Taylor, Isaac, Archie and Elias. Love you all.

Thessa, my star and mega-assistant. Thank you for manning my Facebook page and keeping me in check. Thank you for all the edits you make me. But mostly, thank you for encouraging me with every project I take on. Achille loves you just as much as you love him.

Kia, as always a HUGE thank you for editing this book for me. It was a different kind of book for us, but we made it through!

Neda and the ladies at Ardent PRose. I am so happy that we decided to join forces—world domination is the goal! Let's toast to this, our first project together. I look forward to many many more! You are all stars! Neda, you know I love you to pieces. You most certainly keep my unorganized self in check!

Liz, my fabulous agent. I love you. Thank you for all the support.

Gitte and Jenny from *TotallyBooked Book Blog*. I have nothing to say but thank you and I love you. This career has given me too many blessings to count. I very much include meeting you both in that list.

Vilma, thank you for giving Achille a chance. Love you lots. And we'll forever have Adele!

And a huge thank you to all the many, many more wonderful book blogs and readers that support me and promote my books. Celesha, Tiffany, Stacia, Milasy . . . Gah! I could go on and on, so I'll just say an epic THANK YOU to all who read my books and support me. You have no idea what it means to me.

Tracey-Lee, Thessa and Kerri, a huge thank you for running my street team: The Hangmen Harem. Love you all!

To my street team members—LOVE YOU!!!

My IG girls!!!! Adore you all!

And lastly, my wonderful readers. I want to thank you for reading this novel. Thank you for joining me on whatever adventure I decide to go on (my genres vary a lot, yet you are always there). I hope you enjoyed your trip to Italy. I hope you fell as hard in love with Caresa and Achille as I did. But more than that, I hope you finished this novel with a smile on your face and love in your heart.

I couldn't do this without you.

Ti amo.

Ti amo per sempre.

Author Biography

Tillie Cole hails from a small town in the North-East of England. She grew up on a farm with her English mother, Scottish father, older sister and a multitude of rescue animals. As soon as she could, Tillie left her rural roots for the bright lights of the big city.

After graduating from Newcastle University with a BA Hons in Religious Studies, Tillie followed her Professional Rugby player husband around the world for a decade, becoming a teacher in between and thoroughly enjoyed teaching High School students Social Studies before putting pen to paper, and finishing her first novel.

Tillie has now settled in Austin, Texas, where she is finally able to sit down and write, throwing herself into fantasy worlds and the fabulous minds of her characters.

Tillie is both an independent and traditionally published author, and writes many genres including: Contemporary Romance, Dark Romance, Young Adult and New Adult novels.

347

When she is not writing, Tillie enjoys nothing more than curling up on her couch, watching movies, drinking far too much coffee, while convincing herself that she really doesn't need that extra square of chocolate.

Follow Tillie at:

https://www.facebook.com/tilliecoleauthor

https://www.facebook.com/groups/tilliecolestreetteam

https://twitter.com/tillie_cole

Instagram: @authortilliecole

Or drop me an email at: authortilliecole@gmail.com

Or check out my website:
www.tilliecole.com

For all news on upcoming releases and exclusive giveaways join
Tillie's newsletter: http://eepurl.com/bDFq5H

36775218R00210

Made in the USA
Middletown, DE
18 February 2019